A Lethal Arrogance

AN ARABELLA STEWART HISTORICAL MYSTERY-BOOK THREE

D.S. LANG

Copyright ©2021 by Debra Sue Lang

First ebook September 2021

Cover design by Karen Phillips

Copyediting by Alyssa B. Colton

Paperback ISBN: 978-1-7368385-8-7

Ebook ISBN: 978-1-7368385-2-5

Chapter 1
Prologue

Ohio—August 1920

Pale fingers of rose and pink painted the gray sky as Arabella Stewart leaned back in the Adirondack chair, sipped her coffee, and scanned her surroundings. Summer was her favorite season, and dawn was her favorite time of day. The combination of the two made everything seem possible. A sigh left her as she savored the peace and quiet that marked morning at Ballantyne, the resort that had been in her family for over thirty years. Ballantyne—her heritage, her home, her hope.

Bella's gaze moved across the horizon. Faint fog hovered over the golf course, tennis courts, dock, cottages, and the creek running through the resort. The haze would burn off before golfers arrived, which was too bad. The mist had seemed magical when she was a child. Despite everything that had happened over the past few years, in some ways, it still did. Her hand tightened on the coffee cup. Some magic was needed if Ballantyne was to thrive again.

The opening of the inn's front door intruded on her thoughts, and Bella turned to see Mac MacLendon. "Good morning," she said to the man who was both her business partner and honorary grandfather.

"Good morning, lass." His wide grin and sparkling gray eyes made him seem almost boyish despite his seventy years.

A smile curved her lips. Mac, who had come to Ohio from Scotland with her grandfather, had called her "lass" all her life. She loved that he still did. Bella had always found the charming and unique speech patterns of Mac and Grampa Stew fascinating. The two had come from a remote village where many residents spoke Gaelic—at least they had when the pair was growing up. They also spoke English, which even then had been the predominant language in their country. From what she'd learned from her Gramma Stewart, the people had their own dialect. As a girl, Bella had yearned to travel to the little Scottish town but, even then, it had been fading away. "Sit down," she said, indicating the chair next to hers. "You're up early."

"As are ye," he observed, taking the chair. "Twill be a busy day with the fourball starting tomorrow. Some players be coming for a final practice round."

"Yes, and we'll have contestants and spectators checking into the inn and cottages. I've heard the hotel in town is filled, too." As Bella spoke, butterflies took flight in her stomach. The fourball golf tournament was a big event, the biggest of the season, and this year's competition was more important than the previous ones because it could make or break their efforts to restore Ballantyne to its pre-war status as a premier resort. It would also affect the nearby village of Moreley, which depended on tourists. She didn't want her hometown to disappear like Mac's and Grampa Stew's had. She cleared her throat. "It's good to be busy."

"Aye, lass, that it is. We've come a long way in the past few weeks," he said. "Business has been brisk."

"Yes, we've been lucky." She didn't want to mention the murder that had occurred in one of their cottages last spring. The killing had nearly undone their plans. Now, they only needed a successful tournament to turn the corner on financial difficulties and head into the off-season without undue worry. She and Mac had planned carefully and worked diligently ahead of this first big event. Planning and work were crucial, but luck was important, too. The jangling of the telephone broke into her thoughts. "I'll answer," she said before scurrying inside.

When the operator revealed that Ida Byington was on the line, Bella smiled. Hearing from her best friend was always a treat. At least it usually was but, after they exchanged pleasantries, Ida dropped a stunner.

"I'll be coming to play Ballantyne with Cecil Laheene today, and I wanted you to know," Ida said. Her soft voice held a note of anxiety.

The revelation sent shock hurtling through Bella. Her palms grew damp as she gripped the earpiece and candlestick base. Had she understood Ida correctly? Unsure, she made a statement of fact. "We're getting ready for the men's fourball, and most of today's players are competing in it."

"I know. That's why Cecil is coming. He's substituting for someone who had to withdraw. He plans to tell Mac today."

Confusion evolved into consternation, and Bella's stomach clenched as earlier optimism shriveled. She had known and disliked Cecil Laheene for years. That put her in the majority, since Cecil was snobbish and overbearing. Her initial memory of the man came from when he'd first played at Ballantyne, a decade earlier. He'd run afoul of her father by taking a swing at a young caddy. Several years later, Cecil had once again been chastised by Archer Stewart, that time for cheating and nearly coming to blows with another contestant. Nothing Bella had heard since then improved her opinion. Along with those troubling thoughts, she wondered why Ida would be with a man like him. "I see." But she didn't. Not really.

For several moments, only the crackling of the long-distance line was audible. "You and I haven't chatted for a while, so you don't know that Cecil and I have been courting for a few weeks."

Fresh shock filled Bella. Ida was stepping out with Cecil Laheene? Once again, she wondered if she'd heard her friend correctly. "I see," she repeated, although the whole situation seemed murky. Of all the eligible bachelors around, why would Ida choose to see Cecil?

A faint, perhaps nervous, giggle was Ida's immediate response. "You're probably surprised."

"A little," Bella admitted, although that was a complete and total understatement.

"He isn't so bad, you know," Ida hurried to say. "He's been good to me and my parents."

Absorbing the observation proved difficult, and Bella had trouble forming a logical reply. Finally, she said, "If that's the case, I'm happy for you." Perhaps, Cecil had changed. Bella hoped so. She cleared her throat. "When will you be here?"

"In about an hour. I'm staying at my aunt's house during the tournament, and I'll be leaving here soon. I'm sure Cecil is already on the way from Cleveland."

"Wonderful." Not her true feelings, but Bella didn't know what else to say. "I'll keep a lookout."

By the time they wrapped up their chat, Mac was walking into the lobby. After replacing the earpiece, Bella faced him.

He took one look at her and frowned. "Be ye all right, lass?"

Flustered by her friend's call, Bella wrapped her arms around her waist and struggled to marshal her thoughts. When she replied, her voice sounded as shaky as she felt. Even worse, once Mac heard the news, his craggy features darkened.

"Laheene be a mischief-maker and a rascal."

"He has been in the past, but he may have changed. Ida seems to think so." Mac's gray gaze narrowed, and she knew he was weighing her words. Did he realize they expressed more hope than reality? Cecil's demeanor had always been abhorrent. Why would it improve now?

"The last time Laheene played in an event here, ye father escorted him off the course and told him to stay away if he can nay behave like a gentleman. Perhaps, the man should have been banned, but tis too late now."

The old pro's comments reignited Bella's anxiety. She recalled, all too well, Cecil's fury at her father. "Dad could be on the course every day, but we've half as many workers as we did then. We had others to be alert for trouble, too. Now, there's only a handful of us working. Not only that, the Moreley constable's office is very shorthanded these days." Once again, she was reminded of how important a successful tournament was to the resort and nearby town. Funds were sorely needed.

"Aye," Mac agreed. "As ye say, Laheene may nay be bad now, but I'll call Jax when I get to the shop. The lad may have some ideas. Do nay fret, lass." His features relaxed, and a smile formed. "Twill all be well." With that, the old pro went on his way.

When the screen door slammed shut behind Mac, Bella dropped into the nearest chair. Two of his words *call Jax* echoed in her heart and mind. Jackson Hastings, the local town constable, had once been a fixture at Ballantyne, but now came only when necessary. She and Mac had briefly discussed precautions with him more than a week earlier. Any big event meant more vigilance, and Jax had ticked off a few concerns. Security hadn't been an issue in the past, but crime had increased everywhere since the end of the war, and Moreley had experienced two murders in the past seven months. They hadn't known about Cecil Laheene coming then, so it was probably a good idea for Mac to speak with Jax.

Because she had so many other tasks to handle on this Wednesday morning, Bella shook off the doubt. Until they heard from the constable, she needed to focus on last-minute preparations for guests.

***

An hour later, Jax parked his Chevrolet Chummy and walked down the narrow path to the golf shop. Bittersweet memories washed over him. Growing up, all his free time had been spent at Ballantyne with his best friend, Matt Stewart, and often, with Matt's little sister Bella trailing after them. Back then, he'd thought his future was here, as well, but the Great War had changed that, had changed him.

Jax took a moment to look at the first tee. Currently, it stood vacant, but he could easily imagine Matt—tall and lanky, his dark hair and dark eyes so much like Bella's—standing there, bag over his shoulder, waving and calling for Jax to hurry. A lump formed in his throat. He would give everything he had, everything he would ever have, to see Matt there again, but that was impossible. Nothing could bring his friend back. Not wishful thinking or aching guilt. Matt rested in a French grave, one that should have belonged to Jax.

He fought off faded recollections and lost dreams to concentrate on the next few days. Both the resort and Moreley, only two miles away, would benefit if the tournament went all. With contestants and spectators flocking to the area, security was important, but Jax had felt confident about handling the crowds...until he'd learned about Cecil Laheene's presence. The man was a nasty, aggressive snob who could cause trouble, as he had at two previous Ballantyne events, and at other places. Jax planned to make sure that didn't happen, which was why he'd come to talk with Mac face-to-face. He wanted to assure the older man that extra protection had been arranged and field any additional questions.

Jax had barely stepped inside the small shop when a deep voice drew his attention. He turned to see a familiar, and unwelcome, figure.

"Jax Hastings. What a surprise." The tall man smiled, but it didn't go beyond his thin lips. His pale gray eyes, as cold as lake ice in the dead of winter, narrowed on Jax's badge. "I heard you were a copper now."

Tension gripped Jax. While he'd known Laheene was coming today, Jax hadn't expected him quite so soon. He schooled his features before replying. "Cecil Laheene, I'm surprised to see you, too. Aren't you a bit far from home?" Jax's voice was as glacial as Laheene's arctic stare, but it had little impact. Although the same height as Jax, the man seemed to be looking down his patrician nose. The haughtiness was typical.

"I'm a last-minute substitute, and my partner and I wanted to get a practice round in. And you? Have you found another partner?" The humorless smile became a sneer.

A stab of undiluted pain shot through Jax. Even if he could play in the event, he wouldn't. No one could ever take Matt Stewart's place, not as a partner or as a friend. But what did Laheene know about friendship? Nothing. He'd never partnered twice with the same person. Either they moved on or he did. "I'm not considering one," Jax replied in a stony, stark tone that would have made most men flinch. Of course, Laheene was not most men.

"I heard you were wounded in France. A bad show that." Laheene's expression lacked any trace of interest or empathy.

Jax gritted his teeth. "It was worse than a bad show." Somehow, he cloaked his anger. Laheene had no idea of how bad. His father, an influential industrialist, had kept his son out of legal trouble and out of uniform, far from the trenches. Far from the death and destruction.

"Yes, I suppose it was. Too bad about Matt Stewart. He had a great future ahead of him. Of course, volunteering for the National Guard was a poor choice, but he was always one for duty, honor, and all that folderal. Of course, so were you."

Fiery anger threatened to melt Jax's self-control. Laheene's insensitivity and ignorance knew no bounds. Matt had been more, much more, than an outstanding golfer. He'd been a man of character. "Matt Stewart was a loyal friend, a devoted son, a loving brother. He was an extraordinary officer, too." Someone like Laheene could never understand. Nor could the man fathom the hole that Matt's death left. Jax was about to tell him so when Mac stepped into the breach.

"Young Matthew be greatly missed here." The pro's usually warm Scotch brogue was hard and flat and cold.

Laheene's gaze moved to the old pro. "I'm sure he is."

"He is, and he always will be," Jax added, his own voice far less measured than Mac's.

"Of course," Laheene said as he looked back at Jax. "Maybe you'd like to join us. We're only a threesome."

Even if his game was at its pinnacle, playing with Laheene was something Jax had never done or would do voluntarily. "I can't."

"Really. I hope it's not your wounds."

The smirk on Cecil's darkly handsome face didn't surprise Jax. Any genuine compassion was beyond the man. "No, it isn't. I'm here in an official capacity. We want to ensure no trouble occurs during the tournament."

A humorless laugh left Laheene. "I'm sure you do," he said before turning back to Mac. "Can we tee off now?"

"Aye," the older man replied.

With that, Laheene paid the green fees and nodded to Jax on his way out. When the man was gone, Mac spoke again, "He has nay changed, and tis sorry I am that Floyd Ettinger's original partner needed to back out."

"I am, too," Jax admitted. "We've already reviewed the incidents at other tournaments over the past few years, and Laheene was involved in several." Jax folded his arms across his chest. "Even though I wasn't expecting to see him, I'm glad I was here."

"Aye. Tis good ye will be here over the weekend, too."

Jax nodded. "After I spoke with you, I thought we needed more help, so I called the mayor. He witnessed the last confrontation between Bella's father and Laheene, so he agreed with me. Then, I called Richard Jenkins. He'll be in town tomorrow." The retired senior constable had helped several small police departments during the war when many men were in France, and he'd assisted Jax in solving two murders in the last seven months. "He can spend all day here during the tournament, and I'll be out as much as possible. Nolen Rogers will cover our usual duties until the final day, when he'll mostly be on the course, too. We'll juggle, as needed."

"We appreciate the help, lad. Tis wonderful that Jenkins can come and that your deputy will be on duty, as well. We have so few workers."

"I know you and Bella are keeping expenses down." Jax shifted from one foot to the other. "Evidently, she was surprised to learn about Ida and Laheene stepping out." Bella and Ida had been college roommates, and they'd served together as United States Signal Corps operators in France. The two were very close, so Jax wondered if Bella was truly taken aback by Ida stepping out with Laheene, as Mac had said in their telephone conversation. Did the old pro suspect she knew more, as Jax did?

The older man's gray gaze grew troubled. "Very surprised. She seemed upset, but the lass is nay as happy-go-lucky as before the war. Losing her parents and Matthew has taken a toll."

Jax's heart constricted. The elder Stewarts succumbed to Spanish flu only a few months after Matt's death in the trenches. "I know it's been hard." Much worse than hard, he was sure. Devastating.

"Aye, and she frets about keeping the resort. If the fourball be successful, twill be a relief."

"We'll do everything to make sure it is," Jax told him. "It's important to Moreley, too, but I think we're past the worst problems." Heaven knew, he hoped so.

***

Jax said goodbye and headed to his vehicle. As he walked toward the parking area, annoyance joined with worry. Laheene was standing beside his Cadillac roadster while Ida was exiting her Buick. As he got closer, he noticed Ida pulling her clubs out of the trunk. Laheene did nothing to help her. Not that Jax was surprised. The man had few manners, despite his privileged upbringing. Briefly, he considered continuing to his Chummy, but he didn't want to ignore Ida. They had known each other for many years, and she didn't deserve to be slighted. With that thought in mind, he joined her. "Let me help with those." Jax indicated her bag and clubs.

"Thank you, Jax," she said with a smile. "That's very kind. Bella was telling me..."

Laheene interrupted her. "That's Hastings. Kind to the core, just like Stewart was."

Jax slipped the strap from Ida's bag over his left shoulder, but only addressed her. "It's good to see you again."

"It's good to see you, too," she replied with a smile. Her hazel gold eyes sparkled with genuine pleasure. "I'm glad you're here this morning."

Before Jax could reply, Laheene spoke. "Yes, even though he can't play, he's still hanging around."

"Cecil," Ida said, dismay in her voice.

"Cecil, what?" His tone was harsh and stinging. The pale gray eyes narrowed on her. "I suppose you like the serious type. After all, you planned to marry Alan Brewster, and he was a dull stick."

The color drained from Ida's face as a gasp left her. "I need to put my golf shoes on," she said in an indistinct murmur before stepping away.

"You oaf," Jax spit out in a voice too soft to carry to Ida. "Brewster was a fine man." Perhaps, not as fine as Ida thought, but Alan—despite his flaws—had been far superior to Laheene.

A low snicker left the other man. "You say that like I'm not."

Rage simmered inside Jax. "Alan died carrying one of his men—a boy, really—back to the trenches. He gave his life for someone else." Sorrow muffled his rage. Alan Brewster hadn't been perfect, but he had died a hero, and he deserved to be honored and respected.

"How foolish of him." Laheene released another humorless chuckle. "He and Stewart were both simps."

Everything in Jax urged him to knock the smirk off the other man's face. Only the greatest self-discipline kept him from doing so. Nothing would be gained by stooping to Laheene's level. Nothing would be improved by a show of violence. Heaven knew, he'd seen enough of that to last him a lifetime and beyond. Besides, Laheene enjoyed baiting people and then, watching them get into trouble for reacting to him. Jax wouldn't fall into his trap. He hoped no one else did during the tournament. But that's why he was ensuring strong security was in place.

Another car pulling into the lot drew his attention. He didn't recognize the young man driving the Dodge roadster, but Laheene did.

"Your young friend Guy is here," he called to Ida.

When she came back to stand beside the two men, Ida—her eyes wide with alarm—turned to Laheene. "Let's go, Cecil."

"My partner isn't here yet," Laheene said in a cold, clipped tone, "and I don't take orders from you."

Ida looked from Laheene to the newcomer and back again. Her lips trembled and her eyes filled with tears. Wondering why she was so upset, Jax turned to see the driver emerging from the car.

The young man, misery blanketing his youthful face, gazed at Ida before turning an angry glance on Laheene. "What are you doing here?"

Laheene released a humorless laugh. "What do you think, kid? I'm here to prepare for the tournament, so you might as well beat it. Like your brother, you don't have a chance when I'm in the field."

Fury flashed in the younger man's eyes. "Alan was a fine player and a fine man, which is more than anyone would ever say about you."

Those observations made Jax give the newcomer a closer look. With that look came recognition. The boy was Alan Brewster's younger brother, Guy, who clearly detested Laheene. The kid could have more than one reason for his resentment, but Guy was probably upset by witnessing Ida with Cecil. As Jax looked from one man to the other, he realized young Brewster was a powder keg and Laheene would love to apply a match to him. With grim resolve, Jax stepped forward. "Guy, it's been a long time," he said as he put out his hand.

For a moment, the youngster hesitated. Then, his tension seemed to drain away and Guy accepted the handshake. "Yes, it's been a while. Good to see you again."

"Hello, Guy," Ida murmured.

The younger man's expression indicated confusion and sorrow when he looked at the woman who should have been his sister-in-law. "Hello."

When another automobile roared into the parking area. Ida turned back to Laheene. "Your partner is here, so I'll meet you at the first tee." She bid goodbye to Jax and Guy, took her bag, and hurried away. Laheene grabbed his own clubs and walked to where his partner was emerging from his vehicle.

Tension still simmered in the air, especially around Guy Brewster, who again looked angry and upset. As soon as Laheene was out of earshot, Jax said, "I assume you're playing a practice round. Will your partners be here soon?"

He shrugged. "In a few minutes. I'm early. I wanted to talk to Mr. MacLendon."

"Great. He'll be glad to see you." Jax hesitated only briefly before continuing. "Don't let Laheene get to you. He enjoys baiting people."

Guy nodded. "I know. He's done that with me in the past, but I won't be so quick to react again."

"I've heard about troubles at other tournaments this summer. Were you at any of them?"

The younger man's hands balled into twin fists. "I was. Laheene and I have been at odds all season. This isn't the first time we've had words."

Anxiety dug deeper into Jax. "Bella and Mac don't need trouble during the fourball, or at all. Mac had to close the inn and cottages after Bella's parents died. They've reopened now, but the tennis courts are still closed, and so is the boat dock. If this week goes well, they may get the resort back to normal. That would also help Moreley, since the town relies on visitors who come for activities here. We can't afford to have any incidents that might create bad word of mouth." Would the explanation move Guy? Jax hoped so. A great deal was riding on the next few days.

"I wouldn't do anything to hurt Ballantyne," Guy assured him. He ran one hand over his face. "Laheene is a cad, though."

"I know," Jax admitted. "He gets to me, too."

The younger man glanced at Jax's badge before meeting his gaze. "Really?"

"Really. He made some nasty comments about Matt Stewart a bit ago, and it was all I could do to stay composed. Just remember. Laheene usually wins when he makes someone lose control."

Guy nodded. "I'll be careful around him."

Since the younger man seemed sincere, Jax nodded. "Great. Enjoy your round, and good luck in the tournament."

"Thanks."

Jax watched the kid go into the pro shop before turning toward his Chummy. The sight of Bella on the inn's porch made him pause. Had she seen Ida and wondered why her friend went to the first tee without saying hello? Maybe he should explain what happened and find out if Bella knew more about her friend's new suitor.

As Bella stood on the front porch, she watched the scene in the parking area. Although unable to hear what was said, she sensed tension among the small group there. Once it dispersed, she saw Jax pause and wondered if he planned to leave without a word to her. When Jax headed toward the inn, she relaxed until he got close enough for her to see his strained expression. "What's wrong?"

"Nothing serious," he replied.

Bella searched his chiseled features but found no real clues. "Do you have a few minutes? I'd like to know what Ida said to you. It's not like her to hurry off without even a wave in my direction."

"I can fill you in."

Jax mounted the steps two at a time but stopped several feet away. Close enough for Bella to see wisps of blonde hair beneath his constable's cap. Close enough to see his grass-green eyes. Despite their proximity, a barrier—one Jax had erected after Matt died—stood between them. Before she got swept into the past, Bella looked away. "Let's sit down."

Once seated, he spoke again. "I was surprised when Mac told me about Ida calling you this morning. I guess you were surprised, too."

Something in his tone indicated that Jax might not believe how stunned Bella had been, so she hurried to emphasize the point. "Very much so. Evidently, they've been stepping out for a few weeks. I was so shocked that I didn't ask for details. I've been busy this summer and haven't spoken with her for more than a month." Bella paused before adding, "I really don't understand what she sees in him."

"Evidently, neither does Guy Brewster."

Confusion filled Bella. "Guy. Alan's brother?"

"He was the young man talking with Laheene and Ida."

"From here, it looked tense. Was it really bad?" Bella's fingers dug into the chair arms as she braced herself for his reply.

"Laheene criticized Alan, which got to Guy. Evidently, the two have had run-ins at other tournaments this year."

Fresh anxiety filled Bella. "Always about Alan?"

"Mostly, I think. I had the impression that Guy doesn't like Ida seeing Laheene, and that may be a sore point."

Bella chewed on her lower lip. "That's understandable. Ida got close to all of Alan's family, so it has to be hard to see her move on."

"I suppose," Jax murmured. "In any case, I spoke with Guy about not letting Laheene get to him. I don't want the two of them coming to blows here."

The observation eased Bella's mind but only a little. "If Guy was upset this morning, I'm worried there will be trouble between Cecil and him."

Jax met her gaze. "I wish I could say you have no reason to worry, but I'm afraid Laheene is spoiling for a fight, and he knows he can provoke Guy by criticizing Alan. Even worse, he may try to incite the kid by flaunting his claim on Ida." Jax shook his head. "I don't understand what she sees in Laheene, either, but it's her business."

Bella nodded. "I agree."

Jax hesitated. "Laheene gets to me, so I can understand the kid's issue with him."

Bella's dismay returned. Surely, Jax wouldn't let Cecil upset him. "You have a lot of self-control, far more than most people."

Jax didn't immediately reply. Instead, he briefly glanced away before looking back at her. "That's essential for a constable."

He had been restrained long before going into police work, but Bella withheld the observation. "I hope Guy pays attention to your advice."

"I'll speak with him again, but he reminds me a lot of Alan, and Alan had a cool head. Don't worry, Bella. The Ballantyne Fourball is the only major tournament in the state that's eluded Laheene. If he wants it badly enough, he'll avoid any shenanigans. Besides, he knows Mac would disqualify him in a minute if he caused trouble."

"You're probably right," Bella replied, "but disqualifying the man might cause a bigger problem. I wonder if he still holds a grudge since my dad tossed him out of a couple tournaments here."

"I don't know, but I've made some additional security arrange-ments. After Mac called me, I spoke with Richard Jenkins. He'll be here tomorrow and stay through the tournament. As you already know, Nolen will work full-time all week, which is a big help, too."

Relief allowed Bella to slump back in the chair. "That's good news." The young deputy usually worked only part-time except during big cases or busy times, and having retired Senior Constable Jenkins on hand would add an extra layer of protection.

"Try not to worry, Bella. Everything will be fine—in town and at Ballantyne."

"I hope there's no trouble anywhere." Once again, concern filled her. Jax, Nolen, and Richard would do their best to maintain calm during the tournament, as would the regular resort employees, but Cecil was a real creep.

"I hope not, too, but we're forewarned and forearmed." He offered a reassuring smile. "Now, I should get back to my office, and I know you have plenty to do, too."

Bella nodded. "Thanks for coming out this morning. It's probably good that Cecil saw you and knows you'll be here during the tour-nament." Relying too much on Jax wasn't a good idea, but he was fulfilling his role as constable. For that, she was grateful, yet anxiety remained. For most of her life, Bella had savored every moment of the various events at Ballantyne. Now, she only wished to get to Sunday evening without a hitch.

Chapter One

F our days later

Thursday, Friday, and Saturday had passed quickly for Jax. He was relieved that no problems arose while players and spectators jammed the town, but he remained on edge. Not only was the course at Ballantyne filled with people, but the establishments in Moreley were also all doing brisk business. Happy residents also flocked to the hotel restaurant, the café, and shops. People spilled into the streets each evening. The town council had revived the summer tradition of having a weekly concert in the park off Main Street. Jax was as pleased as anyone that tournament week was going well, but he would only relax when it was over.

He wasn't aware how obvious his worry and weariness were until hours before Sunday's final round when Richard Jenkins, a muscular man in his fifties, entered the constable's office. After one long look at the Jax, the older man said, "Son, you need to take a couple of days off after the fourball ends. You look exhausted." He paused for a moment. "Jenny was planning a big breakfast for us this morning, but you were gone when we got up. It's barely light even now."

"I woke up early. Since there was no sense in tossing and turning, I came to work." Jax forced a smile. "I'm sorry to have missed Jenny's home cooking, though." Richard's wife had come along, as she had the previous December when Moreley had its first murder.

Richard's gray eyebrows lowered a fraction. "She says you could gain a few pounds, so she's making some meals to get you through the coming week, at least."

"That's very kind of her," Jax said, ignoring the comment about his weight. He'd lost twenty pounds in France and hadn't gained more than a few back. Since the local bakery had reopened, his normal breakfast consisted of doughnuts and coffee, although he had to admit having Jenny cook eggs, ham, potatoes, and biscuits for the past few mornings had been a treat. As was having company.

"You were kind to let us stay in your home. It saved us driving back-and-forth to Karston every day. Not to mention that Jenny has enjoyed going to the tournament and seeing Bella."

"I'm sure Bella has enjoyed seeing her, too." Before the older man could mention Bella again, Jax hurried on. "Most of the players and spectators will leave right after this afternoon's round. The rest will leave in the morning, since the resort will close for a few days. Once everyone is gone, I'll take a day off myself."

The older man nodded. "Things have run smoothly, so there's no reason to be overly concerned. Yet, you appear to be."

Jax took another sip of coffee before answering. "Cecil Laheene bothers me. He and his partner are in contention for the tournament, and that's when he's at his worst." He had filled in the senior constable earlier in the week, so Richard had already heard about the troublemaker.

The older man frowned. "I've only seen Laheene in passing. He's got a terrible attitude that's obvious even in brief encounters. I can see why he riles folks up and gets them to act out. To this point, he hasn't tried to egg on young Brewster, has he?"

Jax shook his head. "No, and Guy has steered clear of Laheene, as far as I know."

"Your warnings worked. You've done everything you can to ensure the tournament is successful and that no harm is done to Ballantyne's image. Or to Moreley. You'll be at the course all day, and so will I. Nolen will stay in town for a while, but come out later. If Laheene gets angry at a caddy or competitor, we'll deal with it quickly and decisively. With his reputation, I don't think anything he says or does will have a lot of effect on the resort or the town."

The senior constable had said as much when they'd met on Thursday morning, but Jax couldn't shake his apprehension. "Guy and his partner are matched up with Laheene and his partner in the afternoon round, which concerns me. I plan to follow the group, so I can keep a lid on things, if necessary."

"That's a good plan."

"Even so, I'll be glad when today is over."

"We all will," Jenkins agreed. "Men like Laheene are everywhere, unfortunately. It's particularly hard when people feel free to act out because they have power and money."

During their initial pre-tournament meeting, Jax had revealed how Laheene's family connections helped him avoid consequences for his past behavior. His young deputy had been appalled, but Richard—although also disgusted—hadn't been surprised. "It is hard," Jax concurred, "and I suppose Laheene bothers me more because he's said nasty things about Matt Stewart and Alan Brewster. Not only that, he also had two run-ins with Bella's father, and Laheene is the type to hold a grudge and try to get even." The man's criticism of his best friend bothered Jax most of all.

"If he does anything, we'll be there to handle it. Right now, try not to borrow trouble," the older man advised.

"Good advice," he replied. And it was. But no advice would quell his disquiet. Only getting past the tournament with no problems would accomplish that.

On Sunday, as she had for the past few days, Bella rose quietly to avoid waking her friend. But Ida was already out of the narrow bed in the alcove of

Bella's room. Although Ida had originally planned to visit with her aunt, she'd accepted Bella's invitation to stay at Ballantyne.

"No need to creep around," Ida said with a smile.

"I guess not," Bella agreed. "Why are you up so early? You must be tired after walking the course morning and afternoon these last few days. On top of that, you've helped us when you weren't watching Cecil play."

Ida shrugged. "The fresh air and exercise are good for me. I've picked up a bit of weight since getting home from France, and Cecil has said he prefers slender girls."

Bella bit her lip to keep from saying Cecil's opinion was ridiculous. No one else would be foolish enough to think slim and trim Ida was too plump. Once again, Bella wished she understood why Ida put up with the man. Laheene wanted her to cheer him on him but, as soon as his round was over, he left her at Ballantyne and headed back to the hotel. Not once during the week had the man even asked her to join him for dinner. Only a few days ago, Ida had said Cecil was good to her and her parents; Bella had witnessed nothing to support the claim. "You still don't need to get up this early."

Her friend ran one hand over her auburn bob. Clearly, she hadn't been up long since her usually smooth locks were somewhat askew. "I didn't sleep well," Ida admitted, "so I thought I might as well help you get breakfast going. I appreciate you letting me stay here. It's nice bunking with you."

"It's like old times, and I've enjoyed your company."

"I've always envied you living in the inn. It's such a big, beautiful place and the view from your room is spectacular."

Warmth spread through Bella. She loved every inch of the three-story Georgian structure, which had been built by a wealthy industrialist some fifty years earlier. When he'd fallen on hard times, he sold the entire property to her paternal grandfather and Mac. The pair had been working in Cleveland as assistant golf professionals after emigrating from Scotland. Once they'd saved money, they'd searched for a place to build a resort with a golf course as the centerpiece. They'd found both the grand house and lovely grounds in north-central Ohio, only a few miles south of Lake Erie. "I was lucky to grow up here, and it's fun to have a roommate again, even for only a few days."

"We have roomed together a lot. Three years in college and two in France." Ida glanced around the suite. "The accommodations weren't nearly as lovely as this.

"The décor was Mother's doing." Bella followed her friend's gaze. The spacious suite had been hers since she was ten. Her favorite color had been pink. Her mother had suggested that dashes of a complementary rose would wear well over the years, and she had been right. The room was as appealing to Bella now as it had been fifteen years ago. Pretty and peaceful, it was a refreshing sight at the start of a day and a welcome retreat at the end of one. Just as importantly, the space reminded Bella of her mother's grace, care, and taste. More than anyplace else on the property, she felt Eliza Stewart's presence in this room.

"She had great taste," Ida agreed, "and this is a large suite. So nice."

"Our college dormitory room was crowded," Bella agreed, moving past bittersweet memories by a change in topic, "but our last billet in France made it look like the lap of luxury." At first, they'd had quarters in an elegant Paris hotel taken over by the YMCA. Later, they'd been close to the front where comfort wasn't a consideration. Working long hours, they'd spent little time in their cramped room, but the worst part had been hearing the booming artillery guns and knowing young men were fighting and dying only miles away. A shiver went through her. As always, when she thought of the war, Bella was reminded of Matt. Her beloved big brother's death had left a hole in her heart. The losses of her parents had left two more.

"I won't argue about that," Ida said with a smile. "Why don't I go down and make coffee? I'm not a very good cook, but my coffee is fine. I could also set the buffet and dining room table." Ida held up one hand before Bella could protest. "Please don't say I'm a guest. We're best friends, and I want to help as much as possible."

A rueful smile touched Bella's lips. "All right." She was lucky to have a loyal, caring friend like Ida. With her parents and brother gone, Bella valued Ida's support more than ever. The pair weren't related by blood, but they were sisters of the heart and soul.

Richard and Jenny Jenkins arrived about an hour after Bella went downstairs. As she had for the past three mornings, the senior constable's wife immediately put on an apron before greeting the other women. "Good morning, ladies." A bright smile tipped up the corners of her mouth and sparkled in her cornflower blue eyes.

"Jenny, you don't have to help us again this morning," Bella told her. "You should go out on the course and be a spectator today."

"I'll go out later, but I enjoy being part of this team," the older woman replied.

"We enjoy having you," Mary Rogers told her. The cook-housekeeper, tall but thin, had already been hard at work for over an hour. Her cheeks were pink from bending over the stove while wisps of gray-streaked hair escaped from her usual French twist.

In only a few days, the two older women had struck up a friendship, which pleased Bella. Mary and Jenny were of a similar age, although Jenny, with her blonde bob and stylish clothes, seemed younger and livelier. But she hadn't lost her husband and fallen ill with influenza herself. Although Mary had survived the disease, it had greatly weakened her lungs. Even now, Bella worried about her overdoing as did Nolen, Mary's son. She turned her attention to Jenny. "We all appreciate you assisting in the kitchen these past few mornings." She glanced from Jenny to Richard. "Can I get some breakfast for you?"

"No, thank you," he replied. "We already ate. Right now, I want to get on the course. Jax is already out there, and Nolen is in town until the last spectators leave for here."

"The final groups of this morning tee off in the next thirty minutes," Bella said. "There hasn't been trouble in town, has there?"

Richard shook his gray head. "No, not at all." He offered a reassuring smile.

Bella nodded, but anxiety remained. So much had gone awry in the past few years that she was always braced for another loss, another problem, another obstacle.

"Everything has gone well," Jenny said. "I'm sure today will go smoothly, too."

"I agree," her husband put in. "Now, I'll be off, but I plan to come back around mid-afternoon. I'll see you about three o'clock, my dear." His final words were directed to his wife. Then, he nodded to the others and went out the back door.

A half-hour later, Ida went to follow Cecil while the other women prepared lunch. With so many spectators, the dining room and large wraparound porch had been full each day.

By eleven-thirty, Bella and Jenny were serving their guests while Mary manned the spacious kitchen. Once the noon meal was over, Mary Rogers shooed Bella out. "You've worked very hard. Now, go watch the tournament. Mac will expect you to be ready for the awards ceremony later."

"Yes, dear," Jenny added. "I'll stay and help Mary

clean up."

"I thought you were going to go out on the course with Richard," Bella said.

"I will. But he and Jax are staying around the first tee until the last foursome goes off."

Fresh anxiety hit Bella full force. Cecil and Guy were playing together. As far as she knew, the pair hadn't exchanged words during the tournament. With luck, that would continue. She realized her worry was evident when Jenny spoke again.

"Things have gone well so far," she said.

Mary quickly agreed. "They certainly have."

Bella knew the older women wanted to reassure her, so she smiled while making a silent wish for calm to continue. Only a few more hours before the tournament ended. Then, if nothing went wrong, they could all look back on the event with pride and relief.

"Go ahead and enjoy some of the afternoon," Jenny said.

"Thank you. I will," Bella replied. At least, she would try.

After cleaning up and changing clothes, Bella headed outside. As she briefly stopped on the porch, she gazed out at the course where both players and spectators filled the grounds. Many events had been held at the resort since its founding, but the men's fourball was the oldest and biggest. Over time, the championship had drawn the best golfers in the tri-state area and even beyond. Most years, there were more entrants than slots—that was, until the Great War had taken many players to France, something that had forced Mac and her parents to cancel the event after 1916. Over the following three years, influenza had beset the area. On its heels had come a post-war economic downturn across the country. With fewer and fewer visitors, Ballantyne had become a faded lady. Sadness gripped Bella as she thought about the recent past before allowing her mind to go further back to happier days.

How many times had she stood in this same place on the last day of an event? So very many. On each occasion, awe and excitement had filled her. When she was small, Bella had cheerfully tagged after her father, grandfather, and Mac as they did their work, and she'd loved watching all of them com-pete. As she and Matt grew up, both had taken part in Ballantyne events. With very little effort, Bella could imagine her brother and Jax on the course. She could imagine, heart in throat, silently cheering them on, and she could imagine them supporting her when she took part in a ladies' event. One or the other had caddied for her many times. On a number of occasions, they'd celebrated winning. On others, they'd commiserated about losing. The good, the bad, and the mediocre were all better when shared. That thought sent regret surging through her. Those days were over. The economy would improve, but her parents and brother were gone forever.

With determination, she focused on the present and future. Everything had gone smoothly, and Bel-la hoped with all her heart that it would continue. While she desperately missed her parents and brother, Bella knew they would be proud of how hard she and Mac were working to restore Ballantyne. Perhaps, they were even looking down and sending good wishes.

As she descended the porch steps, Bella got caught up in the escalating excitement. She spent some time walking around the holes closest to the inn before heading to the eighteenth green. Around her, the gallery hummed with anticipation. With Cecil Laheene and Floyd Etting matched head-to-head against Guy Brewster and Sam Gardener, anything could happen, especially when the Ballantyne Fourball Championship hung in the balance.

Now, the four were the only golfers left on the course. Bella listened to the buzz of conversation from the gallery and felt a knot form in her stomach. She didn't want Cecil to win or cause trouble. Evidently, the latter hadn't happened yet, or she hadn't heard about it.

Match play could be exciting and dramatic. Most competitors kept their emotions in check as they directly faced their opponents. But Laheene wasn't like other players. Many people referred to golf as a gentlemen's game. As an avid golferette herself, Bella always added *ladies* to the description. Whether the contestants were male or female, proper etiquette was important in tournaments. Unfortunately, Cecil didn't care about good sportsmanship or proper manners. He only cared about himself.

After the final foursome hit off the eighteenth tee,

Bella saw Ida walking hurriedly down the rough. When her friend got close enough, Bella waved. Ida responded in kind.

Alarm filled Bella as she saw Ida's flushed face and glittering gaze. "Are you all right?" she asked. The two women stood together as the group got in place to hit their shots into the green.

"Yes, but I can't listen to Cecil berate Floyd any longer. Cecil played poorly on the front nine, and Floyd kept them in the match. Now, Floyd has three-putted three times on the back nine, and Cecil has acted horribly." She shook her head. "If they lose this hole, they'll lose the match and the tournament."

Bella's insides seemed to slosh around like boats bobbing in rough waters, which created roiling nausea. She swallowed hard. If Cecil came so close to winning and didn't, would he raise a ruckus? That seemed all too likely since he had in the past.

Preston Cherry, one competitor who had finished earlier, nodded as he came to a stop beside the two women. "Yes, they will. They need a whole point to tie Guy Brewster and Sam Gardener. If they manage to halve the hole and gain a half-point, they'll tie us for second place. Then, Guy and Sam will be the champions."

Mac, who had been greeting groups as they left the last hole, joined them in time to hear Cherry's proclamation. "A close tournament makes for an exciting end," he observed, but no smile formed on his lined face.

Excitement could be good, but not the kind that Cecil often evoked. "Where is Jax?" Bella asked as she looked around.

"I imagine he's on his way here since this be the last group, lass."

Bella swallowed over the lump in her throat. Watching instead of participating had to be hard for Jax. She scanned the gallery but didn't see him, so she turned her attention back to the fairway. Surely, he was nearby.

All four players reached the green with their second shots. Two were on the front edge, and the others were within fifteen feet of the pin. Applause erupted after each shot, but only Laheene's and Etting's opponents acknowledged the greeting.

"Cecil should stop chastising Floyd," Ida repeated, dismay undergirding every word. "It isn't helping."

Apprehension played along Bella's nerves as she noted the harsh expressions on both Laheene's and Etting's faces. As they got closer, it became apparent that they were involved in a heated exchange. Time seemed to tick away more slowly as she waited for the group to finish.

The crowd around the green grew silent as Etting lined up his putt. His young caddy stood behind him and gestured at a point by the cup. "Sir, there's not as much break as you might think. You'll only need to play the ball just outside the hole." His voice, although not loud, carried easily through the stillness.

Laheene, who was only a few yards away, snorted. "What the heck do you know?" The boy's eyes widened as if in surprise, but he had no chance to reply because the man spoke again. "Get out of the way." Laheene crossed the green to stand behind Etting. "Don't listen to the fool. You need to play three inches to the left of the hole."

"Cecil, step away," Etting, who stood a head shorter than Laheene, said in a voice that only spectators closest to him could hear.

Bella's heart thudded in her ears, and she crossed her fingers.

"Don't tell me what to do," Laheene shot back, his voice carrying far farther than Etting's had. "You haven't putted worth a darn all day and now you're listening to some kid who's probably never played in his life. I don't know why you hired someone from around here anyhow. Hick town with dumb hayseeds."

Those close to the exchange gasped, while Bella had to restrain herself from shouting at Cecil to shut up. What an awful, awful man. Once the tournament was over, she planned to talk with Mac about permanently banning Laheene from Ballantyne. How dare he insult her hometown and its residents?

"Get back, Cecil, or I'm picking my ball up right now." Again, Etting spoke in hushed tones, but his stony expression was evident.

"What? You wouldn't dare. Despite how badly you've played, we still have a chance to win." Anger flashed in Laheene's gaze.

"I meant what I said," his partner told him again. His voice rose with each word.

Bella, who was close enough to hear everything, felt another surge of nausea. Not now, she thought. Not when the tournament was almost over. Her gaze shifted to Guy Brewster, who, red in the face, looked as if he was struggling to keep from going after Cecil. Sam Gardener laid one hand on Guy's shoulder and said something that Bella couldn't hear.

Laheene swore under his breath, but he moved several feet back. Bella saw Etting inhale deeply before signaling to his caddy. The boy stepped back beside Floyd. This time, player and caddy whispered. She took a quick glance at Laheene, whose eyes gleamed with fury, and her trepidation escalated.

Bella was right to worry. As soon as Etting's ball spun around the cup to sit on the edge, Laheene loudly cursed his partner and the young caddy. Etting handed his putter to the boy. Before the caddy could put the club away, Laheene grabbed the putter and broke it over his knee. The sound of the hickory shaft snapping into two splintered pieces made Bella flinch. At the same time, a gasp went up from the gallery.

Mac immediately stepped onto the green. "That's enough. Get off the green, Cecil, and leave the course. Ye nay be welcome here any longer."

"I have no intention of ever coming back, old man," Laheene bit out. "Rinky-dink course, rinky-dink tournament. You might as well sell the place because you're never going to make it."

Bella joined Mac, but Jax suddenly appeared. "Do as Mac said, Laheene, and do it now."

"Go to hell, Hastings." Laheene's voice rang with disdain.

Jax's jaw tightened. "Laheene, Mac told you to

leave. Hit the road before you make an even bigger fool of yourself." A dark flush rose in Jax's face as he spoke. When another low buzz rippled through the gallery, Bella felt a sick, sinking sensation in her stomach. Jax needed to keep his head. Normally, she wouldn't worry about him losing control, but Bella had never seen Jax so furious, although he was clearly trying hard to restrain himself. What about Guy Brewster? Once again, her attention went to him, but he was shaking hands with Sam. Hopefully, celebrating their victory would keep Guy away from Cecil.

Laheene released a low sneer. "You and Stewart and Brewster were the fools. They're both dead, and you're too broken to play anymore."

"Cecil, please stop," Ida said as she hurried to his side. Pink colored her cheeks, and pain clouded her gaze. "Let's go."

Laheene wheeled on her. "Be quiet," he hissed.

"I won't," she replied in a soft, but firm voice, although her hands trembled. "Matt, Alan, and Jax are heroes. I won't listen to you degrade them."

His gaze narrowed on her. "You don't want to listen to me?" he asked in a cold, clipped tone.

"Not if you're going to be nasty." Ida lifted her chin and returned the stare.

Bella moved closer to her friend. She appreciated Ida's efforts to quell Cecil's fury, but the man's ire seemed to grow with every passing moment.

"Speaking the truth isn't being nasty," he shot back. "And you're the one who needs to be careful about what you say. I know things about your family that others don't, and I wouldn't forget that if I were

34

you."

The color drained from Ida's face, and she laid a hand on his arm. "Please, Cecil..."

"Now, it's *please?*" A humorless laugh escaped him. "I can ruin your family, and you better remember that." Then, he turned away, tossed his putter to his caddy, and stalked off.

Bella slipped an arm around her friend, who looked to be on the verge of tears. "Are you all right?"

"Yes," she murmured.

Jax followed Laheene, but Bella reached out and laid a hand on his arm before he got past her. "Let him go. The sooner he leaves here, the better." Beneath her fingers, she felt the tension in him. When he replied, Bella relaxed.

"You're right, but I need to get back to town in case he causes a hubbub there."

"I understand," she said, wishing and hoping nothing else happened.

Once Jax was gone, Bella turned back to Ida, who remained pale and shaken. "Maybe you should lie down for a while."

"I'll be fine," she said, "but I think I'll go to my aunt's house for now. I'll gather my things and be on my way."

"You're leaving?" Bella asked with disappointment.

"Yes, I think that's best. I'm sorry, Bella. Sorry for the scene and for Cecil acting so awful."

"It isn't your fault," she assured her friend. "And you don't have to leave." In fact, Bella hoped Ida would stay because she wondered how Laheene could ruin her family. Mr. Byington was a successful, respected businessman, and Mrs. Byington was involved in several charity organizations. How could Cecil hurt them? It made no sense.

"I appreciate that, but it would be for the best. I'll talk to you again soon. Thank you for your hospitality." Ida hurried off.

Torn between her duty as one of the co-owners of Ballantyne and her impulse to follow her best friend, Bella felt undecided and upset. Ida would be fine at her aunt's house, so Bella needed to fulfill her responsibilities as hostess of the tournament. She could call her friend later.

In the incident's wake, Mac stepped on the green to briefly speak with the three players left there. They putted out and headed off the course without further incident.

Although there was a low buzz of conversation between the last group finishing and the awards ceremony, the trophy presentation took place without a hitch. For that, Bella was grateful. She was even more appreciative when many of the players took time to say they had enjoyed playing the course and participating in the tournament. Despite Cecil's tirade, the event had been a success.

After the flurry of check-outs, their small staff—the Ironton twins and the two Molitor brothers—all admitted to fatigue, so they took sandwiches and cookies instead of staying in the kitchen to eat.

Carl Molitor had worked at the resort for more than fifteen years. His younger brother Curt joined him after returning from France. The brothers handled all course maintenance, along with caring for the grounds around the inn and cottages, which meant working long hours even without a special event. Dick and Dale Ironton, sixteen-year-old orphans, had only been employed since April, but they did many odd jobs and filled in where needed.

Since everyone else had left, Bella and Mac—as tired as their help—ate quickly with little conversation. Afterward, Bella suggested going to bed early. The old pro readily agreed.

After heading to her own suite, she settled on the window seat and gazed out at the property that was now hers and Mac's. A light mist had set in well ahead of dusk and, along with it, fog. Now, steady rain was falling. The cottages weren't visible, and Bella could barely make out the towering trees outside her window. She wondered if the low visibility would keep any of the players in town. Only a handful remained at Ballantyne, all in one cottage. For a time, she simply stared into the gathering darkness and let her mind rest.

At some point, she glanced at the nightstand clock, which read nine-thirty. Once she changed into her nightgown, Bella climbed into bed and settled back against the pillows. Fatigue overtook her, and she fell into a deep, dreamless sleep.

Chapter Two

When Monday morning dawned, Bella felt better—rested, restored, and relaxed. Despite Laheene's antics, the tournament had been a success. With the income from it, they could refurbish other parts of the resort, like the boats and tennis courts. They could even consider opening for the Christmas holidays, something that hadn't happened for several years. She hummed while dressing and went downstairs as the grandfather clock in the wide lobby struck eight. Although she was up later than usual, the inn remained quiet.

She headed toward the kitchen, only to be halted by the telephone ringing. Bella detoured to the front desk. She exchanged pleasantries with the operator, and when Jax came on the line, she greeted him warmly. "Good morning."

A brief silence preceded his reply. "I don't know how good it is." His voice was rough with something more than fatigue.

Abruptly, her buoyant mood evaporated. "What's wrong?"

Several seconds of silence ensued. "A couple of hours ago, Laheene's car was found at the bottom of the ravine off the main highway. He's dead."

"Dead?" Bella echoed as shock filled her.

"I'm afraid so."

Bella gripped the candlestick base and earpiece tighter. Although Cecil Laheene was a cad and a snob, she didn't like to hear about anyone dying. "How awful," she murmured. How long had he been in the vehicle? Overnight? Just since early today? "Did he leave this morning?"

"No," Jax replied. "According to Thaddeus Cooper, Laheene checked out of the hotel around dusk. By then, rain had started, and fog was still a problem."

Cooper kept careful track of all the guests at his hotel, so he wouldn't have mistaken the time. As she considered the news, Bella's heart pounded hard enough that she had trouble focusing on Jax's words. "Cecil lost control and went off the road?"

Again, Jax hesitated before replying. "I don't know, Bella. We found another set of tire tracks in the soft shoulder. One set is clearly from Laheene's Cadillac because they disappear partway down the creek bank in line with his vehicle. The other set is from a vehicle that got back on the highway. The driver might have forced him off the road. Whether it was accidental or intentional isn't clear, but there was another automobile on the scene as far as we can tell."

"You think someone ran Cecil into the ravine?"

Her anxiety returned with a vengeance.

"I'm afraid that's a possibility," he told her. "Richard was planning to go home this morning, but he's staying to help with the investigation. Right now, he's at the hotel interviewing the remaining guests. Nolen is contacting local boys who caddied to see if they know anything." Jax cleared his throat. "The reason I'm calling is that I need to know how many people who stayed at the inn or in a cottage checked out last night, and I need to speak with anyone who's still there."

Bella was quick to reply. "All the inn guests checked out yesterday. Most right after the awards ceremony, and the rest long before dusk. We didn't even need to serve dinner last evening." She paused for a moment as she tallied the remaining guests. "Only four people stayed overnight in a cottage. They were planning to play at Crystal Lakes later this morning, so they're still here. I'll tell them you want to speak with them. What time do you think that will be?"

"I can drive out now."

"They may not be up yet, but I'm about to make breakfast. If you haven't eaten, plan on having something here."

"Thanks, Bella. I'll do that."

After hanging up, Bella stood by the front desk. She had felt better thinking Cecil was out of the area, but he hadn't made it that far. While Bella would never have wished harm on Cecil, or anyone else, she knew few people would mourn his loss. The knot in her stomach tightened. Although vehicle crashes were becoming more and more common, this smash-up might not be accidental. What if it wasn't? What if someone had meant for him to careen off the road? Any death was dreadful, but could this one have wider repercussions? Business at the resort had picked up, but they weren't in the clear yet, and they didn't need another murder, if that's what this was.

When Mac came into the kitchen a few minutes after Bella's conversation with Jax, he was beaming. "Good morning, lass."

The knot in Bella's stomach doubled. She hated to spoil his merry mood, but he needed to know what had happened before Jax arrived. "Good morning. I have coffee made and muffins left from yesterday. I'll fix whatever else you want for breakfast—eggs, bacon, sausage, oatmeal."

"Curt and Carl will nay work today since the course be closed, so dinna bother with oatmeal. The twins are nay up, and I nay expect them to be soon. Muffins and coffee sound fine for now. Eggs and bacon will be good once ye have coffee, too."

Bella took a plate of muffins and two cups of coffee to the table and sat down. "Jax will be here soon, and I invited him for breakfast. I'll wait until he arrives to make the rest."

Confusion filled Mac's gray eyes. "I twould think the lad twould want to take it easy this morning. He had a long week coming out here while also taking care of his regular duties."

She cleared her throat. "He probably won't be taking it easy for a while."

A look of surprise crossed the old pro's face. "I hope they dinna have trouble in town last night."

"Not in town," she replied. With real reluctance, Bella summarized what Jax had told her.

Dismay replaced surprise on Mac's lined face. "The lad believes Laheene was intentionally run off the road?"

"He thinks it's possible, and so does Richard Jenkins. He and Jenny were planning to leave today, but he's going to stay and help. In fact, Richard is interviewing hotel guests. I don't know other details, but Jax will share more with us." Despite the hot cup of coffee in her hands and the warm air in the room, Bella felt a chill go down her spine while cold dread squeezed her heart. A questionable death could spell trouble.

Jax arrived minutes later. He tapped on the kitchen door before stepping inside. Bella immediately noted his drawn features and bloodshot eyes and hurried to offer him coffee.

"Thanks. That sounds good," he replied.

After getting a cup for him, Bella said, "Sit down. How about bacon and eggs? I was about to fix breakfast for Mac and me."

His weary gaze met hers. "That would be great, too. Richard and I left my house very early, and we've both been busy ever since. We grabbed doughnuts and coffee at the bakery, but that was hours ago." He crossed the room to join Mac at the table. The two men exchanged greetings before Jax went on. "I imagine Bella told you what happened to Laheene."

Mac nodded. "What do ye know about it?"

A heavy sigh left Jax. "We know another car was involved because the shoulder is very soft there, and another set of tire tracks is quite clear. On top of that, the back end of Laheene's car is visible and there's damage like it was scraped or bumped by another vehicle. It's possible that a driver tried to pass and lost control. Or Cecil could have been passing another automobile and done the same thing. It's hard to say until we gather more evidence. We can't see the front bumper or the car's passenger side due to the water level."

"Then, it could be an accident," Bella said as she placed the food, plates, and cutlery on the table before pouring more coffee and sitting down herself.

"It's possible, but the other driver had to know Laheene went off the road, yet he or she didn't stop," Jax responded before taking another sip of coffee.

"*He or she?*" Bella repeated his words in dismay. "Do you have suspects already?"

Jax shrugged. "I was at the hotel with Richard for a while after we got back from the scene. Laheene left last night. His car wasn't noticed until shortly after dawn today. No one passing in the dark would have seen the broken shrubs and trees, so that's not surprising." He took a bite of his eggs before continuing. "The crash probably occurred shortly after he left the hotel because there would be no reason for him to dawdle on the road. The weather was getting bad. Even in town, you couldn't see more than a few hundred feet ahead."

"Do ye know if anyone left around the same time Cecil did?" Mac asked.

"From what we've learned so far, several people checked out about then. I was at the hotel long enough to find out that Floyd Etting and Guy Brewster did." Jax cleared his throat. "According to Thad Cooper, Guy was checking out when Laheene came down, and they had words again. People heard their voices, but no one got all of what was said. Floyd came down shortly after Laheene got in his car. Their voices were raised. Again, people got only bits and pieces. Bits and pieces indicating they both thought Laheene should reap what he's sown. That was the general summation, not an exact quote."

"So, you have two suspects," Bella noted with increasing dread. She didn't want to think either Guy or Floyd would have harmed Cecil. An accident seemed better, but why hadn't the other driver stopped? Surely, the person must have known Cecil went off the road.

"No, we have at least four." Jax moved his attention to his coffee and stared into the brown liquid. Seconds ticked away before he continued. "Ida didn't go straight to her aunt's home when she left here yesterday. She showed up at the hotel later to speak with Laheene. We don't know where she was between the time she left here and got there. Also, Thad wasn't sure when she left the hotel because he got sidetracked helping his wife prepare box meals for guests who were checking out and wanting food to take with them. Ida could have taken off thirty minutes before Laheene, or right before he did. Bertis, the desk clerk, said Ida was crying when she arrived, and he heard them arguing in the hall before she went into Laheene's room. He couldn't make out their words, though. Unfortunately, Bert went off-duty not long after she arrived, so no one was at the front desk for a while."

As Bella listened, her trepidation increased. Everything Jax said tied the accident to someone who had been at the fourball. Even worse, her best friend was on the list of suspects. "I can't believe Ida would try to harm Cecil, or even be in an accident without reporting it. I can't believe Guy would, either." Or maybe she simply didn't want to believe either one would force Cecil off the road or drive away from a crash. Ida had been terribly upset with her suitor. Had she tried to pass him in the rain? Had he tried to pass her? Both seemed possible and, if either had happened, Ida might have panicked. The same could be true for Guy. Leaving the scene of an accident was bad, but certainly not as bad as forcing another driver into a ravine.

"Ye said ye have four suspects. That be only three," Mac observed.

Jax laid his fork down. "I spoke with several players at the hotel this morning. One was Preston Cherry. He knew more about this year's incidents involving Laheene and a lot about a major one last summer." Jax leaned back and folded his arms across his lean waist. "He actually witnessed Laheene raising a ruckus at a couple of tournaments. We already knew something about those. Much worse, Preston also told me about Laheene going after a caddy at his club last summer."

Shock and dismay assailed Bella. "Why?"

"For no good reason," Jax replied. "The boy took a shortcut from one hole to the next. He had to walk across some stones in the creek, and he slipped. Most of the clubs ended up in the water, and Laheene went on a rampage. He cursed and chased the boy, who fell a couple more times. Laheene's playing partners forced him to stop."

"Is the lad all right?" Mac asked, his own disbelief clear in both his tone and expression.

"No. He was badly injured from falling into the rocks. From what Preston told me, the kid uses crutches to walk," Jax said, his tone and expression somber.

Bella gasped. "That's terrible. Was Cecil charged with assault?"

Jax's jaw tightened. "You know his father is very influential, so he stopped any charges. In any case, charging Laheene would have been doubtful, since he didn't actually touch the kid. Of course, that was mostly due to the other men in his group. After he was threatened with suspension from the club, he paid the boy's medical bills, but that's all. Nothing for more assistance."

"Is he so badly hurt that he needs continuing care?" Bella asked. Threatening anyone, especially a young boy, made her sick at heart.

"Unfortunately, it seems that way. From what Preston heard, Chipper couldn't go back to school.

Evidently, he has trouble walking, even with crutches," Jax replied. "Preston didn't know all the details, but the boy got his injuries from falling, so Laheene said he wasn't at fault. If he didn't come from a wealthy, powerful family, he might have gotten charged. Hard to say."

"That's just awful. The boy probably wouldn't have fallen and been badly hurt if Cecil hadn't chased him," Bella murmured. "Aren't the Laheenes going to give them more money? They should."

"Aye, the man needs to make sure his son's victim has proper care," Mac agreed.

With one finger, Jax traced the rim of his coffee cup. "I agree, and they might have." When he glanced up, a troubled expression covered his face. "Preston said Mr. Smith, Chipper's father, attacked Cecil. He was arrested and convicted of assault. Now, the elder Smith is in prison."

Bella gasped. "That makes the whole situation even worse. I'm sure he was very upset about his son, but Cecil couldn't have been hurt as badly as Chipper. He could play golf, and he looks fine. Looked fine," she corrected. It was hard to think of him being dead.

"No, Laheene wasn't badly injured, but Mr. Smith went looking for Cecil, caught him off-guard, and got in some punches before he was stopped. Once again, old man Laheene used his influence—this time, to get Smith charged and tried," Jax revealed with a frown.

"I ken Smith's anger," Mac put in, "but nay his actions. Going to prison dinna help his family."

"I agree," Bella added. "It's terrible, but what does

it have to do with a fourth suspect?"

Jax looked from Bella to Mac. "One of the caddies who came from Cleveland is the kid's older brother. His name is Chaz Smith. He and Laheene had words in the lobby shortly after the tournament. When I left the hotel a bit ago, we hadn't been able to determine when Chaz left."

The news only added to Bella's apprehension. "Having his brother be badly injured and his father go to prison certainly gives him the motive to go after Cecil, especially if they argued. Do you know if the boy drove to Moreley or did he come with someone else?"

"Thad said Chaz has his own vehicle, an old junker," Jax replied. "The kid may not be a good suspect, but I need to talk with him. Hopefully, tomorrow. Today, talking to your help and guests is enough. On my way back to town, I'll stop at the accident scene, too. The water is high due to last night's heavy rain, but that bend of the creek goes down almost as fast as it rises. Seeing more of the Cadillac could help, especially if there's additional damage from a collision. We only have the barest facts right now, but a lot of them. Putting them into some semblance of order is necessary, and extra details could help. I took notes already, and I'll add Richard's information later." As Jax rubbed his right bicep and shoulder, a pent-up breath left him.

Bella watched him with concern. Was his shoulder in such bad shape that taking a few notes bothered it? His war wounds were an impediment in several ways. Of course, as Mac had observed only a short time ago, Jax had already had a hard and long week, which certainly didn't help.

When he spoke again, his voice was rough with exhaustion. "You said everyone checked out of the inn well before dusk." He scribbled in his notepad between bites of bacon and eggs.

"Yes, that's right."

Jax nodded. "That will eliminate them, although I'll probably have Nolen call each one later. If you could make a list of names and addresses, I'd appreciate it."

"Of course," she replied.

"Thanks, it's not a top priority. Unless one of them was waiting for Laheene, it's doubtful they know much. The crash had to be an hour or more after they left here. I want to talk with the four remaining guests as soon as possible, though."

"They need to come here to check out. That could be soon since they indicated they wanted to leave around nine-thirty, and it's almost that now. Do you want to use the library to interview them?" Bella asked him.

"If you don't mind," Jax replied.

"Of course not." She hesitated for a moment before continuing. "I can take notes for you again."

"That seems like a fine idea, lass." Mac's voice broke the silence.

Jax nodded. "If you can spare the time, Mac is right. It's a good idea."

His quick acceptance telegraphed the depth of his discomfort and fatigue. Jax never accepted help unless absolutely necessary. Even then, he often hesitated. "We're closed for the next three days, so I have nothing but time," Bella said. "Mrs. Rogers and two ladies from town will be here around noon. They'll clean the rooms and such. The twins will help with the heavy work." Although she would pitch in later, Bella didn't want to miss what was said during the interviews. Participating in two previous investigations had only increased her interest in detective work.

"If you two don't mind, I'd like to ask you both a few more questions before I speak with your guests." After Mac and Bella readily agreed, Jax glanced at her and said, "I'll take notes while I ask you, Bella. Then, you can take over when I talk to Mac and the guests. The same with the twins. Talking with Curt and Carl can wait a bit. I know they spent most of their time on the course."

She simply nodded.

"You already told me that only four people spent last night here. Did any of those who checked out yesterday mention Laheene?" Jax asked.

"Not to me," she replied. "The twins helped carry bags to cars, so I didn't speak with each guest separately."

"Is there anything or anyone standing out to you regarding Laheene?" Jax asked. "Something said or done."

Bella bit her lower lip as she searched her mind for clues. "I'm sorry, but nothing I observed after the awards ceremony was related to him."

"That's fine." Jax handed the notepad and pencil to her before turning his attention to Mac.

"What about you? Did you see or hear anything related to Laheene? Anyone who stayed late after checking out? Anyone who mentioned a personal gripe with him?"

Mac narrowed his gaze as if he was focusing on the events of the previous evening. "I can nay say that anyone stayed much beyond check-out. The twins and I went back to the pro shop after the awards ceremony. A few players stopped to comment favorably on the condition of the course and such, but all of that was closer to the end of play. Nay much after that because I closed the shop around seven."

"Did any discuss Laheene?" Jax asked.

A frown formed on Mac's weathered features. "Only a couple brought up the incident on eighteen green."

Bella briefly stopped writing and looked at Mac. "Who talked about it?" Anxiety played through her. She didn't want any guests, competitors, or spectators leaving Ballantyne with bad feelings or negative comments.

"Floyd Etting be one of them. He apologized for Cecil's behavior," Mac replied.

"What did he say exactly?" Jax posed the question.

Again, Mac looked pensive before answering. "He said he'd nay partner with Laheene again, and the man should be barred from tournaments. Floyd also said twas unlikely to happen since old Laheene provides a large donation any time Cecil causes a problem. That keeps the welcome mat out for him."

"Was Floyd upset, or did he simply offer the information?" Jax wondered.

A low, humorless laugh left Mac. "Still pretty mad. He faulted himself for letting Cecil take his original partner's place. Said winning should nay be so important to him, and he'd learned a good lesson."

"Who else mentioned the incident?" Jax's expression remained tense.

"Preston Cherry. He was sorry Cecil made a scene and indicated he was just as fed up with the man's behavior as Etting. Preston was nay as emotional as Floyd, though," Mac told Jax.

He pulled out his pocket watch before looking back at Bella. "Are the twins around?"

"Yes, but Dick and Dale are still sleeping. I can get them. Go ahead to the library," Bella said. The boys lived in the former housekeeper's room just off the kitchen.

"Thank you," Jax said before looking at Mac. "Thanks to you, too, and don't worry. We'll get to the truth as soon as possible."

Bella knew Jax wanted to reassure them, but another worry came to mind. "Does Cecil's father know about the accident?"

A line formed between Jax's brows as he nodded. "I called him as soon as I got back to the office from the crash scene." He put two fingers to his forehead as if trying to stem a headache. "We spoke briefly."

"What did he say?" Bella asked when he didn't continue.

"He plans to hire a detective agency. He's giving me until the day of the funeral to find the killer." Jax's voice was emotionless, but his gaze blazed with green fire.

"There's no need for that," she hurried to say. "You've already solved two murders, and we don't even know that Cecil's death wasn't accidental."

A harsh breath left Jax. "Mr. Laheene insists it had to be murder. He's sure the culprit is someone who hated his son."

"Twould be a long list," Mac added.

"That's true, but no detectives are needed." Bella looked at Jax. "You're investigating."

Jax shrugged. "Mr. Laheene thinks I'm biased. Evidently, Cecil telephoned the man, told him about our encounter a few days ago, and made it sound like I issued a threat."

Bella shook her head. "That's ridiculous. You only saw him for a few minutes in the parking lot." Had Cecil called his father mainly to complain about Jax? Or did the two speak often? She supposed it didn't really matter, but she felt aggravated on Jax's behalf.

After glancing at Mac, Jax returned his attention to Bella. "The two of us spoke in the pro shop before then."

"I don't believe you threatened him," Bella asserted.

"Ye be right, lass. Jax and Cecil exchanged a few words. Nay more."

When the men traded a long look, Bella wondered what they weren't saying. "What happened?"

"Laheene wondered if I was playing in the tournament," Jax hurriedly replied.

Too hurriedly to Bella's way of thinking. Was he hiding the content of their conversation? If so, why? She looked at Mac, who was nodding. Perhaps, despite his self-control, the query had bothered Jax, but the grim expressions on the two men's faces gave her pause. What weren't they revealing? Slowly, an idea emerged. "Did he mention my brother? Did he say something bad about Matt?"

Jax's green eyes glittered with some emotion. "There's nothing bad to say about Matt."

His expression and voice were as hard as steel. When Bella looked at Mac, she saw his countenance appeared much the same. "Neither of you would let a negative comment stand. Not even a minor one." When a flush rose in Jax's lean cheeks and Mac smiled, Bella knew she was right. "Thank you," she murmured, her throat suddenly clogged with emotion.

A low, audible sigh left Jax. "Matt wasn't only my best friend; he was like a brother to me. Plus, he was one of the finest men that I've ever known or ever will know."

Bella managed a tremulous smile. "He felt the same about you."

Jax frowned. "I'll wait in the library while you get the twins." Then, he left the room.

After a moment, Bella turned to Mac. "Jax doesn't like to talk about Matt."

The old pro nodded. "When your Grandfather Stew died, twas hard for me to discuss him for a long, long time. Ye were a wee one, so ye probably dinna recall."

"Not too much," Bella agreed. She remembered her grampa's death, but not the reactions of Mac, her parents, or her grandmother.

"Twas difficult to lose him. Still tis," he admitted. "But ye dad, ye grandmother, and I were with Stew when he left us. Jax dinna have that gift."

Tears pricked the backs of Bella's eyes, and she

blinked hastily to clear them. "No, he didn't, but I'm so glad Curt was there." Curt Molitor, her brother's platoon sergeant, had held Matt as he was dying. Now, he helped his own brother as the assistant greenskeeper at Ballantyne. Both were good workers, which was important, but more than that, Bella welcomed any tie to Matt.

"As am I, lass. As am I."

With one hand, Bella swiped away any lingering moisture. "I'd better get the twins," she said before hurrying away.

Jax headed to the library. The talk about Matt had gotten to him, as any reference to his best friend did. Regret rose hard and fast but faded much more slowly. Luckily, he had about ten minutes before the twins arrived with Bella. By then, he'd rallied his defenses. As they entered the room, both boys, their almond brown hair tousled, looked sleepy.

"I'm sorry to get you two out of bed, but I need to ask a few questions that might help with the current case," Jax said. He started to provide an explanation but was cut off.

"Bella told us," Dale replied. "I didn't even see Mr. Laheene yesterday. Neither of us did."

"That isn't important, and it's not why I want to speak with you," Jax told the boy. "What I need to know is, did either of you see or hear anything about Mr. Laheene or the incident around the last green?" Jax kept his voice well-modulated in order to offer reassurance that he didn't suspect them of wrongdoing.

"A couple of men who come into the shop to talk with Mac did. I didn't hear all of it, but they said they was sorry Mr. Laheene shot off his mouth." Dale glanced at his brother and back at Jax. "Mostly, we was helping folks get their clubs in their automobiles and running back and forth to the inn for suitcases and such."

"Did you hear anything more, Dick?" Jax asked.

"Some friends who caddied told me about the set-to. They said some other stuff about Mr. Laheene," the boy replied.

"Like what?" Jax asked. He hoped the pair might provide a clue to move the investigation forward. With old Laheene's warning hanging over him, he felt pressured to solve the case. Laheene had also threatened to besmirch Ballantyne and Moreley if someone wasn't arrested for murder within the week. Jax hadn't revealed that part of the conversation to Mac and Bella because they didn't need the added burden. Nor had he disclosed the industrialist's threat to get Jax fired.

"That he's mean and talks terrible to the caddies and even his partner." Dick grimaced.

"I see," Jax murmured. As clues went, it wasn't much, but it confirmed what he already knew. "Anything else that might be helpful? Anyone say something threatening?"

Dale and Dick exchanged a glance before shaking their heads. "No, sir," Dick replied.

"Nope," was Dale's answer.

"Thanks, boys. I appreciate your time," Jax said.

"Is that all?" Dale inquired in clear confusion.

"Yep. You're free to go back to bed," Jax said with a smile. "If it's okay with Bella."

"It is," she put in. "The work can wait until later or even tomorrow."

The boys, their youthful faces now slack with relief, nodded in response before leaving the library.

"They didn't know much," Bella observed.

"No, but Nolen is contacting all the local kids who caddied."

"That's a good idea. The caddies often see and hear things that the rest of us don't."

Their conversation was interrupted by a tap on the door. "The four gentlemen who stayed overnight be about to check out, but I said ye want to speak with each of them, lad. I can send the first one in if ye be ready," Mac said.

"Please do," Jax said.

Chapter Three

Those interviews did not take long. The group had been together all evening, and each man served as an alibi witness for the three others. While they had observed the scene on the eighteenth green, none had any additional knowledge about Cecil's previous clashes, nor had any of them had personal run-ins with the man.

"No suspects among these men," he commented to Bella. Jax leaned forward to pull at the bottom of one pant leg and then, on the other.

Bella's attention followed his action. For the first time, she realized his pants were damp from the knees down. "Did you go into the ravine this morning?"

He nodded. "I wanted to closely examine the car, which wasn't really possible. As I said, the creek is way up. Nolen and I got Laheene out. That was a bit of a chore with the front end and passenger side underwater."

"You and Nolen carried him up the bank?" No wonder Jax bowed to accepting help so easily. Undoubtedly, his shoulder and arm were hurting after hauling Cecil out of the vehicle. Her thoughts returned to when he'd lifted and carried her after she'd been kidnapped by a killer in April. Doc Smedlay had suggested a sling, but Jax balked—as he probably would now. "Wasn't that a strain for you?"

For several moments, he remained silent. Finally, he said, "The driver-side door was clear, so we managed pretty well."

Since he wasn't apt to admit if additional damage had been done to his arm, Bella moved the conversation back to the case. "Earlier, you said Mr. Laheene is threatening to hire detectives after the funeral. Did he say when the service would be?"

"Thursday."

She studied his troubled expression. "That gives us a few days, and maybe Mr. Laheene will change his mind. After all, you're investigating as quickly as possible."

"That doesn't matter much to Laheene. He expects people to ask *how high* when he says *jump.*"

"No wonder Cecil was such a loathsome person. His father sounds just as bad, maybe worse."

"I met him a few times, and worse sounds about right." Jax glanced at his pocket watch. "Richard will be finished at the hotel soon, and I want to talk with him and Nolen about putting our information together."

"Do you think having Richard Jenkins will be enough help? It sounds like you'll have to interview a lot more people, maybe in Cleveland."

"We have a big job ahead of us, but he'll make a real difference. He did with the last two cases."

His reply didn't address her last statement. Bella considered reiterating it but hesitated. Richard, not Jax, had supported her involvement in the two previous cases. Perhaps, she'd be wise to rely on his support now instead of asking Jax about going along to Cleveland. "Yes, he did," Bella agreed. "Is Jenny helping, too?"

"She went to the hotel with Richard to take notes for him." Before Bella had a chance to speak, he hurried on. "Why did Ida decide to leave yesterday? I thought she'd stay until this morning, at least."

Bella closed her notepad and studied his face. Something in his expression disturbed her, and his question added to her discomfort. "Why did you think she'd stay?"

"Answering a question with a question isn't really answering at all," he pointed out.

The response further annoyed Bella. Why was he questioning her friend's actions? She knew Ida well, and she couldn't be responsible for Cecil's crash. Could she? Bella wouldn't have thought Ida would ever step out with a man like Cecil Laheene. Had grief changed her friend? Bella shook off her doubt. "Why are you asking?"

"That's another question," he said with a chuckle.

Any other time, Bella would have welcomed his amusement. Unfortunately, his query seemed far from casual. "Honestly, Jax, you can't possibly think that Ida forced Cecil off the road."

His humor fled. "I don't want to think so, but he

could have been following her and tried to pass. After all, they argued and we both know Laheene had a hot temper. If Ida was ahead of him, he might have wanted to show off or scare her. In the rain and gathering darkness, he could have lost control."

Bella folded her hands together at her waist as anxiety rose again. "If that happened, with Ida or someone else, would the other driver be in trouble for taking off?"

Jax ran one hand through his blonde hair. "Some trouble. Leaving the scene of an accident is a felony in New York. The penalty in Ohio isn't as severe. Certainly not as bad as purposefully running him off the road." His gaze narrowed on her. "You haven't answered my question. Do you know why she left immediately, why she later went into town, or why she was so upset?"

The questions made Ida seem like a serious suspect, as did Jax's tone, which Bella considered his *constable's voice*. "I'm not sure. From what I witnessed, Cecil treats her terribly. When she called the other morning, Ida said he was good to her and to her parents. I didn't ask what she meant, but I was hoping he'd changed." Uncertainty gripped her. Surely, Ida had done nothing wrong.

A frown furrowed his forehead. "That doesn't make sense. He threatened to ruin her family. What do you think he meant?" Jax asked.

"I have no idea. Like I just told you, she made it sound like he'd changed."

His eyebrows rose a fraction. "Really? You're her best friend, and you have no idea of what he meant."

Annoyance hit Bella hard. "Do you think I'm lying

to you?"

His green gaze moved away and back. "I didn't say that."

"No, but you intimated as much. I know we aren't as close as we once were, but I wouldn't withhold important information from you." Briefly, he looked as if she'd struck him. But why would her honest admission hurt Jax?

"I know you wouldn't. I just thought...I mean, sometimes, we keep secrets for our friends because they want us to."

The urge to ask if Jax was keeping confidences for Matt rose in her thoughts. What could her brother possibly have wanted to keep a secret? Was it another friend who had confided something to Jax? After a moment, Bella brushed the foolish questions from her mind and concentrated on the present debacle. "I don't know why Ida hurried to leave. Maybe to go to the hotel and break off with him."

"But she didn't go straight to town. According to what Thad Cooper said, she showed up a while later. Closer to when Laheene left."

"I know nothing about the delay, either, but I still think she went to break things off. After the way he acted, I would have." Not that she'd ever get involved with a man like Cecil Laheene.

"I suppose that's possible. You're certainly right about how he treats—treated—her. However, even if they parted ways, it doesn't mean I don't need to speak with Ida."

"I understand." The statements were undeniable, but another idea rose to mind and came out with no forethought. "At least he didn't die here," Abruptly, heat bloomed in her cheeks. "Oh, that sounded awful."

Laughter rumbled out of Jax. "Awful, maybe, but definitely true."

After a moment, Bella couldn't help but chuckle, too. "Don't tell anyone what I said."

He winked. "It's our secret."

Her heart lifted. His reaction was typical of the old Jax. For a moment, she simply enjoyed the lighter atmosphere and his good humor. "How about more coffee and some muffins? Curt and Carl should be along in a short time. Last night, they planned to come up by eleven o'clock. You could wait for them in the kitchen."

"That sounds like a good idea," he said, stifling a yawn.

A frown furrowed her forehead. Before she considered the wisdom of her words, they were out of her mouth. "You look completely spent, Jax." When he opened his mouth to reply, she hurried on. "Please don't say you aren't. It's obvious. You don't take very good care of yourself." His fatigue was only one issue. Helping haul Cecil out of the ravine could have done more lasting damage to his arm. Didn't he have any concern for his own well-being?

"I hope the town council and mayor aren't as observant as you are. If they think I'm not up to the job, they may fire me."

Bella shook her head as worry filled her. "They don't care if you work yourself to the bone." Or injure himself crawling into a ravine and carrying a dead body. What if he'd done more harm to his shoulder and arm? Had he given a moment's thought to that possibility?

Suddenly, his gaze—steady and warm—met hers. For several moments, neither of them spoke or moved. "And you do?" Jax asked.

The question, made in a rough murmur, hung heavily in the air between them. All nonchalance disappeared. Her heart jumped into her throat as Bella realized how her comment might sound. Too personal. Too interested. If she could, Bella would retract her words. But it was too late.

A knock on the library door interrupted her train of thought and their stilted impasse. "Come in," she called, grateful for the intrusion.

Mac stuck his head inside the room. "Lad, Constable Jenkins is on the phone. He'd like to speak with ye."

"Thanks, Mac. I'll be right there." Briefly, he turned to Bella. All traces of emotion had fled. Once again, he was the staid and stoic lawman. "Thank you for taking notes and thanks for the offer of coffee and muffins, but I should get back to town. If you can type up the material, I'll have Nolen pick up your transcription when he drives his mother out later today. He can also interview Curt and Carl. I don't know that they'll have a lot to add, but he can see."

Abruptly, without providing a chance for her to respond, he was gone. Bella's regret about expressing concern for him multiplied. They got along, for the most part, but they weren't close anymore. Not like before the war. Not like before Matt died. Despite Jax's intention to be a substitute big brother, stated months ago, he was mostly absent from her life. Usually, she felt like she'd come to terms with the change. Then, they'd be together, and he'd be like his old self before withdrawing, as he just had.

Bella took a bit of time to gather pad and pencil before regaining her composure and leaving the library. As she did, she reminded herself not to express deep concern again.

When Bella entered the lobby, she found Jax still on the phone. She waited until he finished and then, asked, "Any news?"

"Not a lot," was all he said.

His terse reply and stony expression irritated Bella because she felt sure there was some news. She was just as sure he would not share it. Not now, at least. Why had she gotten personal? Should she fall back on his plan to be like a sibling? If Matt was still alive, Bella would fret about him. Should she make the comparison? The green ice in Jax's gaze froze that budding idea. Her brother had never given her so chilly a look. "I see."

"I need to get going." Jax turned away but stopped when she spoke again.

"Let me put some muffins in a basket. Even if you don't want any, Nolen and Richard might." She sounded as distant as he had and, instead of giving him a chance to answer, Bella hurried to the kitchen.

Once Bella was gone, Jax felt Mac's gaze on him and

shifted from one foot to the other. He cleared his throat but didn't know what to say, so he remained quiet.

"Have the two of ye had another spat?" the pro asked.

The older man's question made Jax feel like an errant schoolboy. "Not really." That was true. He and Bella hadn't disagreed. Instead, she'd shown real anxiety for him, and he'd allowed himself to briefly savor it before realizing how imprudent that was. What had he been thinking to ask if she cared about him? That question slipped out before Jax regrouped. Any sign of interest from her was appealing but dangerous. Dangerous to the barrier he'd built between them. To regain control, Jax had been cold and dismissive. But what other choice was there? He'd given up any hope of a future with Bella when he'd let her brother die.

"Then, what? Tis clear the lass is upset with ye."

Jax ran one hand over his face. "I didn't do anything to cause it," he protested, although that wasn't precisely true. It was more his foolish question and quick regret over it. He'd compounded the situation by saying he didn't want a snack anymore. Discouraging her had been his intention, but Bella seemed to take his response as a personal rejection. It wasn't. Being at Ballantyne every day for the past week had made Jax yearn for the old days and his dead hopes, which left him far too vulnerable to her compassion. Even if Matt was still alive, Jax had no future at Ballantyne or any place else—not as a golf pro. Not with the damage to his arm and shoulder.

Mac's gray gaze narrowed on him. "Why do I nay

believe that, lad?"

A hot flush rose in his face. He'd never been able to get anything past Mac. Neither had Matt. By the time the two of them had turned ten, they'd given up. Why was he trying now? "Bella is the soul of kindness, which is a wonderful trait, but I don't deserve it." There, the admission—at least part of it—was out in the open.

For several moments, Mac simply looked at him. When he finally spoke, his voice was soft and subdued. "She cares about ye, Jax, and I think ye care about her."

The observation from the old pro wasn't completely new, but Jax's pulse pounded wildly. Was he so transparent? If so, he needed to repair the damage before it got worse. The two of them had no future, but he couldn't explain why to Mac. Or to Bella. They would be sickened by his behavior. He certainly was. "Of course, I do. She's my best friend's little sister. Bella and I have always had a good relationship. Besides, Matt wanted me to look after her." The words sounded hollow even to his own ears. The last was the truth, but not the entire truth.

Mac shook his gray head. "Maybe ye want to fool yeself. I dinna ken why."

Jax's shoulders slumped with defeat and dismay. Unable to maintain eye contact with Mac, he looked at the closed kitchen door. "Things happened in France. If she knew…if you knew. I doubt either of you would welcome me here."

Mac's gray gaze narrowed on Jax. For several moments, he studied the younger man's face. "Lad, I'm not asking ye to share it with me. As I said, the lass cares for ye as more than her brother's best friend, more than as a replacement for Matthew, and she has for some time."

The observations made Jax squirm. "It's not only that." With thumb and forefinger, he pinched the bridge of his nose. "Bella needs someone to be a full partner in the resort. You need someone like that. I can never fill that role, Mac. Not now."

"Ye still have nay seen the surgeon."

A harsh breath left Jax. "I've talked to him, and I will see him. The surgery probably won't solve the entire problem. He said as much on the telephone."

"I ken that getting all the shrapnel out is nay likely."

Fresh frustration gripped Jax. What he'd learned from Doc Smedlay's friend wasn't surprising since the man had echoed the prognosis provided by doctors in France. "It's not only shrapnel. I caught some right before the armistice, but a few weeks earlier, I got hit in my upper arm. A bullet tore into my right bicep. The muscle was damaged." Since coming home, he hadn't admitted the severity of the first injury to anyone except Doc Smedlay. Until now.

For long moments, the old pro gazed steadily at Jax. "Does the lass know?"

"She knows I was wounded twice. The first time was only days before Matt died, so she had other things on her mind."

Mac nodded. "Ye have nay told her how bad the wound to ye arm was?"

"It wasn't so bad really, just did damage to the

muscle." A lot of damage. Too much for him to ever play golf competitively again. Making that major admission proved to be difficult.

"Bad enough to keep ye from pursuing ye dreams."

"It's not only my wounds in the way of those," Jax admitted.

"I know ye are nay ready for a tournament now, but maybe next year."

Jax looked at Mac in surprise. Only days ago, he'd as much as said he wouldn't partner with anyone new. Once again, a lump of sorrow formed in his throat. "Even if I get back to the game, I couldn't play without Matt. It wouldn't be right." Just the suggestion made him feel slightly ill.

For a moment, the old pro studied Jax's expression. "I know ye two were very close, but there's nay right or wrong about going ahead with ye life, lad. Ye are here, and Matthew will nay be again."

Jax's attention went to the photograph above the fireplace mantle. He stared at the image of Matt and himself, taken right after they had won the 1916 fourball. Guilt and regret were overt forces as he studied his friend's grin. "I couldn't play with another partner." The words were barely audible, even to his own ears.

Mac laid one hand on Jax's shoulder. "If ye were in a French grave and Matthew be here, I'd tell him the same thing." He paused for a moment, as if letting the idea sink in. "We always remember and treasure those who are lost, but we have to continue with our lives, too. In fact, we live for them when they're gone. Tis what I do for Stew, and now for

Archer and Matthew."

A heavy sigh left Jax as he looked at the older man. The warm weight of Mac's hand grounded Jax in a way that he hadn't experienced in three years. His usual urge, to move away from any emotional discussion, ebbed. Mac had suffered many bereavements in his long life. His best friend and partner, Stew Stewart, died too young, as had Stew's son Archer and grandson Matt. Bella's mother had also been gone before her time. Before those deaths, Mac's young wife had perished. A man who had lived so long and lost so many might understand Jax's internal battle.

Abruptly, the urge to reveal his role in Matt's death hit Jax with potent force. For several seconds, he considered the idea before dismissing it. "You and Stew were as close as Matt and me," he observed, focusing on what Mac had said.

"Aye, lad. Like brothers. When he died, I wanted to sell my share of the resort to Bella's parents and leave, but Archer said he needed my help. He asked if I could stay long enough for him to get settled into running the place alone. He was Stew's son, but the closest I had to one myself, so I agreed." He chuckled and stepped back, releasing his hold on Jax's shoulder. "Then, one reason after another came up, and I stayed longer. Finally, I realized this be my only home, and Stew's family be my family. I think twould make him happy that I nay left, and I think twould make Matthew happy if ye reconsidered ye future."

Jax blinked in confusion. "I'm not sure what you mean, Mac."

"Think about it, lad. It will come to ye." He smiled a cryptic smile. "Ye need nay play a lot of golf to be a club pro."

The words were so much like ones uttered by Bella last spring that Jax wondered if the partners had discussed him. Ever since then, her offer—to work at Ballantyne and be the next head professional—came to mind far more often than was wise.

Reconsider his future. Was that advisable? Jax had settled for being the town constable. Could he resurrect some of his old dreams? Should he try?

Any further conversation was cut off by Bella's return. She brusquely thrust the carrier at Jax. "Have Nolen give the basket to his mother. She can bring it back with her."

Her blank expression and flat tone stung him. She was hurt, and he was at fault. Despite what Mac had said, Jax wasn't ready to tell Bella the truth—not about his injuries and not about Matt's death—and he wasn't sure he ever would be. And he'd made promises to his friends, both Alan and Matt. So much was on his shoulders. The burden was getting heavier, but Jax didn't know how to lay it aside without creating a burden for Bella, which was something he would never do. He swallowed hard and forced a smile. "Thanks, Bella. We all appreciate it."

Jax took the basket, nodded to Mac, and walked out before he said more.

Chapter Four

Mrs. Rogers drove herself to Ballantyne that afternoon, which meant Nolen wasn't there to take the notes back. Bella figured Jax probably didn't need them right away, so she arranged for the older woman to perform the task at the end of the day.

Part of Bella wanted to take them herself because she wondered if there was more news about La-heene's death. However, she didn't want to know badly enough to ask Jax. His sudden dismissive attitude earlier had hurt, especially since he was the one who asked an emotionally laden question. Of course, that had come after her too personal comment. Why hadn't she simply said, *Of course, I care. I cared about Matt's welfare, and I care about yours.* Jax wanted a sibling relationship, and Bella had agreed to it. Too bad she hadn't realized the pitfalls along the way.

Aggravation and weariness dragged on her like

leaden weights. The fourball, while successful and exciting, had taken a toll. Bella had felt better first thing this morning, but Laheene's suspicious death added anxiety. So did her friend's odd comments and involvement, not to mention the friction with Jax.

While Mrs. Rogers and the two hired women got to work on chores, Bella went to her desk. She didn't have a lot of paperwork, so finishing it in a short time would be easy. And, just as importantly, it would fill her mind with matters other than the cause of Cecil's death and the repercussions.

As the clock in the lobby struck two, the telephone rang. Bella exchanged greetings with the operator, who quickly connected the call without revealing who was on the line. Usually, the woman did. "Ballantyne Inn. How may I help you?"

"Bella, it's Jax."

Sudden suspicion assailed her. Had Jax asked the operator not to say who was calling? Did he think she'd hang up on him? Annoyed, Bella waited for him to speak again. When he didn't, she was forced to continue. "How may I help you?" Repeating her greeting made it sound like she was talking to a stranger, but she didn't care. He acted like a stranger at times.

Something that sounded very much like a sigh echoed over the telephone line. "Nolen just told me that his mother drove herself to work, so he didn't get your notes. I hate to bother you, but could you bring them to the office this afternoon? I thought Nolen would talk to Curt and Carl while he was there, but we can postpone that. Right now, we have a lot of other leads to follow, which means none of us is free to drive out to Ballantyne today. I could really use your typed transcription, though."

His insistence seemed strange since not much had been learned during the interviews. Bella wanted to say she was too busy to rush into town, but she didn't want to hinder a police investigation out of personal pique. Especially one related to the resort. Even so, Bella let a moment pass before she responded in a flat, disinterested tone. "Yes, I can do that."

"Thank you," Jax replied. Silence filled the line for what seemed like an eternity. "I need to interview Ida. I just called, and she said this afternoon would be fine." He cleared his throat. "I wondered if you could go with me. Not only would it help if you took notes, but I also think she'd be more comfortable with you there. She's still at her aunt's house, so it wouldn't take us long. We'd most likely be gone less than two hours, and it would help if you did some of the driving."

Realization hit her. This was his real reason for calling. Jax wanted her to go with him to see Ida. As she twisted the phone cord around one index finger, Bella considered her reply. Once again, she wanted to refuse, but he was right about her friend being more at ease if Bella went along. "Yes, I can go."

"Thank you, Bella."

"It will be a half-hour before I get there." Her voice remained chilly.

"That's fine. Take your time," he assured her.

Bella said nothing more. Still annoyed with him, she simply hung up the phone without a goodbye.

Thirty minutes later, Bella pulled her Model T into the open parking spot next to Jax's Chummy. Surprise rippled through her when she saw him standing on the car's passenger side.

"I thought you might like to drive both ways," he called as she got out of her vehicle.

Bella hesitated on the sidewalk for a moment. She'd expected him to take the wheel for part of the trip since it wasn't far, but he knew she enjoyed driving. Jax had let her get in the driver's seat once, and she'd exclaimed about how much fun it was to drive his sporty Chevy roadster instead of her sedate Model-T sedan. The knot of resentment that had tied her insides in knots since morning loosened. Maybe he wanted to make up for his abrupt withdrawal. Whether or not he did, driving the Chummy was a treat that Bella couldn't resist.

"Yes, I would love to." Jax hurried to the driver's side and opened the door for her. "Thank you," she murmured.

Within moments, they were headed out of town. Driving the roadster was pure pleasure. Bella sped up once they reached the main road. The wind whipped her short bob, but she didn't mind at all.

The breeze was wonderful, and she felt completely carefree. "I'm glad you put the top down." It was hard to stay aloof when she was having so much fun.

"I am, too. It's not something I do much anymore. I've thought of selling the Chummy since a sedan might be more fitting for a constable."

Her gaze skittered briefly to him and back to the road. "I think the Chummy is perfect, but if you decide to make a change, maybe we could trade."

A low laugh left him. "Maybe," Jax replied, but he didn't sound very interested in the idea.

Bella relaxed. Perhaps the trip would be more pleasant than she figured. If she didn't express any personal concern toward him, they might manage better. With that in mind, she went on. "Have you gotten any other leads?"

"Not really," he replied. "We made a list of people to interview in person. Some of them aren't likely suspects, but they may have important information. I called Guy this morning. He was playing golf, but his father said he'd be there tomorrow. I didn't say why I was coming, and Mr. Brewster didn't ask."

"Interesting," Bella murmured. "Was Richard able to find out anything more about Chaz Smith?"

"He's made some calls, and he's waiting for people to get back to him. He has a friend who retired from the Cleveland Police Department recently. The man may know something worthwhile. Richard will probably spend most of the afternoon in the office and on the telephone, which is a big help. I just wish it didn't take so long to make long-distance calls."

"It's a process, and operators do the best they

can," Bella said.

"I know, I know," he replied. "I'm not blaming the operators, but every call eats up a lot of time, which is frustrating."

"It can frustrate for operators, too. I know I got aggravated at times."

"I'm sure you never let it show."

"No, I didn't," Bella said, "and neither did my sister operators. We knew every call was crucial to the war effort, and we did the work as quickly and efficiently as possible."

"You ladies were much faster than the men you replaced," he observed.

The observation was accurate, and it filled her with pride. Because she didn't want to embark on a discussion of the war, and doubted Jax really did, Bella moved to another topic. "What is Jenny doing?"

"My mother's garden is in terrible shape and has been since I got back from France. The kid who was doing the lawn and checking the house moved away with his family before I returned. Now, I get the grass mowed, but that's about all. Anyhow, Jenny noticed the weeds. I didn't want her working, but Richard says she loves to putter in their yard. Since he's tied up in the office, he doesn't need her assistance this afternoon."

"That's kind of her, and I'm sure she'll enjoy being out on such a lovely day."

"I hope so. It's been nice having them stay with me. The house is big for one person. I'd sell it, but there are still a lot of empty houses in town to let or buy."

A long sigh left Bella. "At least, the hotel and bakery have reopened, along with a few other establishments. If we can sustain our business for the rest of the season, that should help everyone." Success might hinge on figuring out how Cecil Laheene had died. If it was just an accident, someone leaving the scene wasn't such a terrible thing. If the smash-up was intentional, that could cause problems. Especially after two previous murders in less than a year. Bella's first concern was saving Ballantyne, but Moreley depended on the resort, too. Some businesses had reopened, and more planned to do so...if the resort flourished. If not, what would become of the area? The question was always at the back of her mind.

"Probably so. It's certainly what everyone is counting on," Jax said.

As they continued along the main highway, Bella downshifted. "The crash site must be coming up. Do you want to stop and see if the water has receded?"

"I looked after I left Ballantyne, and it hadn't gone down much. Let's wait and check on the way back. Another hour could make a little difference."

"All right." When Bella saw broken shrubs and tire tracks, she couldn't help but wonder about the accident. A sick sensation rose inside her. Cecil Laheene had been a haughty cad, yet thinking of him careening into the ravine and to his death made her shudder. She hadn't asked if he might have survived the crash, only to perish in the surging water. "Do you know if Cecil died right away?" she asked in a hushed voice.

A moment's hesitation preceded his reply. "It looked that way, but Doc is doing the autopsy this afternoon. He'll have a better idea afterward. Old Mr. Laheene had a Cleveland mortician call. Of course, he wants the body as soon as possible since the funeral is already scheduled."

"If Mr. Laheene really believes the crash was intentional, you'd think he'd realize that you might need to keep the body longer."

"He doesn't care. Like I said, he expects people to dance to his tune and do it quickly. According to the mortician who called, there will be a second autopsy in Cleveland."

"A second autopsy." Bella shot a glance at Jax before focusing on the road again. "That's not necessary."

"Lionel Laheene thinks it is," Jax replied. "Besides, he'll want a report to give his detectives if he hires some."

The frustration in Jax's voice made Bella frown. "You'll probably solve the case before the funeral." She hoped so.

"Maybe," Jax said, but he didn't sound optimistic.

Chapter Five

During the last part of the drive, neither of them spoke. Weariness and frustration hampered Jax, and he didn't want to do or say anything that would make Bella worry more. Her optimism about the case being solved quickly was misplaced. They had clues and suspects. Too many of the latter for him to be confident.

When they arrived at their destination, Jax hurried to open the driver's door for Bella before following her up the front walk. He stopped on the first porch step as Bella rang the bell. When the door opened, Jax moved to stand behind her as his gaze went to Ida. A tentative smile touched her lips, but she was clearly nervous.

"Please come in," she said in a voice that wobbled. "Can I get either of you anything? Coffee? Tea? Lemonade?"

Both Bella and Jax declined the offer and followed Ida into the small, but tasteful, parlor. A loveseat faced the fireplace, now fronted with a pretty needlepoint screen. Two Queen Anne chairs, their upholstery faded with time, flanked it.

Ida stopped by the loveseat. "Please make yourselves comfortable."

Jax took one of the chairs while Bella settled next to Ida. She patted her friend's hand. "I'm sure all of this came as a terrible shock."

"Yes, it did," the other woman replied in a low murmur. "Someone called this morning to say there had been an accident." Her gaze went to Jax. "When you phoned later and said it might be intentional, I was stunned. The rain was heavy, and the roads must have gotten slippery. Luckily, I made it here before the worst of it, but I'm sure it would have been easy to slide off if a driver was speeding, and Cecil loved to drive fast no matter what the conditions were."

The words tumbled out in a rush, which only reinforced Jax's conclusion about Ida feeling anxious. Not only that, much of her statement seemed to be rehearsed. If Ida had gotten here before the worst weather set in, why was she so sure conditions contributed to the crash? Summer storms were often hit-or-miss. Even if heavy rain had fallen in her aunt's area, how could Ida be certain the same was true around Moreley? Since he didn't want to ask her outright, Jax made a statement. "The evidence at the scene leads us to think it might not be an accident, but we won't make a final determination right away." He paused for a moment. "As I said on the phone, I have a few questions for you, and Bella is going to take notes for me," he concluded in what he hoped was a pleasant, non-accusatory tone.

Ida looked at her friend with a weak smile. "All right."

Bella retrieved the pad and pencil from her bag. She patted the other woman's arm again. "Don't worry, Ida. Everything will be fine."

Jax frowned. While he didn't consider Ida a strong suspect, he wished Bella hadn't offered what could be false encouragement. "You left Ballantyne shortly before Laheene. According to Thaddeus Copper, you arrived at the hotel a while after Cecil did, though, and went upstairs right away. At least one person heard the two of you arguing in the hall before you went into the room. Is that right?"

A slight tremor rippled through the redhead. "I got partway here and turned around. I wanted to talk with him. After what happened on the last green, I knew I couldn't continue courting with him. When I got to the hotel, I went upstairs because he'd already told me his room number." Pink surged into her cheeks as she glanced from Jax to Bella. "I know that seems improper, but I didn't want our discussion shouted to everyone in the place. Cecil can be so loud."

Bella patted Ida's hand. "I understand. No one will think poorly of you."

When Bella shot him a look, Jax added to the reassurance. "No, of course not."

Ida nodded, but the flush remained on her face. "Cecil acted awful when he and Floyd finished their round. Neither of them played well. Even so, they stayed in the match. Cecil put all the blame on Floyd. He was so nasty. You both heard some of it."

"Yes, he was," Jax agreed before waiting for her to continue, but Bella spoke instead.

"That wasn't the first time I've seen him act that way." Bella looked at Jax. "He was just as bad a few years ago when he partnered with Lucius Columbine. The two of them were tied with you and Matt going into the last nine holes. Then, you won on eighteen by holing a long putt."

Her words made Jax smile and, for a moment, he forgot about the intervening years and the task at hand. He and Matt had celebrated with glee. "It was a great day, and you're right. Laheene went after Columbine. I thought the two of them might come to blows; it was that bad." Jax paused briefly. "Laheene wasn't happy with Matt and me, either. He couldn't even congratulate us."

"I was there with Alan," Ida put in, "and I remember it, too." Her hazel gaze clouded. "I guess I pushed that from my mind until yesterday."

"It was a while back," Jax said. "I've heard Laheene has acted up at other tournaments this season, and last year, he went after a young caddy who got hurt in the incident."

Ida looked from Bella to Jax. "That was before I started seeing him, and I only heard about it last week. Cecil made excuses, of course. He said a lot of the boy's ongoing troubles were because he tried to run off, fell in the creek bed twice, and wasn't taken to a doctor right away. Cecil made excuses for his behavior at tournaments this year, too. I know I must seem very foolish for getting involved with him. It's just that...well, you heard what Cecil said about ruining my family. That's another part of why

I went to see him. I wanted to reason with him, but he was even meaner at the hotel. He said much crueler things about Alan and about my father." Her eyes filled with tears, and she hastily brushed away a few that slid down her pale face.

Bella squeezed her friend's hand. "Why would Cecil say terrible things about your father? How could he ruin your family? It doesn't make sense."

A shuddering sigh escaped Ida as she glanced from Bella to Jax and, finally, to her clasped hands. "My father lost a lot of money in the stock market. To cover his losses, he borrowed from an unsavory character at a very high rate of interest. His debt quickly escalated. He isn't quite bankrupt, but he's very close. Because of that, he and Mother want to see me settled as soon as possible. They're afraid if people know how impoverished we are, we'll all be shunned. Then, I might never get married. Even worse, without Cecil's money, my father couldn't have paid off any of the loan." She plucked at her skirt. "Cecil is...was...always very gentlemanly in their presence. He was quite charming to me at first, too. My father didn't like him coming around because he'd heard about Cecil's reputation. But Cecil was so ingratiating and pleasant. I thought he might have changed, and, after a while, my parents did, too. Because of our financial situation, I felt pressured to let him court me. Then, he started having tantrums at tournaments and, as I said, I heard about the incident with the young caddy only recently..." Her voice trailed off. "By that time, Cecil had given a lot of money to my father, so I didn't know what to do."

"That's why you said he'd been good to you and your parents," Bella said with sudden understanding. No wonder her friend put up with Cecil La-heene. Desperation did terrible things to people, and her friend had clearly been desperate. "I'm so sorry about your father's money troubles. I had no idea."

"Hardly anyone knows. My parents quit the club, but Father told people he can no longer play because of his health. My mother seldom went unless there was a big social event. She's always busy with her charities, although she won't be able to do that now." Ida bowed her head. "I'm afraid they'll have to sell the house, too. It will be a blow for all of us, but bills have mounted. My parents said it would help if I was married, especially since Cecil would have given them more money, to pay off bills and to find another home. I've only played in tournaments this year when Cecil gave me the funds. Of course, I felt I owed him after that and after he helped my father."

"I see," Bella replied, and she did. Her friend had been and still was in a terrible situation.

Ida folded her trembling hands in her lap. "I should have told you and Guy. I know he felt angry and betrayed when I started to see Cecil. I should have explained that no one could ever take Alan's place." Her voice broke on her deceased fiancé's name.

Again, Bella laid a hand on the other woman's arm. "You can still tell him. He'll understand."

Anxiety filled Ida's hazel gaze. "You don't think Guy was responsible, do you?"

"I don't know. I hope he isn't." Jax paused. He was

already saying too much, but poor Ida needed some reassurance.

"I wish I had broken things off with Cecil sooner," she said in a small, thready voice.

"Is that why you argued yesterday at the hotel?" Jax inquired.

She nodded. "I said I couldn't continue to see a man who acted so badly. He laughed in my face. Right from the first, I had to tell him why I wasn't competing anymore. When I did, he seemed sincerely sorry for me and offered to pay my expenses for the tournaments. There aren't so many for ladies, but going is expensive. Then, my father needed money to pay debts. Neither my father nor I should have accepted the money. Even worse, I should never have listened to Cecil disparage Alan, but because of my situation, I forced myself to ignore the ugly comments. I shouldn't have done that. Alan deserved to be defended and respected."

Jax briefly hesitated before speaking. "He would understand, Ida."

Her tear-filled eyes focused on him. "Do you think so?"

"I know so," he assured her. "He would be sorry to have you in this position, but he'd definitely understand."

Some of the tension drained from Ida as she slumped back in the loveseat. "I told Cecil at the hotel that I didn't want to see or hear from him again."

"What did he say?" Jax asked.

Ida swallowed convulsively. "He said I owed him all the money that he'd paid for various entry fees, as well as my lodging at tournaments. He said my father needs to repay him, too. I told him it would take time, but we would. I've modeled a little again, so I have some pin money, and I'm going to look for a teaching position for the coming school year. I told Cecil that, and he said I better do it quickly or he'd tell everyone about my family's dire straits."

Bella focused on her friend. "Oh, Ida. I'm so very sorry. I wish you had told me about your family's situation."

Ida shrugged. "I'm embarrassed, Bella. My parents are embarrassed, especially my father. He feels like he's let Mother and me down. He never really liked Cecil, despite Cecil trying to be pleasant to him and Mother. It's been hard for Father to see our courtship."

"There are other eligible men," Jax pointed out.

Ida's hazel gaze went from Bella to Jax. "Yes, but Cecil said he'd pay off Father's debts, which are substantial, and he'd started to do that. Few other men have that kind of money," she replied with sad certainty.

"I can't argue with that," Jax said. Few families were as wealthy as the Laheenes.

"Do you have other questions, Jax?" Bella asked.

"No, I don't." Jax turned his attention to the other woman. "I may need to speak with you again, and I'd like to talk with your aunt, just to verify that you got home when you said."

Ida's eyes, still wet with tears, widened in anxiety. "You don't believe me?"

"It's not that. It's my job to get the facts, all of them. I can't skip that because you're a friend, Ida.

I hope you understand." When she nodded, Jax continued. "When do you think your aunt will be home?"

"Around supper time," Ida responded.

"I'll call then, but please don't tell her. It's important that she not feel pressured to be less than honest."

Bella scowled at him. "Jax, is that really necessary?"

"I'm afraid so. I want to completely clear Ida." He glanced back at the redhead. "I shouldn't say this, but we've known one another a long time, and I don't think you ran Laheene off the road. Even so, I can't go on with what I think or feel. I have to have solid proof."

"I understand," Ida murmured. "Do I need to stay in the area?"

Jax shifted in the chair. "I think that would be best."

"Why?" Bella couldn't keep the dismay out of her voice. "Ida has done nothing wrong."

Color surged into Jax's face when he met Bella's gaze. "I already said I have to do my job."

The single sentence hung heavily in the now-quiet room until Ida broke the silence. "I suppose I can stay, although I was planning to pack tonight and leave first thing in the morning. My cousin Arnold is coming with his family, and there are only three bedrooms. Aunt Florence insists that the two children can sleep on the floor on blankets, but I don't want to put anyone out."

After a last glare at Jax, Bella turned back to her friend. "You don't have to go home. Why don't you pack and come to Ballantyne? You could stay as long as you like."

"That is kind of you, Bella, but I can't pay, and I won't be a burden." Ida offered a wobbly smile.

"You don't have to pay, and you couldn't be a burden," Bella assured her friend. "In fact, you could help. We're closed for the next three days, but the weekend will be busy."

Ida chewed her lower lip as if in thought. Finally, she spoke again. "If I can really be useful, I'd love to come."

"You really can be useful, and I'd love to have your company for as long as you want to stay," Bella said with a smile. "If you don't want to follow us back now, come later today."

"I'd like to wait until after my aunt returns. She's been very kind to open her home to me, but I feel like a burden here, too. My uncle didn't leave her very well off. She has the house, but not a lot more." She bit her trembling lower lip. "In the meantime, I can pack and be ready to leave right after she gets back."

"Wonderful," Bella replied with a smile. "I just need to take Jax back to Moreley, get the Ford, and head to Ballantyne. I'll be there long before you arrive, so your room will be ready. As fun as it was to share my suite, you'll have your own space since we won't be as crowded for the rest of the season."

The friends hugged. "Thank you, Bella. Thank you so much."

Chapter Six

O nce Bella and Jax were outside, he paused. "That's Ida's car, isn't it?" He gestured toward the Buick roadster at the side of the house.

"Yes, it is. Why?"

"I want to look." Jax didn't wait for her reply. Instead, he headed toward the vehicle.

Bella hurried after him. "Why?" she repeated.

He went around the automobile and studied it from every angle. Because Bella wouldn't like his answer, he hesitated to reply. Finally, he glanced at her. "Because Laheene's car probably collided with the other vehicle. You already know there's a dent on the rear fender. I'd like to see if this roadster has damage." He continued his appraisal but was aware that Bella stalked back to the Chummy. When he finished a thorough examination, Jax joined her.

She started the car and got back on the road before speaking. "Was there damage?" Her clipped, cold tone dripped icicles.

"No," Jax admitted.

"What do you think now?"

Neither her voice nor expression softened. Didn't Bella understand he disliked being the bad guy? Or that he especially hated questioning her best friend? Evidently not. Or maybe she was still peeved about their earlier contretemps.

"I haven't changed my mind, and what I said to Ida is what I think. I am highly doubtful that she's involved, but my opinion can't enter into the investigation. That's why I have to be especially careful, Bella. I knew Laheene, Ida, and Guy fairly well. I've also known Etting on a casual basis. I don't want anyone saying I've played favorites. If someone is charged and goes to trial, I don't want him getting off because I did something wrong."

Silence echoed around them before she replied. "You're right. I know it can't be easy for you, either."

"The whole job isn't easy for me," he admitted with a rough sigh.

Again, Bella paused before speaking. "I know it isn't your first choice of careers."

A low, humorless laugh left him. "There's no sense in pretending it is, but I'm lucky the mayor and council hired me. I honestly don't know what else I could do." As soon as the words were out, Jax regretted them. Before Bella reiterated he could be a club pro, he hurried on. "I still want to stop at the accident scene, if you don't mind."

"Of course not."

Relief filled him when she didn't mention the job at Ballantyne. "I'd like to see the water level. I'm sure it hasn't completely receded, but I'm hoping the front end will be visible soon. If possible, I'd like to look at the vehicle while it's still in the ravine, since pulling it out might disturb useful evidence, like dislodging the fender."

"I suppose it will be a hard task," Bella observed. "How do you plan to try?"

"I already spoke with folks at the filling station. They've looked and agreed that it won't be easy, but they can do it. Maybe not right away, though, which is a concern. The water level is a big issue. I know Laheene's father will insist on having his detectives see the accident scene. He may want us to leave the vehicle there, but I can't wait on his whims." Irritation underscored each word.

"He hasn't hired anyone yet," Bella pointed out, "and he may not."

"Maybe not," Jax replied, but he figured Laheene would do whatever he wanted, whenever he wanted, just like his son.

Within a short time, they approached the crash site. As they did, Bella shifted into a lower gear. Jax spoke before the Chummy came to a complete stop. "Wait here. This won't take long."

Before Bella could respond, he jumped out and darted across the road. Annoyance flickered through her, but she ignored his statement and followed him to the opposite shoulder. "I just want to look. I won't get in your way," she said when he gave her a sidelong glance.

"There isn't much to see." With one hand, he gestured at the car, laying nose down and tilting to the passenger side. "The water is down about half a foot since early this morning, but the front fender is still submerged and maybe stuck in the mud. The water will need to recede more to be sure."

As Bella gazed at the vehicle, she understood why hauling it out would be difficult. While the gully was only thirty feet deep, the creek was running high and fast. In addition, it had a muddy bottom that only dried out after a long arid spell. "Getting Cecil out of the car and up the embankment couldn't have been easy." Again, a shiver ran through her. What a terrible task for Jax and Nolen. Both men had seen dead bodies in France. Both, she knew, had gone into No Man's Land to fetch fallen comrades. Had retrieving Cecil brought back ugly images? Another glance at Jax revealed the hard set of his jaw. When he turned toward her, the bleakness in his eyes and rasp in his voice answered her question.

"It wasn't easy, but everyone should be respected in death. Even Cecil Laheene, so leaving him there wasn't an option." Jax clenched his jaw. "There's nothing to be done here at the moment. We'll have to wait until tomorrow to examine the scene in more detail and remove the Cadillac. The water should be close to a normal level by then. Unless we get more rain."

As Bella continued to study the vehicle, she noticed the dent in the rear fender. With one hand, she gestured toward it. "You said another car could have hit Cecil, but it's hard to tell from here if there was a hard collision."

Jax followed her gesture. "Nolen and I looked more closely when we were down there. The damage is from some light impact with another vehicle, but we don't know for sure that the dent wasn't there before Sunday night. So far, no one we've interviewed can say whether it was or wasn't. We've gotten some clues, but a lot of questions still need to be answered."

"Maybe some important evidence will arise tomorrow."

"That's my hope."

When Jax absently massaged his right bicep and shoulder, Bella realized climbing into the ravine and getting Cecil out had taken a significant toll on him, whether or not he admitted it. Recalling their earlier exchange, when he clearly hadn't appreciated her concern, she withheld the observation and walked back to the Chummy. Once Jax settled in the passenger seat, Bella drove on. "Do you really think seeing the front end of the car will help?"

"I don't know, but we may find marks left by another vehicle. If we could match up dents and dings, that would help a lot. Hopefully, there's not too much damage to the Cadillac from crashing down the embankment."

"Still a lot for you to investigate," she murmured.

"Exactly," he replied.

His tone clearly telegraphed exasperation that echoed inside Bella. Solving the case before Cecil's funeral didn't seem as likely as she had earlier thought.

Within a few minutes, they were back in Moreley. After she parked the Chummy on Main Street, Bella turned to Jax. "I might as well transcribe my notes before I go home."

Jax nodded. "That would be good. Richard and I plan to go over all the information yet today. Having the ones from Ida's interview will be useful. Then, it will be easier for me to fill him in."

When they went into the office, Jenkins and Nolen were behind the counter. The older man had a notepad in his hands. "I'm glad you're back."

The strained expression on Jenkins' face troubled Jax. "Is something wrong?"

"I'm afraid so," the man replied. "My wife's mother fell and injured her ankle. It may be a break. As far as we know, it isn't bad, but we need to head home as soon as possible. I'll try to get back tomorrow, but I can't stay and go over the case notes. Jenny needs to be with her mother, and she probably won't be with me when I return."

Both Bella and Jax expressed their sympathy. Then, Jax went on. "Don't worry about anything here. We'll manage."

"I will be back, son. If not tomorrow, the next day—unless my mother-in-law has complications. Right now, it doesn't sound like it's bad. Jenny will stay with her, but once they're settled, I'll be free to help you wrap up the case. I know you need to go to Cleveland tomorrow to speak with young Brewster and possibly others. That means Nolen won't be free to help with the investigation since he'll have to do the regular duties. I'm sorry for that because it puts a lot of pressure on both of you. On the plus side, I got some new information that might be useful. I was just jotting it down, but I have time to go over it with you right now if you like."

"Good," Jax replied. "Bella is going to transcribe the notes from Ida's interview."

Jenkins smiled at Bella. "You are so much like Jenny. Taking notes and knowing shorthand are helpful, of course, but you also have great insights like she does. You were certainly instrumental in solving the Schwarz and Monticello cases."

Conflicting emotions hammered Jax. While what the senior constable said was true, it was also unsettling. Managing Bella's participation was difficult enough without Jenkins heaping praise on her. Since Richard had offered similar compliments in the past, Jax felt the man was knowingly promoting Bella. He just wasn't sure why. In the spring, he and Richard had spoken briefly about Bella. Jax had revealed as little as possible about any feelings he harbored, but the other man was astute.

Bella smiled. "Thank you."

Jenkins smiled back at her. "My wife considers her help to me as an avocation."

"I hadn't thought of it that way," Bella said in a thoughtful tone.

The exchange bothered Jax. "You already have a job running Ballantyne with Mac. If you wanted a second vocation, you could be a French teacher like you planned to do when you went to college. Of course, you also have experience as a phone operator." He recognized the tartness in his voice, but Jax didn't like the idea of her getting involved in dangerous situations, which he'd said more than once. Jax couldn't believe she'd completely put last April's kidnapping behind her. Although a repeat was unlikely with this case, she ought to be a little less anxious to get entangled in a homicide case.

She gave him an odd sidelong glance. "I'm not looking for another job. I just want to help, if I can."

"That's commendable," Jenkins told her. "I know we all appreciate it." As he said *we*, his gaze went to Jax.

Jax felt properly chastised. Richard had stopped short of suggesting Bella accompany him to Cleveland, something Jax was considering. Having her with him was preferable to leaving her to do her own digging. "I'm sure you want to get on the road, so why don't we go over your new information?" He turned toward his office, but the senior constable's next comment stopped him.

"I can tell you right here. One of my friends who retired from the Cleveland Police Department called back a short time ago. After Laheene chased and threatened Chipper Smith last year, the boy's father, who was evidently a heavy drinker, sought Cecil out and attacked him. We knew Smith was arrested for assault, tried, and convicted but, according to my friend, the man couldn't afford a decent attorney. Otherwise, he might have gotten off. At least that was the talk in the department."

"More confirmation that Laheene's father used his influence in getting Mr. Smith convicted," Jax observed.

"My friend says his contacts think that's highly likely. Evidently, it wasn't the police as much as the prosecutor and judge who pushed the case," Jenkins told him. "The other item of interest was that the elder Smith was let out early. My friend isn't sure why."

"So, we may have another suspect." Jax shoved both hands into the front pockets of his uniform jacket. He'd hoped to eliminate suspects, not add more.

"Possibly. My friend didn't know where Smith is now, but you may get more information tomorrow. Were you able to contact the pros at both of the courses where the son caddies?"

Jax nodded. "I did that right before we went to see Ida Byington. Preston Cherry gave me the names of both clubs, but only one of the pros was in today. He said Chaz had been there a lot lately. I called the other course and neither the assistant nor caddy master has seen Chaz for the past month, so I may not need to go there at all."

"You've made significant progress already," Jenkins observed before pulling out his pocket watch. "I'll try to get back as soon as I can, but I really should leave now. If my friend learns anything else, he'll call me, and I'll pass it along to you."

"Thanks," Jax replied. "Before you go, we stopped at the accident scene on the way back. The water is still too high to see much more or to get the car out. I'll look again tomorrow."

Richard frowned. "That's all you can do. The front bumper may have damage that gives us a better idea of what happened. That's a big reason not to try towing it now. I'm afraid it may catch onto something and pull loose. If it got stuck in the mud, we may not get to it until the creek dries up."

"That won't be until fall," Jax said.

"All the more reason to be patient and wait," Richard replied. "I'll be back as soon as I can."

"Don't worry about that. Just take care of your family." That's what Jax would do—if he still had one.

After Jenkins left, Jax turned to Nolen. "Maybe you should make the afternoon rounds now. I'll be here going over the notes for quite a while."

The young deputy nodded. "Mrs. Adams called, and her shed was broken into last night. Once she heard about the accident, she waited to call because she knew we'd be busy. But she would like one of us to look. I can do that after I finish the rounds."

"Good idea," Jax told him. "Make a report and we can discuss it later. I doubt if there was actually a break-in, but she'll feel better if you stop and check."

"She's a sweet lady," Nolen observed, "but living alone seems to be scary for her."

"It's nice of you two to honor her complaints," Bella said.

"It doesn't take much time to put her mind at ease," Jax said before turning back to Nolen. "I still plan to go to Cleveland tomorrow, so you'll likely be here alone for most of the day. With that in mind, you can leave once you talk to Mrs. Adams. I'll get that report from you tomorrow."

Nolen nodded. "I reached a couple of the caddies in Mr. Laheene's group, and I made notes on that," he said with a smile. "I have one more call to make."

"Well done. Make the call and then, get the information together. We can discuss those interviews before you go out." Jax turned to Bella. "Come on, you can transcribe the notes in my office and get on the road after that yourself."

Bella preceded Jax into the office, but she stopped once they were both inside the door. "I can stay and help you."

He ran one hand over his face. Her overture didn't surprise Jax, but his receptivity to it did. Only this morning, he'd foolishly reacted to her show of concern before needing to withdraw, which had led to more uneasiness between them. He needed to shore up his defenses and act like a big brother would. "You have a business to run, Bella. I can't expect you to spend your time here."

She frowned. "I told you that Mrs. Rogers is handling things, and Ida will be there soon, so I'm not really needed right now. I'll call and ask that a room be readied for her," she told him. "I could spend a couple of hours here if that would be useful. After all, you and Nolen already have your hands full."

For a moment, he said nothing. Jenkins' observations flickered through his mind. Along with them came the knowledge that, with exhaustion and pain draining him, he needed help. Rejecting hers would be foolish, and possibly detrimental to solving the case. The last thought combined with his promise to Matt decided the issue. "If you're sure. You already know Jenkins and I were going to review things this afternoon. As he said, you have a knack for this work, and I have to admit, my brain is fuzzy at this point."

"You're just tired," she replied.

"I can't deny that," Jax said with a weary smile.

"Matt used to get addlebrained when he was overtired."

Was she tacitly reminding him of his role as substitute big brother? "Yeah, he did." The last time Jax had seen Matt, his friend was just starting a short, much-needed leave. An image of Matt formed in his mind. Abruptly, Jax stopped his mental rambling. He couldn't think about his buddy now.

"I'll be glad to go over details with you. Then, you and Nolen would only need to hit the highlights in the morning."

"That sounds like a good idea." Jax settled his mind and gestured at the round table in the corner. "Have a seat. I'll lay out all the notes, and we can go over them."

Bella sat down and began to tap away at the old typewriter perched on a small side table. When Jax joined her in the office, he smiled. "You're very fast, especially considering that some keys have the letters and symbols worn off."

Her fingers paused mid-stroke, and she stared at him. "I suppose you only use your forefingers and look at the keys."

A half-shrug lifted one shoulder. "Nolen does most of the typing, and that's his strategy." Some muttered words left Bella, but Jax couldn't make them out. "Neither of us took a typing class."

"You could have. Nolen, too. Mrs. Ingram taught shorthand one semester and typing another. She still does."

Her words and expression seemed sober, which Jax couldn't fathom. "You're kidding, right?"

"I'm not kidding. I'm serious." Her dark gaze narrowed on him.

"No guys ever took those classes," he pointed out.

"If you had, you'd know how to type. That would be helpful now, wouldn't it?"

"We only have a lot of notes when there's a big case, and there have only been three since I took the job last summer."

A smile lifted the corners of her lips. "Luckily, you've had me to help you out."

Her sudden amusement made Jax realize Bella had only made the observations to emphasize her role in solving the previous cases and to promote her assistance in this one. He couldn't help but grin in return. "You're right, Bella."

The smile intensified. "I love to hear you say that."

"I'm sure you do." Some of his tension seeped away. "There's a lot to go over, and I doubt if much of it will be really useful. I'd like to get a second opinion, so why don't you leave the rest of the typing for Nolen?"

"Let me finish this page," she replied. When she was done, Bella extracted the paper and laid it on the desk before glancing at the stack Jax had put on the table.

Jax studied the notes he'd made earlier. "My

mother would be appalled at my chicken-scratching. Good penmanship was something she not only taught at school but at home, too. I'm sure I practiced more than other kids."

"Your writing was always beautiful," she commented. "Nicer than anyone else's, even mine."

He shrugged. "It isn't now."

"If you have the surgery, it might be. Of course, I'd hate to lose my chauffeuring job."

Briefly, he'd thought she would again suggest he could return to his golf career. When she didn't, Jax relaxed. "Luckily, you have other careers to fall back on," Jax said. Nolen's tap on the door interrupted their conversation. "Come on in and sit down," Jax called out. "I'd like to hear what you found out. Then, you can go back to your regular duties."

The deputy nodded as he took a seat at the battered table. "I spoke with Danny Preswick and Benjie Bondy. They had a few things to add. Preswick caddied for Laheene and Bondy caddied for Etting. That was Danny's first time, and he said it would have been his last. The man paid decently, but his demands and complaints were more than the kid wanted to handle. Benjie said Laheene chastised him more than once, too. Like saying to get out of his line or stop moving when he was ready to hit, even though Benjie said he wasn't doing any of that. He had no complaints about Etting. However, he said that Etting was fed up with Laheene and said he hoped the guy *gets what he deserves* more than once during the final holes. Both of the caddies left shortly after the last round. He also overheard Guy

Brewster saying much the same about Mr. Laheene to his partner, Sam."

"Etting, Brewster, and Chaz Smith queued up in wanting Cecil to reap what he sowed," Jax observed. "Now, we've got three potential suspects who told witnesses they hoped Laheene got what was coming to him, and the elder Smith, who undoubtedly feels the same way."

"At least Ida never said that," Bella pointed out.

"I wouldn't blame her if she had," Jax replied, "but you're right. She didn't." He looked at Nolen. "Bella and I are going to go over the case notes, so you can make the rounds. Like I said, end your day early. I can handle any calls that come in."

"Thanks, Jax," Nolen replied before hurrying out of the office.

Chapter Seven

Jax went into the outer office with Nolen but returned in moments. He sat down, leaned back in his chair, and studied the notepads on the battered table. "We might as well get started. As I told you, Jenkins and I planned to go over the primary suspects and discuss what we learned about each one. I know you don't want to believe Ida was involved but, until I talk with her aunt, I can't rule her out. Since it's almost five o'clock, I just called. She isn't home yet."

"You said you didn't believe Ida ran him off the road. Besides, her vehicle had no dent or dings, and she never threatened him." Her voice held a critical note.

Jax took a long breath before he spoke. Why Bella felt the need to remind him, he didn't know. Her loyalty to her friend was understandable, but he wished she better understood his position. "Both your comments are true. Nonetheless, I want to hear from her aunt before removing her from the list. Loose ends have to be tied up. That's part of my job." When Bella opened her mouth, he held up one hand. "I know you don't agree with me, but let's not argue about it. We don't have to discuss Ida since we have other suspects." He took a stack of papers and laid them across the table. "Floyd Etting and Guy Brewster are still suspects, and Chaz Smith could be, too. As far as we know, they all had means, motive, and opportunity. Even Mr. Smith is a possibility." Several moments of silence ensued. During that time, Jax braced himself for another defense of Ida but, when Bella spoke again, she asked a question.

"What are your plans for tomorrow?"

The comment was probably a prelude to suggesting she accompany him, but he didn't respond. As usual, he felt torn about having her along. "You know I spoke with the pro and caddy master where Smith caddies now, and he was on the course today. Evidently, he's been caddying there most days. Since they said he usually arrives before noon, I'm planning to stop at the course after I see Guy Brewster. If I can catch young Smith off-guard, that would be best. Then, he won't have excuses prepared beforehand. I'll ask him for his home address and see the father, too, if I can."

"You're very clever, constable." A lilt was in her voice and gaze.

Some of his tension ebbed. "Not so much, but I'm learning," he replied with a low laugh. Then, he sobered. "Let's go over the basics regarding each of the three. We don't know enough about Mr. Smith to discuss him, but as Richard said, I might learn more tomorrow." He tapped the short stack of papers in front of him. "According to witnesses, Guy threatened Laheene at the hotel, and there was a lot of tension between the two of them a few days ago as well as on the course yesterday. That bothers me because I talked with Guy, and he assured me he would ignore Laheene, yet they argued after the tournament. I followed their group, and there were some terse words at times. Guy tried really hard to maintain his composure, and his partner Sam helped a lot in that regard. Even so, there was hostility beneath the surface, which makes me wonder if Guy might have finally lost control."

"I'm bothered, too," Bella admitted. "I didn't think so much of it when Guy was upset over Cecil berating Alan at the course, but there was arguing at the hotel after Guy and Sam won the tournament. That's more troubling. Guy should have been focused on celebrating. Besides, I was surprised Guy and Sam left Ballantyne so soon. Winners usually stay longer to show off the loving cup and accept congratulations."

"I agree. On top of that, Laheene kept disparaging Alan, something he's evidently done for a long time. We both know Guy took that to heart. He idolized his older brother, so it isn't a surprise that he detested Laheene or even made what could be idle threats. I don't know Guy well enough to say if he lets his emotions rule his behavior or not." Jax picked up a pencil and tapped it against the table. "He looks like Alan, but that doesn't mean he shares his older brother's placid personality."

Bella's teeth caught her lower lip. "Alan always seemed quite mature, restrained, and responsible. I mostly knew him through Ida, and she held him in high esteem. He would have been a loyal and loving husband."

Jax briefly caught her gaze before looking away. "I suppose," he murmured.

Bella's brows pulled down as she studied his face. "You said the war changed you. Did it change Alan, too?"

His fingers tightened on the pencil until his knuckles were white. Of course, as astute as she was, Bella would read between the lines. "I also said it changed most of us, and you agreed. That has nothing to do with this case or with Guy." Jax hurried on before Bella could comment further. "The kid doesn't have a reputation for being volatile, but Laheene knew how to get to him. However, Guy's dislike of Cecil is a motive to harass the man, if nothing else."

Bella gazed at him a moment longer. Finally, she nodded. "I know Ida and Guy stayed in touch for a while after Alan died. Guy often said he felt like they were already brother and sister. After we got home from France, she visited with the Brewsters a few times. Guy was at college, but they corresponded. It had to be devastating when she started seeing Laheene. Guy might feel betrayed, and strong emotion can lead to dangerous behavior."

"I don't disagree, and it had to upset Guy a lot when Laheene lashed out at Ida. I doubt if he knew it was about financial trouble in the Byington family, but if he felt like a brother to her..." His voice trailed off.

A sigh left Bella. "He might have wanted to protect her. If that was his goal, do you think he only wanted to harass Cecil or show him up?"

"I don't know," Jax said. "I don't want to think Guy is involved at all, but I can't overlook him. He has too much motive to be ignored as a potential suspect. Laheene would have recognized Guy's car. Maybe Guy thought that would be enough. The driving conditions were poor, and he might only have wanted to make a point by passing him really close and speeding off. I might have a better grasp of Guy's involvement, or lack of involvement, tomorrow. When I called, his father was pleasant. Other than that, I don't know much about Mr. and Mrs. Brewster."

"Did his father say what time Guy got home yesterday?"

Jax frowned. "Unfortunately, the Brewsters were at the lake until very late last night. Guy was home when they got there. However, the time frame gives him plenty of leeway to have run Laheene off the road."

"Which isn't helpful," Bella observed. "We know he left ahead of Laheene, and Guy was alone. He could have waited, I guess, and forcing Cecil off the road wouldn't have taken very long. That doesn't seem positive for Guy, does it?"

"No, but he isn't the only one with no known alibi." Jax pushed that stack of papers aside and looked at the next pile. "We might as well talk about Chaz Smith, even though we don't know as much about him."

"We know he had every reason to hate Laheene. More reason than Guy or Floyd Etting, I'd say. Certainly, a lot more than Ida. Of course, there's the older Smith." Bella observed.

"Yes, he's a wild card. When Preston Cherry told me about the Smith boy's injury and his father's attack on Laheene, he said the man was in prison. Evidently, Preston doesn't know Smith was released. I'll call him later and see what he can find out. Preston knew Laheene's father gave some money to the family, but said it was a pittance. If the boy never walks normally again, he'll need a lot more to get along and funds for surgery might help."

Jax narrowed his gaze as if he was focusing on the likelihood of that scenario. "It's conceivable, I suppose, and I'll definitely look into it. Chaz could have easily found out in advance that Laheene was playing in the fourball and then, taken a caddying job for the tournament to be here, too. A group of caddies came from out-of-town, so it wouldn't be odd that he did. If he's in touch with his father, the pair of them could have worked together. You never know. Revenge is a powerful motivator," Jax observed. A frown shadowed his face. "It's a terrible miscarriage of justice that Mr. Smith was sent to jail and Laheene went virtually scot-free for what happened to the boy. I don't agree with people taking the law into their own hands, but it isn't hard to understand why Smith did."

"It certainly isn't," Bella said in agreement. "I feel so sorry for young Chipper and the whole family. I hope the Smiths weren't involved, either. But, with two distinct sets of tire tracks on the shoulder, someone must have known Cecil went off the road, perhaps accidentally but possibly intentionally."

"Both are still conceivable and, even if another driver ran Laheene off the road, the person might not have planned to kill him." Jax tapped his fingers on the table. "Keeping an open mind is important at this point."

"The other driver should have stopped," Bella said, repeating what they'd already discussed.

"True. In order to know why he didn't, we need more information." His lips twitched. "But no more suspects."

Bella grinned. "I don't know that we can control that part."

"Unfortunately, we can't," Jax admitted in frustration. "Let's keep looking at possibilities. Talking them out can help."

"What about Etting? Laheene humiliated him after their round, but is there anything to indicate he's the vengeful type?"

Jax looked at the next paper. "You heard Nolen say he talked with Benjie this morning since he caddied for Etting. As a local boy, he didn't know Floyd before the tournament. But, according to Richard's notes, a couple of caddies from Cleveland said they'd seen Etting do small things to get even with men who crossed him. More practical jokes than revenge, though."

"What do you mean?"

"Last year, there was an incident with the pro who refereed Etting's final match in a district event. Floyd thought the guy gave his opponent a big break by letting him have a free drop instead of assessing a penalty. Later that week, the pro discovered all of his car tires were flat." Jax frowned.

"It's childish behavior for a grown man, but that doesn't make Etting prone to violence." Bella paused briefly before asking, "The caddies from Cleveland really think Floyd Etting did that?"

"Evidently so." Jax stopped to scan the notes again. "They said everyone at the club thinks so, too. They also said that another member had all the spikes in his golf shoes loosened. The man didn't notice the issue until he got on the first tee in a tournament. He had problems. Again, Floyd is the likely culprit because the man had accused him of not counting all his strokes on a couple of holes when they played together earlier that week. The names of the caddies are in the notes. If Etting turns out to be a strong suspect, I may need to interview them, too."

"I suppose so, but those are childish tricks. They wouldn't cause serious harm to anyone."

"That's true. However, we don't know that the other driver meant to cause Laheene actual harm. Someone might have wanted to scare him. Or the person might have wanted to pass to show off. I think one of those ideas would have been Guy's only intent if he was involved. But it may have been Etting who wanted to play a practical joke that went wrong. The same could be true for Chaz or Mr. Smith. You know how Laheene was about every-thing. He had to have the newest, most expensive equipment and clothing, as well as the costliest and fastest car. If anyone tried to pass him, I can see him speeding up and cutting them off."

"Your theories make sense. With a wet road and soft shoulder, a prank could have turned into a tragedy," Bella suggested.

"That's a prospect that I plan to pursue with all the current suspects, along with other potential scenarios." The phone ringing in the outer office interrupted. Jax rose to his feet. "Excuse me. That may be Ida's aunt returning my call." A few minutes later, he came back with a smile on his face. "Good news. Mrs. Wilson said Ida got back when she said she did, so there's no way she could have been involved in the incident. Ida was at her aunt's house before the accident could have happened. The housekeeper got on the line and confirmed that fact for me."

Relief flooded Bella. "I knew she wasn't involved, but I'm so happy to have it verified. Would you mind if I use the office phone to call her?"

His grin widened. "I already did."

"That was very kind," Bella said, her voice soft and gentle. "I'm sure Ida appreciated the gesture."

A shrug twisted his shoulders. "I wouldn't let any potential suspect feel uneasy and uncomfortable when I've cleared them, but I especially wanted to tell Ida as soon as possible. As you say, she's had too much to handle already. She doesn't need to worry about being charged with a crime she didn't commit."

"You are a good constable, Jax."

Her kind words pleased him, but he couldn't afford to let that show. Finally, he said, "I'm learning on the job."

"I am, too." She smiled. "I never planned to run

Ballantyne. As much as I love golf, I always thought Matt would end up doing that, and I would teach French. Of course, I would have spent summer vacations here, but I didn't count on the responsibility of the whole place. I don't know how Mac managed alone after Mother and Dad died while I was still in France."

He studied her face for a moment. "That's why I hate to impose on you. You've got plenty to do." Of course, her safety was still a concern to him but, wisely, he didn't mention that. She'd been fearless as a child, fearless as an operator, and she seemed fearless now, which was not necessarily an asset in his mind. An image of her bound, gagged, and unconscious in the trunk of a killer's vehicle floated before him. Four months had passed since then but, to Jax, the image was as clear as if it had happened last night. He couldn't let her be in such danger again, not when he'd promised her brother to look out for her. Not when he couldn't live with himself if something bad happened to her.

Bella smiled. "I enjoy helping with these cases. Besides, we're closed until Thursday. You know that. Even then, Mrs. Rogers is more than willing to work extra hours, and Ida may stay the rest of the summer."

Jax blinked to clear the ugly image lingering in his mind. Clearly, Bella had no idea of his thoughts. Had she completely set aside what happened at the end of the last murder investigation? He hadn't, and he probably never would. "Having her stay for the summer would be helpful? I mean, I know you and Mac have been careful about adding employees."

Bella nodded. "Yes, we've been cautious, but the fourball was very successful. We get a lot of play Thursdays through Sundays, the inn is almost completely booked every weekend, and we often have guests who stay several days. We can afford to pay Ida a stipend and, of course, she'd have room and board. Having her there would allow Dick and Dale to oversee the dock. We've mostly had fishermen, but a couple of the boats are in good enough shape for people to use. The boys could handle that, and I'd have more free time."

"You should use some of that free time to do fun things, like play golf yourself."

Bella nodded. "Ida and I will probably play a few evenings, but solving cases is fun, too."

Jax couldn't help but smile. "You're a combination of both grandfathers," he observed. "The golf pro and the lawman."

A laugh escaped her. "I suppose I am." She hesitated before speaking again. "As I said, we won't be busy again until the end of the week. That gives me the rest of today and the next two days. You're very short-handed. On top of that, both you and Nolen worked a lot of hours last week. I could go to Cleveland with you tomorrow and take notes. I could even drive since it's a long trip."

Her suggestion wasn't a surprise. For a moment, he scanned her face. Having her drive and take notes would remove a big burden. Helping Nolen get Laheene out of the car and up the embankment had wreaked havoc with Jax's shoulder and bicep. As much as he hurt and as tired as he was, Jax doubted his ability to handle the trip alone. If

Richard had stayed, Jax would have asked Nolen to go along. Now, that was impossible. As long as Jax was cautious, Bella wouldn't get hurt. Interviewing Guy wouldn't be a hazard, and he'd talk to Chaz at the golf course where she'd be perfectly safe. Besides, if she stayed around home, she might go out looking for clues herself. "You would be a help," he finally admitted. "It's a long drive and shifting gears still causes problems for my arm and shoulder, not to mention my writing is terrible, as you know."

Her expression brightened. "Would we take the Chummy?"

The question and her good humor made him chuckle. "I'm not sure if you're more interested in helping solve the case or in driving my fast car."

"I'm not sure myself," she said with a lilt of amusement.

As they wrapped up plans for their trip, Jax said, "A big concern is Chaz running if he recognizes me. I don't remember seeing him, but he might've observed the quarrel on eighteen green or the exchange between Laheene and me."

"You're not wearing your uniform tomorrow, are you?" Bella asked.

Jax paused before answering. "I hadn't really thought about it. I'm used to wearing it now, but I wouldn't have to. After all, we won't be in my jurisdiction."

"If we both wear golf clothes, we'd blend in," she suggested. "Then, no one, including Chaz Smith, is likely to be suspicious when we arrive at the golf course."

A grin curved his mouth. "That's a good plan,

116

Bella."

Once that was settled, they agreed on a departure time and Bella headed home. Jax still felt ambivalent about involving her more in the case, but he brushed it away. Although her safety wasn't a big concern on the trip, maintaining distance for an entire day could tax his restraint. But he'd be cautious in word and deed. Very cautious.

Chapter Eight

When Bella got to the inn, Ida was already at the front desk. "I feel so much better," Ida said with a smile. "I'm glad Jax could eliminate me as a suspect."

"I am, too," Bella agreed as she crossed the large lobby and leaned against the counter. "Now, we can talk about you staying for the rest of the summer."

"Are you sure, Bella?" Ida's auburn brows furrowed as she spoke, and uncertainty clouded her gaze. "I don't want to take advantage of your hospitality."

"You wouldn't be taking advantage; you'd be a big help, especially right now. Jenny and Richard Jenkins had to go home. Her mother fell and maybe broke an ankle. Richard will be back as soon as possible, but Jenny won't. That leaves Jax and Nolen short-handed, especially tomorrow." She paused for a moment. "Jax is going to Cleveland to talk with suspects and witnesses. The long trip would be hard on his arm and shoulder, so it would be a big help to him if I could drive and take notes. I already said I would."

Ida looked pensive. "I didn't realize his wound was so serious."

Bella saw genuine concern in her friend's gaze. After her fiancé's death in early September 1918, Ida had struggled to do her job as an operator. Ida had known about Jax's wounds but, perhaps, grief made memories of that time hazy. Bella, too, had been confronted with loss when her brother died shortly after Alan. Perhaps, her memories weren't sharp, either. "He has shrapnel, which isn't uncommon, and he was back on the line within a few days. Evidently, that was his decision. I'm not sure the doctors agreed because he never really says exactly what occurred. A while back, Jax told me he knew the armistice was coming, and he wanted to be with his men, so maybe he went back too soon, since the end was in sight."

"I can understand his feelings," Ida murmured. "But it's been almost two years. Do you know why it still gives him problems?"

"The doctors in France didn't get all the shrapnel out, so he has pain, maybe swelling, too. I don't know much about the long-term effects, but shifting gears in the car is a problem, and so is a lot of writing." Bella hesitated briefly before voicing what was in the back of her mind. "Jax was also wounded shortly before Matt was killed. I never got any details. I was too caught up in grief to ask." And badly hurt by Jax's dismissal when they'd crossed paths right after her brother's death. Bella had never told Ida about that day, and she hesitated to do so now. Should she? Indecision held her tongue. So did the image of the pretty French nurse who had walked away with Jax.

"Maybe the worst wound was the first one. Why don't you ask him about it?"

Bella shifted restlessly as she considered the query. A clear question deserved a direct answer. "More times than not, he clams up when the war, his wounds, or my brother are mentioned."

"That's not surprising. Most men don't want to look weak or vulnerable, especially to someone close to them."

Uneasiness flickered through Bella. For several moments, she considered how to respond. Before a good comment came to mind, Ida spoke again.

"Don't say you and Jax aren't close anymore."

"We aren't, Ida. He wants to take Matt's place as a big brother, but Jax stays away most of the time, and actions speak louder than words."

Ida's expression softened. "You said it was hard for him to come here and know he can't live out his dream. You shouldn't take that personally."

With one hand, Bella massaged her taut neck muscles. "Last spring, after the murder was solved, I offered Jax a job here. As co-professional with Mac now and as the head pro when Mac retires."

A soft exhalation left Ida. Her hazel eyes grew round as she stared steadily at Bella. "I'm assuming he turned it down."

Because a lump rose in her throat, Bella only nodded.

"What did he say, exactly?"

Bella swallowed hard before replying. "He can't play in big tournaments, or much at all, although I know he's gone to Crystal Lakes Golf Club a couple of times just recently."

"Did he play eighteen holes?"

"I'm not sure."

"If he has trouble writing and shifting gears, I doubt he did," Ida observed in a thoughtful tone.

"I suppose that's true," Bella admitted.

"But you're upset he didn't come here to play."

"Not upset, really. I just don't understand why he completely dismissed the idea of working here. Before the war, he was an assistant golf pro at Crystal Lakes, which was his dream for years. From the time he first came to Ballantyne with Matt, that's all Jax wanted. It's all he talked about. He lived, breathed, ate, drank, and slept golf. His goal was to get his own head pro job. He and Matt planned to work together here after Mac and my dad retired. Jax admits being constable is far from his first choice, but he turned me down."

Ida laid one hand on Bella's forearm. "He didn't turn you down. He turned the job down."

The reassuring touch sent some of Bella's tension scampering away. "But why? He admits being constable is hard."

A half-shrug lifted one of Ida's slender shoulders. "There's a certain expectation that head pros at places like Ballantyne will represent the course at major tournaments and play in events on-site. Didn't your Grampa Stew and Mac do that? I know your dad did."

"Mac hasn't competed for a long time," Bella said,

although that same point had been summarily dismissed by Jax.

"No, but when Mac stopped, your dad and Matt still played as representatives of Ballantyne."

Bella considered her friend's comments, which were much the same as Jax's had been. "Competing doesn't have to be part of the job. Mac agrees."

"Jax might change his mind at some point, but I wouldn't count on it. Pride can be hard to overcome, and that may be part of what's standing in his way."

"I suppose so," Bella admitted. "He gets frustrated with his job, though. Like now, Cecil's father is threatening to hire a detective agency if the case isn't solved by Thursday, the day of the funeral. That's not much time, which puts a lot of pressure on Jax. The town council only approved hiring him by one vote, and everyone in town knows he always swore he'd never follow in his father's footsteps. If Mr. Laheene hires a detective, that could look bad for Jax."

Ida patted Bella's arm. "Then, it's good you're helping again."

The lighter note in her friend's voice wasn't new to Bella. Both she and Ida had always striven to lift the other's spirits when needed. The change in tone also served to table a difficult topic. For now, at least. Ida was apt to bring the subject up again once Bella had a chance to mull it over. They knew each other well and gave one another space at just the right times. Bella needed that space now. "I suppose so."

"And he'll let you drive that cute Chummy?"

Amusement sparkled in Ida's hazel eyes.

A low laugh escaped Bella. "Yes, he will. He let me drive home from Toledo last spring, and yesterday, to and from your aunt's house."

Ida gave her friend a speculative look. "A man doesn't let just anyone drive his sporty roadster."

Warmth crept into Bella's cheeks, but she shook her head. "It's a matter of necessity." Of course, Jax wasn't incapable of driving, but it was a strain on him. The same was true of writing. He only needed her help, which was clear to Bella despite Ida's view to the contrary.

"If you say so," Ida replied, but she didn't sound convinced.

Bella ignored the comment. "If you're here, I'll feel better about being away. Mrs. Rogers is willing to put in more hours, so it should work out well."

"That sounds fine. I hope you and Jax get some information that will solve the case. Even though Cecil wasn't a nice person, I hate to think that someone intended to do him harm."

Since her friend had been completely cleared, Bella shared the plausible theories. She wrapped up by saying, "Once the water goes down, any additional damage should be visible." Bella didn't mention Jax looking at her friend's vehicle for dents and dings.

"So, it could have been completely accidental."

Bella nodded. "Yes, but why didn't the other driver stop? He had to know Cecil crashed into the ravine."

"That bothers me, too. It's especially troubling that Guy argued with Cecil more than once."

Ida's observation reminded Bella of Jax saying he knew little about Guy and his parents. She didn't, either, but her friend probably did. "I don't know Guy very well. Is he much different from Alan in personality?"

"He's somewhat more sentimental than Alan. Part of that could be from losing his big brother. Cecil criticizing Alan really upset Guy. He idolized Alan and wanted to partner with him in golf events after the war." She blinked hastily, as if to keep tears from filling her eyes. "The whole family is grief-stricken. I doubt if they'll ever get over the loss."

Ida didn't need to say she'd been equally distraught because Bella had been there when news of Alan's death came. "That's understandable."

"I hope Guy wasn't involved in Cecil's accident. I can't believe he'd run anyone off the road, but he might have wanted to jolt Cecil." Her worried gaze narrowed on Bella. "I'm afraid that's a big reason why Mr. Laheene wants to hire private detectives. He saw at least one argument between Cecil and Guy."

Surprise rippled through Bella. "When?"

"At a tournament about a month ago, Cecil kept accusing Guy of playing slowly and disturbing his game, which was ridiculous. I walked around with Cecil's group, and they never waited on Guy's foursome. Mr. Laheene started criticizing Guy, and there were some hard words between them, as well." Her hazel eyes filled with unshed tears. "I never should have started seeing Cecil. Now, I'm worried that might have caused Guy to lash out. If Guy gets arrested, I'll never forgive myself."

Bella reached out to pat her friend's hand. "Even if that's what happened, and I'm not at all sure it is, you aren't at fault. You're entitled to go on with your life, even if some people disagree."

Tears trickled from Ida's eyes. With the back of one hand, she swiped them away. "I suppose so, but I don't want Alan's family to suffer anymore."

"I don't believe I ever met Mr. and Mrs. Brewster. Are they pleasant people?" Perhaps she could get some details to share with Jax.

A smile lifted Ida's lips. "Yes, they're lovely. I would have been very happy to have them as in-laws."

"How do you think they'll feel about Jax and me visiting tomorrow to talk with Guy? Jax spoke briefly with Mr. Brewster when he called to set up the meeting. He said Guy's father was nice."

"He would be. He's a wonderful man. Nothing like Cecil's father. Mrs. Brewster is sweet and kind. She'll be very hospitable to both of you."

Her friend's observations eased Bella's mind. She'd share them with Jax on their way to Cleveland in the morning. "What about Cecil's mother? Do you know her?"

"She died when Cecil was small, so I never met her. I only saw his father a handful of times. I can't say I ever enjoyed the experience."

"Jax didn't say much about the man except that he seems demanding and that he's sure someone meant to harm Cecil."

Alarm flickered across Ida's face. "What if Jax discovers evidence indicating it was an accident? Would the other driver be in trouble for not stopping?"

"Jax said it wouldn't be nearly as bad as forcing Cecil off the road."

"What if Mr. Laheene influences the outcome? You know, get detectives to say it was intentional."

"His power doesn't reach this far, so don't worry about that," Bella replied, although a niggling finger of concern touched her heart. Jax had withstood scrutiny through the two previous murder cases and gained a bit more support, but he didn't need any added burdens.

Ida nodded. "I know Jax wouldn't bow to pressure. He'll do the right thing no matter what, but Mr. Laheene might make things tough for him, and he might try to pin the crash on Guy."

"Richard Jenkins will support Jax, and he has a strong reputation as a good lawman. They'll follow the evidence and stand by their conclusions. They won't let anyone get railroaded, so don't fret about Guy being wrongly arrested."

Relief blanketed Ida's face. "All right."

While Bella was glad to see her friend relax, she still felt tense. Richard would—as she'd told Ida—back up Jax, but the Moreley mayor was far more likely to cave in to pressure.

Chapter Nine

Jax wasn't surprised to see Nolen already in the office the next morning. His deputy had picked up his habit of arriving early. Once again, Jax hoped the younger man would be hired on a full-time basis. Nolen already worked much harder and longer than was necessary for his half-time position.

"Good morning, Nolen."

The deputy shrugged. "Maybe not so good."

Jax stopped in his tracks. A negative comment was completely unlike Nolen. "What's wrong?" he asked immediately.

"Mayor Cawlings stopped on his way to town hall. He wants you to call him right away."

"Did he say why?" The mayor seldom went to work this early, which put Jax even more on edge.

"Cecil Laheene's father called him at home first thing this morning. He asked the mayor if we've found the guilty party and said he's talked to a private detective. Mr. Laheene plans to hire the man if we don't have a suspect in custody by the time his son is buried."

A ragged breath escaped Jax. "Laheene said the same to me already." The man probably figured he'd exert additional pressure by contacting the mayor.

"It's barely been twenty-four hours since the body was found. I don't see how anyone can expect an arrest this soon," Nolen said, dismay was clear on his freckled face.

Jax crossed the outer office and leaned against the counter. "Leonard Laheene is a powerful and rich businessman. From what I know, he runs his company with an iron hand, and he expects his will to be done in a lot of other settings, as well."

"But why is Mayor Cawlings worried about what he thinks? Laheene doesn't live here or have influence."

"He knows a great many people in northeast Ohio, including at least one newspaper publisher. Laheene could instigate bad press for Ballantyne and for Moreley. Things are just turning around, so I'm sure Cawlings is worried about offending Laheene."

Trepidation replaced dismay on Nolen's face. "We used to get a lot of visitors from northeast Ohio, almost as many as from the Toledo area. I guess Mr. Laheene could cause problems."

"He'd try. I'm not sure he'd succeed, but I'd rather not test him," Jax said. "I'll call Cawlings right now. How about if you make the rounds a bit early? Bella will be here soon, and I want to get on the road right away."

"Sure thing."

Once again weighted down by frustration, Jax picked up the telephone and waited while the operator connected him to Cawlings. The mayor's admonitions to hurry on the case didn't surprise Jax. Nor did the man's concern about potential damage to both town and resort if the case wasn't closed soon.

Early Tuesday morning, Bella got ready for her day trip. She had spoken with Mrs. Rogers the previous evening and confirmed that the woman would work more hours until the Laheene case was solved. The cook-housekeeper was pleased with the idea and equally glad to hear Ida would help for the rest of the summer.

Bella was pulling clothes out of the armoire when Ida tapped on her door, entered the suite, and stopped in the middle of the bedroom. "You're not going to wear that, are you?" A look of dismay blanketed her face as she stared at Bella.

Before replying, Bella glanced at the brown skirt and beige blouse in her hands. "Yes, I am. Among other interviews, Jax and I plan to go to the golf course where one suspect caddies. I suggested we dress like we were there to play a round. Then, our suspect won't immediately recognize us, and we won't stand out to anyone else, either."

Ida nodded. "Okay, I see the wisdom in wearing golf attire, but that outfit is old and dated. Very pre-war."

A half-shrug lifted one of Bella's shoulders. "I haven't gotten any new golf clothes since I returned from France because I don't play enough to need any."

Her friend's hazel gaze skimmed the outfit again. "Maybe not, but it's quite old-fashioned." Ida plucked at the skirt. "This will hang to mid-calf." She tugged at the plain beige blouse. "And this color is so dull. It does nothing for your lovely complexion."

Bella grimaced. "Ida, I'm helping with an investigation, not appearing in a style show."

The other woman pursed her lips as if she found her friend's observation as sour as a lemon. "You're helping a handsome, eligible man," her friend pointed out. "You don't need to go looking like someone's elderly spinster aunt."

Warmth rose in Bella's cheeks. "Oh, Ida." To herself, she admitted she didn't want to look bland and boring. And certainly not like an old spinster aunt.

"I know you're going to say the two of you are now like brother and sister. We don't need to argue again. Even so, you may see some other bachelor today. Someone who might come to Ballantyne. After all, you are going to a golf club." She grinned. "I have a couple of outfits that I haven't worn yet. You could wear one."

Bella was unconvinced. "You're thinner than I am, Ida."

"Not much thinner. The tops will fit fine, and one pair of knickers is a bit big for me. I think they'll fit you perfectly." Ida smiled in pleasure at her plan.

"Knickers?" Shock filled Bella and echoed in her

voice.

"Yes, you've seen me in them. They're in style now. Other women in the gallery had them on during the tournament. You must have noticed."

"A few did." Very few, so Bella was unconvinced. While she was hardly a shrinking violet, Bella didn't want to be a spectacle in terms of attire.

"The few who are stylish," Ida said with certainty.

"I don't think I'd feel comfortable in knickers, especially since we have other places to go besides the golf course." She didn't again mention going to the Brewsters' house since she didn't want to upset Ida with a reminder of Alan.

Ida looked pensive for a moment. "I suppose you're right. I also have a cute outfit with a skirt. It hasn't been worn, and it's more stylish than your choice. Wait a moment." She hurried from the room and returned with a two-piece knit dress and a coordinating headband.

The band was navy, with an amber flower that perfectly matched the navy and amber top, but Bella hesitated when she studied the skirt. She couldn't ignore the obvious. "The skirt seems very short."

"It's certainly shorter than your old ones. Haven't you noticed that hems have been rising?" Ida sounded rather surprised and somewhat dismayed.

"Not in the village of Moreley," Bella pointed out.

"They will," her friend assured her. "Besides, this will still fall below your knees, and it's perfectly acceptable to wear at the golf course or in town. In fact, most young women in the city will wear skirts shorter than this one."

Bella felt dubious, but her friend's enthusiasm

was contagious. Not only that, this was the first time Ida had acted like her old self in quite a while. Bella didn't want to quash the other woman's enthusiasm. Besides, she loved the jaunty outfit. "Let me try it on and see how it looks."

"It will look fabulous," Ida assured her.

Bella stepped behind the dressing screen in the corner of her bedroom and hurriedly put on the ensemble. When she came out, her friend clasped her hands together. "Perfect! Look at yourself in the mirror."

As she turned to follow Ida's instructions, Bella couldn't help but smile at her reflection. She looked sophisticated.

"Let's put the headband on." Ida adjusted it and stood back. "I'm glad you had your hair cut. The bob is wonderful with this ornament. So cute."

Bella had hesitated to cut her hair, but Ida had encouraged her. While still billeted in Paris, the two of them had gone to a salon after seeing photographs of Coco Chanel, who bobbed her hair during the war. Others followed suit, especially women in France. Besides, the short style was much easier to maintain than long hair, particularly when they'd been busy with their work as operators. Both had continued the cuts ever since. "It looks nice."

"Nice," Ida echoed. She reached into her pocket and pulled out a long strand of beads. "Here. These are very trendy and will set off the entire ensemble." Ida slipped the necklace over her friend's head, adjusted them, and grinned.

"We're going to the golf course. I wouldn't wear beads to play. Or a headband, either, for that matter."

Ida rolled her eyes. "You aren't actually playing, though. Besides, you look fabulous."

Bella gazed into the mirror again. "Beads still seem a bit much."

A sigh of exasperation escaped Ida. "Just keep them on. The overall outfit is great on you."

Bella wasn't half as convinced as her friend, but confidence filled her as she went on her way. Even if no one else noticed, she felt elegant in the new attire.

Mrs. Rogers was already in the kitchen when Bella and Ida went downstairs. She smiled and said, "You look lovely, my dear. That's a stunning set."

Once again, Bella felt warmth rise in her face. Maybe being stylish was too much out of character for her. If the older woman had such a strong re-action, what would Jax think? Bella feared looking silly. "Thank you. Ida is letting me borrow it. She says my clothes are very pre-war."

"I'm not letting you borrow it," Ida said. "I'm giving it to you. I'll never wear it, and Mrs. Rogers is right. You look very modern."

Bella ignored her friend and looked at the older woman. "You don't think the skirt is too short?"

"Not at all. It's very much in style. If I was a few years younger, I'd shorten my dresses to that length myself. As it is, I have hemmed some of them. Even women my age like to be in fashion." The older woman winked at the younger ones. "Besides, shorter skirts make it easier to move around, which is nice. I like not having my hems around my ankles."

"That's true," Bella replied. She certainly was for anything that gave women more freedom.

"See," Ida said as she turned to Bella. "I told you that this is stylish and tasteful, not to mention practical. Times are changing and, even though you've never taken much interest in the latest fashion trends, you are a very modern woman."

"Both of you are," Mary Rogers said. "It took a lot of pluck to go overseas and serve as operators. I'm not sure I could have done it. Of course, I'm not fluent in French."

"That was our major asset. When we went to training back East, the lady in charge said it was easier to train fluent French speakers to operate a switchboard than it would be to train operators to speak fluent French," Bella said.

"We were lucky to be among the two hundred chosen," Ida agreed.

"From what Nolen told me, the soldiers were lucky you girls took over from the male operators. He said you were much, much faster," Mrs. Rogers observed.

Ida and Bella exchanged grins before they said almost simultaneously, "Yes, we were." During the busiest periods, female operators connected calls six times faster than the men who preceded them in the job.

The three women chuckled before Bella looked at the clock on the kitchen wall. "I appreciate the gift, but I should be on my way. We want to be at the golf club before noon."

"Have a wonderful time," Ida said with enthusiasm.

"It's a police investigation, not a social occasion," Bella protested.

Ida and Mrs. Rogers exchanged a look before both laughed. "Maybe, maybe not," her friend said.

Anxiety assailed Bella as she drove into Moreley. By the time she pulled the Model T to a stop next to the Chummy, Bella had enough butterflies in her stomach to feel slightly ill, and she fought to settle her nerves. What was wrong with her? She was simply wearing a more up-to-date outfit. Styles changed and, as they did, women adapted to them. That was all she was doing. As Mrs. Rogers had said, Bella and Ida were modern women. Dressing accordingly was an outward manifestation of their new roles in the world.

Even so, she took several slow breaths. Bella was just calming down when Jax exited the constable's office. He smiled and waved, but she only waved back. Her uncertainty made smiling impossible.

All too quickly, he was at the side of her car and opening the door for her. She had no choice but to step out. As she did, Bella grasped the side of her skirt, so it didn't ride up. Although she wore stockings, Bella felt cool morning air hit her calves, and the garment seemed shorter than ever. For a moment, she focused her attention on keeping the skirt from revealing more leg than was seemly. Knickers might have been a better choice.

When she finally looked at Jax, Bella saw him staring. Her uneasiness multiplied. Did she look ridiculous? Or worse, coquettish? Her butterflies seemed to multiply. So much for her pep talk about simply updating her wardrobe. She felt like she was on display and not in a good way. Unsure what to say with his green gaze riveted on her, Bella stepped away from her vehicle and closed the door. "Are you ready?"

Jax studied her face. Then, his gaze skimmed over the headband before looking into her eyes. "You look nice this morning," he observed in a low voice. "Not that you don't always," he quickly said. "You do." Abruptly, he stopped as color rose in his tanned face. "That is, I mean to say...that's a pretty outfit, and you look very nice in it."

Bella couldn't help but smile. Jax's inarticulate mumbling clearly indicated that he was as nervous as she was. How could a change in her clothing style make them both feel so awkward? "Thank you," she said again. His discomfort made her feel a bit more confident, so she continued, "I was about to put on one of the golf skirts that I usually wear, and Ida said it was long out of style. She insisted I wear one of her outfits. First, she tried to get me into a pair of knickers, but I didn't think they'd be appropriate."

Suddenly, his gaze glittered with amusement. "You used to wear Matt's pants when they got too small for him. You weren't worried about being appropriate then."

She pursed her lips in disapproval. "I was a little girl."

A low laugh left him. "You were fifteen the last time. Hardly a little girl, and I'm sure you would have kept wearing his old stuff if your mother hadn't insisted you dress like a lady."

Some of her discomfort seeped away. The exchange was reminiscent of the days before the war, and of what her brother might have said. "It's ungallant of you to mention that," she said with mock reproach.

"Probably so, but it is true." Amusement remained in his tone and expression.

Bella liked the current good humor between them, but she didn't want to admit he was right. "Shouldn't we be going?"

His lips twitched. "No comeback for that, huh?"

"Let's go," Bella said, but as she turned away, she was smiling, too, especially when she recalled donning Matt's castoffs. Knickers provided even more freedom than a shorter skirt. Maybe she would wear Ida's knickers soon and see how she liked the more stylish ones made for ladies.

They were barely out of town when Jax spoke. "Slow down when we get near the accident scene. I want to see if the front bumper is visible now."

"You're not climbing down there, are you?"

"That ravine isn't deep. If the water is low enough, I might be able to see the fender. I won't investigate and get muddy if that's what bothers you. I'm sure you don't want to be seen with a guy in dirty, damp clothes." He injected a note of levity, partly because he wanted to keep things casual. His reaction to her outfit had caught him off-guard. Even worse, he'd sounded like a dazzled schoolboy instead of a big brother.

Several seconds passed before Bella replied. "No, of course not."

He went to the edge of the ravine and gazed down at the Cadillac. While the water level was lower, the bumper wasn't visible. As he'd feared, it was sunk into the mud. Getting the car out wouldn't be easy.

Resigned to that not happening today, Jax turned back toward Bella. Briefly, his steps faltered. She was standing on the edge of the road, grasping her beads. Once again, he took in her attire. The headband held her dark hair back from her lovely face. Jax was no fashion expert, of course, and no matter what she wore, Bella was pretty. Very pretty. He swallowed hard and went to the passenger side of the Chummy. "The fender is really stuck in the creek bottom. We won't be able to see it or the front end until it's out of there. The guys from the filling station will help us. With luck, that will happen tomorrow."

After a last look at the tire tracks and ravine, Bella asked, "It was a bad crash, wasn't it?"

Jax turned to look at her. "Everyone says Laheene drove very fast, so speed was likely a major factor. And the weather conditions, of course. I spoke with Doc Smedlay late last night, and he said Laheene probably died right away. Unfortunately, that doesn't tell us who else might be involved, or how the accident happened."

When they were both inside the vehicle, Bella spoke again. "We may uncover something really crucial today."

Jax slumped back in the seat as Bella put the Chummy in gear and got going again. "With luck, we might. If we can narrow the number of suspects down, it would help."

Once they were on the road, Bella made an observation. "I hope Mrs. Brewster won't be offended when we show up in golf clothes. I know it's a good idea to see Chaz before he runs away from us, but I wonder if she'll think we're too casual."

"After you left yesterday, I called and told Mr. Brewster that we'd stop at The Woods after we see Guy and we'd be in golf attire. He said they're a casual household. Besides, your outfit is very stylish. The same really can't be said for mine."

Bella glanced at Jax. The ivory flannel pants and matching cable-knit sweater vest combined with a white shirt and brown tie with ivory stripes looked good on him, as most everything did and always had. "And you'll fit in. Many men wear pants instead of knickers when they play."

"I think I still prefer knickers, but they wouldn't look right when we visit Guy or Floyd Etting."

"Maybe not," Bella agreed, but she used to like seeing him in them. Now that she thought about it, until today, she hadn't seen him in anything but a uniform for years. Maybe clothes made a difference because, after the first moments of discomfort, there seemed to be an easiness between them, like in the old days before the war. Because going back in time wasn't possible, Bella forced her attention to the matters at hand. "I haven't been to the Brewster home, but Ida said it isn't far from the course. I also asked her about them. You know, if Guy is much like Alan and how their parents are."

Jax shifted in his seat. "What did she say?"

"Mr. and Mrs. Brewster are both lovely people, and Ida looked forward to being part of their family." Bella's heart ached when she thought about all the losses wrought by the Great War. After a deep breath, she continued. "Guy is usually a lot like Alan. Calm and low-key for the most part. Cecil was the only one who really upset him."

"I'm not surprised. Laheene had a real knack for pushing people to their limits."

Jax's tone and words surprised Bella, who took a quick sidelong glance at him. "Were you close to your limits when Cecil criticized my brother the day before the tournament started?"

Moments of silence ticked away before Jax responded. "Yeah, pretty close."

The three words offered no real insight, so she tried again. "It isn't like you to let someone do that," she pointed out.

An audible sigh left him. "Not usually."

The brief responses only made Bella more determined to discover what had happened. "Neither you nor Mac gave any details."

"You don't need to know details, Bella, just know that Laheene's words could never do anything to tarnish Matt's memory. Not for me, not for Mac, not for anyone else who knew your brother."

The statements, conveyed in a rough murmur, resonated deep inside Bella. Although Jax rarely spoke about Matt, she was touched by his loyalty. "Thank you."

"No thanks are needed." He cleared his throat. "It's good to know that Guy is usually even-tempered."

Briefly, Bella considered pursuing the conversation about Matt, but what more was there to say? Her brother was gone, but not forgotten. Not by her or by Jax. With determination, she again concentrated on the case. "Ida is concerned, though. She's afraid Guy might have wanted to get even with Cecil for criticizing Alan and for courting her."

"It is possible. By the time we're headed home, I hope to have a better idea of exactly what happened and why."

Bella nodded. "It should take us another hour-and-a-half to get to the Brewster house."

Jax pulled out his pocket watch. "Good. We'll have plenty of time to talk with Guy and make it to the course before the Smith kid goes out to caddy."

"I hope we catch Chaz at the course."

"I do, too. I'm afraid he'll take off if he hears later that I was looking for him there. Chaz probably won't recognize me at a distance, but he'd know you, I imagine. Your idea to wear golf clothes was great. It will help us blend in and not alert him right off."

Bella didn't bother to suppress a smile. "Of course, you're right that Chaz may recognize me. I don't recall seeing him, but he could have seen me at some point."

"If you wore street clothes, and I wore my uniform, we'd stand out like sore thumbs. Then, someone could tip him off before we were barely out of the car. It's a good strategy, Bella." He grinned at her. "You really learned a lot from your Grandfather Morton."

"I'm glad to hear you say that. Now, you'll let me help with other investigations." His smile faded, and Bella looked back at the road. Another big case in Moreley was highly unlikely—after all, they'd had three in the last seven months after years of only petty crimes—and he didn't need help investigating the usual minor incidents. "More major cases aren't apt to occur, of course."

"I hope not."

The comment was obviously heart-felt, but Bella had to agree. "Peace and calm would be best for everyone."

Chapter Ten

For the rest of the trip, they talked about Ballantyne, Mac, the course, and other tournaments. As they got close to Cleveland, their conversation turned back to the case.

"The Brewster home is on the next street," Jax told Bella.

Once Bella turned into the driveway and stopped, she took a long look at the impressive house. The white colonial sat on a large lot filled with towering shade trees. Red roses climbed twin trellises flanking the front door. The overall effect was one of grace and gentility, Bella thought as she climbed out of the car and preceded Jax along the brick walk leading to the spacious porch. The scent of roses filled her nostrils. A quick glance revealed a swing at one end and several wicker chairs near it. Despite the attractive exterior, Bella knew heartache dwelled inside.

Jax used the brass knocker, and within moments,

a uniformed maid opened the door. "Good morning," he said to the girl. "We are here to talk with young Mr. Brewster."

"Come in, please," the maid said with a smile.

Although the day was warm, the front hall felt cool and comfortable. Bella and Jax had barely gotten inside when a middle-aged woman, her gray hair swept into a neat bun, hurried toward them. "You must be Arabella Stewart and Constable Hastings," she said with a welcoming smile. "I'm Edith Brewster, Guy's mother."

Mrs. Brewster was dressed in a pale lavender suit trimmed with violet cuffs and lapels. Beneath the ensemble, she wore a white blouse of fine linen. A beautiful broach, studded with amethysts, was pinned to the silk suit's lapel. The entire outfit would have been at the forefront of fashion only a few years ago. Now, the suit seemed overly structured and its skirt was longer than most women currently wore. Despite that, Bella recognized it had, undoubtedly, cost a pretty penny. At the same time, she realized Ida's early morning fashion lesson had stayed with her. She was noticing style without even thinking about it. A smile formed at the thought. Her friend would be pleased.

After exchanging pleasantries, the older woman turned to the maid. "Katie, would you take a tray with coffee, rolls, and such to the patio? I'll see Miss Stewart and the constable out there." She turned back to her guests. "Come along. It's such a warm day that I thought you'd be more comfortable outside in the shade. You'll get the breeze there, too."

"Thank you," Bella said as they followed Mrs.

144

Brewster to a sprawling brick patio that ran almost the width of the house. A profusion of flowers bordered the patio and lined the brick pathways. More roses, like those in front, climbed trellises at each end of the veranda. In the distance, Bella saw a wooden swing in the shade of towering elms. She could easily imagine the family spending wonderful hours here. At least they would have before they'd lost their older son. Again, sadness filled Bella. The Brewsters had endured so much already. She sincerely hoped they wouldn't have to face Guy being arrested. Abruptly, her pleasure at the beautiful surroundings slipped away.

"Please sit down," their hostess told them as she indicated a white wrought-iron table and chairs located in a shady nook at one end of the patio. "Alan mentioned both of you many times, and Guy has, too, of course."

Bella and Jax expressed their sympathies over Alan's death. Mrs. Brewster's smile wavered. "We miss him terribly, but I understand you lost your brother in France, Miss Stewart, so you know how we feel."

"Yes, I do," Bella agreed in a soft murmur. She would always miss Matt and her parents, and she knew the same was true for others who had lost loved ones to influenza and war. Perhaps, it was even more difficult for a parent to lose a child. She'd been in France when Matt died, but her parents must have been devastated. Mac, too.

Mrs. Brewster went on quickly. "I'm afraid I have an appointment, but Katie will be out with refreshments right away, and Guy will be down shortly.

Please make yourselves at home."

After Mrs. Brewster went back into the house, Bella turned to Jax. "Do you think she knows why we're here?"

He shrugged. "She was very calm and hospitable, so I'm not sure. Of course, she may know but feel certain her son isn't involved."

Fresh anxiety filled Bella as she hoped again that Guy hadn't done something foolish. Mrs. Brewster was such a sweet lady.

Further discussion was cut off by Guy's arrival. The younger man looked anxious, but he greeted them warmly. He had just taken a seat when Katie arrived with the tray. Guy thanked her and turned back to his guests. "Father said that you called yesterday and wanted to talk with me. Evidently, you didn't tell him why."

Jax shook his head. "No, I didn't. I'm sure you heard what happened Sunday evening when you played golf yesterday."

Guy grimaced. "Yes, everyone was talking about it." He glanced from Jax to Bella and back.

When he hesitated, Jax cut in. "Do your parents know why we're here?"

A harsh breath escaped Guy. "When Dad passed your message on, I told him about the accident and about my run-in with Cecil last week, but I didn't tell Mother. I don't want to upset her. She took Alan's death very hard, and I don't want her worrying about me being questioned. It's only been in the last few months that she's returned to her regular activities. For months and months, she stayed at home or only spent time with a few close friends. Laheene's death was in this morning's paper, but Mother stopped reading the news after Alan died. She knows the man was courting Ida, and that upset her. Not because she doesn't want Ida to be happy, but because everyone knows Laheene is—was—a scoundrel." He chewed on his lower lip. "I wasn't involved in it, Jax, and I hope you won't have to question Mother."

"I don't see any reason why we should. I already know both of your parents were at the lake house on Sunday evening and that you were already home when they got back," Jax replied.

"Good, she's still quite fragile," Guy said. "I worry about her."

"I have a few questions for you, though," Jax said to the younger man.

"I'm happy to help if I can but, as I said, I wasn't involved."

His noncommittal tone did not reinforce the words. Guy was clearly concerned about his mother, which didn't mean he'd done nothing wrong. After another sip of coffee, Bella pulled her notepad out. Getting the facts down was important but, silently, she willed Guy to provide iron-clad evidence of his innocence.

Jax nodded at Guy. "I'd like to go over a few things with you in light of what we've already learned."

"Of course," Guy said before taking a bite of muffin.

"Several witnesses who were in the hotel on Sunday evening thought they heard you threaten Laheene," Jax observed. "Also, one of the caddies in your group on Sunday overheard you telling Sam that Laheene should get what's coming to him."

Guy's eyes widened. "Yes, I said I hoped he got what he deserved, and I'd like to see it happen. I didn't mean it as a personal threat, and I certainly didn't mean I planned to harm him myself because I didn't."

"But it sounds threatening," Jax pointed out.

"Now that Laheene is dead, I suppose it could," the younger man admitted, "but I honestly wasn't threatening him, Jax. I'm not sorry he's dead, which puts me with a lot of others." He laid what was left of the muffin on a plate. "Losing Alan almost killed my parents. As I told you, my mother is still struggling. I would never do anything to cause her more sorrow. I feel like I need to be an even better son now that Alan is gone." He swallowed convulsively. "I want to make Alan proud, too. I feel like I need to live for him, but I suppose that sounds silly."

While the words didn't eliminate him as a suspect, Guy's rough voice telegraphed a world of pain and loss and confusion. As she scanned his tanned face, Bella was filled with empathy. She knew how he felt. Losing a beloved big brother was a terrible blow.

"Not at all," Jax put in. "Mac has said he keeps going for Stew Stewart. They founded Ballantyne together, but Stew died some years ago." His gaze briefly went to Bella. "He was Bella's and Matt's grandfather."

"Everyone knows about Stew Stewart. He was a fine player. He and Mac both," Guy said.

"They were, and they were not only partners but best friends. Like brothers," Jax said.

Guy seemed to consider the observations. "Alan always said that's how you and Matt Stewart were."

Bella's heart lurched, and she quickly looked at Jax, whose expression remained impassive. However, the set of his shoulders revealed tension, so she waited for his response. Would he be open, as he'd been on their way here, or would he withdraw as he so often did?

"Matt and I were very close. I miss him every day, so I know some of how you feel about Alan," Jax said.

Although Jax seemed calm, his eyes glowed with some suppressed emotion, reminding Bella of their earlier conversation. He had defended her brother to Cecil, something that revealed the connection remaining between them. But Jax had also divulged that he'd been pushed nearly to the edge of his patience by whatever Laheene had said. As she studied Guy, Bella wondered if he had the same ironclad restraint. Perhaps not.

Guy put his forearms on his knees and leaned forward to focus on Jax. "I had to take up for my brother when Laheene went after him. Wouldn't you do the same for Matt?"

"I would, and I have," Jax admitted. "But only verbally."

"That's all I did, too. Believe me, I would have liked to punch Laheene, but I swear I didn't have anything to do with the accident."

Jax nodded. "I definitely understand wanting to hit him."

For long moments, Bella watched Jax. He'd admitted being pushed to the brink by Cecil, but she was stunned that he had considered hitting the other man. That was completely unlike Jax. Had Cecil's comments about Matt been so nasty? Or did grief make Jax react strongly? Since he rarely spoke about her brother, Bella couldn't be sure.

"I have to ask about your reactions, Guy," Jax told him. "It's my job and, since you don't have a strong alibi, I can't eliminate you as a suspect."

The younger man's jaw tightened, but he nodded. "I understand." Guy sighed. "I wish I had someone to vouch for me, but I probably passed the scene shortly before Laheene got there."

"Did anyone else see you on the road? Anyone who might have recognized your car?" Jax asked.

Bella bowed her head and continued to take notes. Although Guy said he couldn't kill anyone, had he caused the crash?

"I'm afraid not." Guy's brow furrowed in concentration. "There was a car coming the other way, but I don't think it was anyone from the tournament. Players and spectators wouldn't be coming toward Moreley at that time."

"What kind of car?" Jax asked.

"A dark Willys Touring car, I think. An older one. Since sunset was falling and there was rain and fog, I don't know if there were passengers or not. Is that any help?" Guy asked anxiously.

"It could be." Jax glanced at Bella. "Zeb Cutter lives out that way, and he has an old Willys. He's the only one who comes to mind. Can you think of anyone else?"

"No, I can't. Do you know if Zeb came to town on Sunday evening?" Bella asked.

"I don't, but I was in the office until late, so I wouldn't have seen him," Jax responded. "Of course, he could have turned off before he got to town." He turned back to Guy. "I'll talk with him later today and ask if he saw your car. He's the most likely local person to have seen you."

"I hope he did, but, like I said, it was almost dark by then, and the rain was getting heavy." Guy didn't quite meet Jax's gaze as he spoke. "And it's possible it wasn't a Willys."

"Your red roadster is rather distinctive, and the color should have shown up better than a dark vehicle, even with low visibility," Jax pointed out. "If Zeb was out there, I think he would have seen it."

"I wouldn't count on it," Guy insisted. "It was hard to see much. Another driver might have noticed a car but being able to identify a particular one would be difficult. The other car looked dark, but I don't know what color for sure. It could have been another kind of sedan. I can't be certain."

Guy's vacillation bothered Bella. Why was he suddenly dismissing the possibility of another driver seeing him? Had there actually been a car, or was he trying to provide a false alibi? His assertion about not wanting to cause more pain for his parents sounded valid, but that didn't mean he hadn't been involved in the smash-up.

"You said you didn't mean your words as a personal threat and that you wouldn't want to kill anyone, but did you consider scaring Laheene?" Jax asked.

The younger man looked at Jax in confusion. "I'm not sure what you mean."

"I mean, it's possible that the accident happened when someone swerved to frighten Laheene, and he could have lost control on the slippery road," Jax suggested.

Guy's eyes widened. "That would be a dangerous trick. Both cars could have crashed."

For a few seconds, Jax studied the younger man's expression. "Yes, they could have."

Guy met Jax's gaze. "I didn't do that, either, Jax. I'm not a fool. I wouldn't put my own life in jeopardy to scare anyone, not even Cecil Laheene."

"What about passing his car to show him up?" Jax asked. "We all know Laheene bragged about having a fast vehicle. Surely, you heard him do that."

"The Cadillac has a powerful engine," Guy agreed, "but my Dodge roadster is just as fast, and probably faster. I don't need to brag about it or try to show someone up, especially on a wet road in steady rain and thickening fog. Like I already told you, I'm not going to do anything to upset my parents."

Jax nodded in response before wrapping up the rest of the interview quickly and getting to his feet. "I'd like to look at your roadster before we leave."

A frown furrowed Guy's smooth brow as he stood up. "Why?"

"Because I'd like to ensure there's no damage to it. Right now, we're not sure how the crash happened. If the Cadillac has dents on the passenger side or front bumper, it's likely the other automobile does, too. And there is a ding on the back fender. If yours has none, that could rule you out."

Guy shifted from one foot to the other. "I was in a small smash-up early last week. I didn't have time to get it fixed before the tournament, so there's some damage."

Renewed apprehension filled Bella as she put her notepad and pencil away. When she looked at Jax, she saw his strained expression. What if Guy had caused the accident? Would it lead to his arrest? If so, Ida would be as distressed as the elder Brewsters.

"I'd still like to look at it," Jax said.

A harsh breath escaped Guy, but he nodded. "All right. It's at the side of the house."

Bella and Jax followed Guy to where the roadster was parked. As soon as they saw the passenger side, the dents were obvious.

Jax squatted down to take a better look. Before speaking, he glanced up at Guy. "I assume another vehicle was involved."

"A guy hit me coming out of a side street, but he drove off, and I didn't get a license plate number. The damage isn't bad enough to hinder driving. I'll get it repaired this week," Guy said.

After standing up, Jax replied. "Don't get it fixed until you hear from me."

Red rose in Guy's face. "I didn't have anything to

do with Cecil's crash. I already told you that. Don't you believe me?"

The plaintive tone in the younger man's voice was clear, but Jax couldn't let it affect him. "What I believe isn't important. Evidence is, so leave the car as is. In fact, I'd prefer that you don't drive it right now."

Moments of silence ticked away before Guy nodded. "All right."

"I'll let you know as soon as I talk to Zeb and also about fixing the dent," Jax said.

"All right," Guy said again.

"Please thank your mother for her hospitality," Bella said.

"I will," Guy said as he followed them to the Chummy. He bid Bella goodbye, but said nothing more to Jax.

Once they were on the road again, Bella asked Jax what he thought.

"I don't know what to think," he admitted. "First, Guy sounded like he could identify another car, which would have given him an alibi witness. Then, he hedged. That's troublesome. A red roadster would be noticeable when headlamps hit it, even in the rain. Even worse, it has a dent and dings. What did you think?"

"I felt the same way. For a moment, I thought he had someone who saw his car. Then, he made it sound like another driver couldn't possibly tell the color or kind. I know the rain was bad. Darkness was falling and fog was forming. But if Zeb passed Guy, I think he would have noticed and remembered seeing a red roadster. As you said, it's distinctive. The damage is troubling, too."

"I wish I'd seen Guy's vehicle up close last week, but I never took a long look."

"Why would you?" Bella asked. "None of us expected a fatal accident."

"True." Jax released a pent-up breath. "I'd like to stop by Zeb's place on our way home. If he was on the road and recalls seeing another car, it would help. As for the damage, it will be easier to tell if that's significant once we see the rest of the Cadillac."

"What if it wasn't Zeb Cutter? It could have been another driver," Bella pointed out. "Guy said he wasn't sure about the make and model."

"I know and, since it's a main road, it could have been anyone," Jax said. "Maybe someone simply passing through the area. The fact that Guy says it was a dark car isn't helpful, either. Not when many vehicles are dark colors. Plus, like you said, he hedged on the brand. I still don't want to believe Guy is guilty, but I can't help but think—despite what he said—he might have only been harassing Laheene or maybe showing off."

"That seems all too possible. Guy was so upset and angry with Cecil. First over Alan, and then, with how Ida was treated. That's a volatile combination," she admitted.

"Yes, and he's still a kid. Of course, so is Chaz Smith."

"Maybe we'll learn something from him that will lead to answers."

"That would be nice," Jax said, but his tone indicated he wasn't counting on it.

Since Bella had been to The Woods several times in the past, she easily drove the short distance from the Brewster home. "It's not noon yet, so we may be waiting for Chaz," she pointed out.

"The pro is expecting us, and I'd like to speak with him," Jax told Bella. "If Chaz isn't there yet, we can use the putting green."

"That would be fun," Bella remarked. "I haven't been here for a few years, but I heard the head pro retired."

"Yes, he did. The new pro took this job about three years ago. He's heard of Ballantyne, of course."

"Is he from this area?" she asked, thinking she might know the man already.

"No, he moved here from Pennsylvania."

As Bella steered the Chummy down the tree-lined boulevard leading to the course, she smiled. The old oaks, elms, and maples provided a canopy for the homes and the street. On such a warm summer day, the pools of shade dotting the road were appealing. "It's a beautiful area, and the course is lovely."

At the end of the winding driveway, she pulled to a stop in the parking area. Two young caddies hurried to the car. "Good morning," the taller one said. "Can we take your clubs?"

Jax pulled some money from his pocket as he got out of the Chummy. "That would be great," he replied as he opened the trunk. Once the young-sters grabbed the bags, he handed some coins to each one. "Thanks, boys."

Bella joined Jax by the back of the Chevrolet. "Should we change our shoes or wait and see if Chaz is already here?"

"Let's see if he's here first."

She nodded. They followed the cobblestone walk to the golf shop. A few other caddies were sitting on a bench to one side, but all of them were too young to be Smith. As she looked farther on, Bella saw a tall, slim man in his early thirties standing in front of the building. Clad in muted plaid knickers, a brown sweater vest, and a white shirt with a brown tie, he looked every inch the golf professional.

When he saw them, he headed their way. "Good morning. Would you be Miss Stewart and Constable Hastings?"

"Yes," Jax replied as he put his hand out.

The other man shook it. "I'm Griffith Biggins, the pro here."

"It's nice to meet you," Bella said.

Biggins smiled at her. "And it's wonderful to meet you, Miss Stewart. I've heard great things about Ballantyne, and I'm so glad the inn re-opened this year. It has a marvelous reputation. The course is well-known as a challenging layout. I hope to play there soon." His pale silver eyes, sparkling in his tanned face, focused on Bella.

"Please come any time and be our guest," she said. "We'd love to have you."

"That's very kind. I hope if I'm able to come, you'll consider being my playing partner." He beamed at her again.

Pink rose in her cheeks. "I don't play much now."

His smile remained in place. "I've heard you were an accomplished golferette before the war. I'm sure it will come back to you quickly."

"I wouldn't want to interfere with your game," she said, but her tone was light.

"You wouldn't interfere. In fact, it would be a pleasure to play with you."

Jax ground his teeth as he listened to the by-play. Bella was always unfailingly pleasant to everyone, but he'd never seen her respond quite like this to a man. Of course, he seldom saw her around eligible bachelors. Jax knew Biggins fell into that category because the man had revealed—in their telephone conversation the day before—that he lived alone above the pro shop. Mixed emotions filled Jax. He wasn't involved with Bella, so she could flirt with other men. One like Biggins had to be of interest. Not only was he a handsome guy and a dapper dresser, but he was also a golf professional, like all the important men in her life had been. Jax didn't want to think too much about why the interaction between them bothered him. After all, he and Bella had a casual, sibling-like relationship now and, due to his bad judgment in France, they always would.

To change the conversation, he said, "Is Smith here?" Even to his own ears, his question sounded brusque and cold. He felt Bella's gaze on him, but he ignored her. A moment of silence passed. Jax glanced around as if looking for the caddy.

"I just checked with our caddy master, and Chaz isn't here yet. That's not unusual, though. He normally comes right around noon. Sometimes, a bit later. While you're waiting for him, do you want to putt or come into the shop?" He turned his attention to Bella. "It's a hot day, but it's cool inside."

"Maybe you and I could putt, Biggins. Then, you could point Smith out when he gets here. Neither of us is sure what he looks like," Jax said, his voice still chilly.

Dismay darkened the other man's gaze, but he nodded. "Sure." When he turned back to Bella, the pro smiled. "You're welcome to join us or wait inside, Miss Stewart."

"Oh, please call me Bella, Mr. Biggins."

"And you must call me Griff. All my friends do."

Once again, irritation filled Jax. "We need to change our shoes," he said in a clipped tone. "Come on, Bella." He turned and stalked off.

Chapter Eleven

B ella followed him but, when she got to the car, she put her hands on her hips and stared at Jax. "What was that about?"

"What was what about?" he asked. He kept his attention on changing his shoes and didn't spare her a glance. He'd probably made an idiot of himself, but Jax didn't want to be chastised. He already felt ridiculous.

"You were very rude to Griff, and he's doing us a favor."

Her assertion was true, but Jax brushed it off. "Sorry, I'm just on edge. I want to get this case solved as soon as possible."

"I know you do," Bella replied. Without another word, she changed her shoes and headed to the pro shop where Biggins waited for them. She didn't even glance back at Jax.

Bella's abrupt dismissal telegraphed her consternation. Jax finished putting on his shoes before joining the pair. He forced a smile. "I appreciate you cooperating with us, Biggins." Jax knew he sounded insincere, but he was really trying to be civil. If Bella liked the pro and Biggins liked her, that was none of Jax's business. It couldn't be.

"Always glad to help a fellow pro," the other man said.

Jax's smile faded. He was no longer a *fellow pro*, but he didn't point that out. Instead, he took his putter from his bag and walked to the practice green with Biggins and Bella.

About fifteen minutes later, the other man said, "Chaz just drove in. He's in an old black coupe."

Jax glanced toward the parking lot and saw a lean young man climb out of the vehicle. He didn't look familiar.

"Do you want me to call him over?" Biggins asked Jax.

"Yes, that's a good idea. Once he gets over here, you can introduce us." Jax started to mentally review the questions he planned to ask the boy.

"What will you do if he runs?" Bella asked.

"Chase him," Jax said.

Bella looked dubious. Did she think he was incapable of running? His arm was wounded, not his legs, and Jax was hardly an invalid.

"We'll both give chase, Bella," Biggins assured her.

Jax wanted to tell the other man to stay out of it, but he resisted. Sounding irritable wasn't apt to help the situation. Instead, he said, "The car looks to be the crank kind. Even if he runs, he'd have to take time to get it going."

Biggins called out to the caddy. "Hey, Smith,

come over for a minute."

The lanky youth headed toward them. As he grew closer, Jax noted he looked calm and unconcerned. That was good. Chaz stopped once he reached them. He looked at Bella and Jax. "In need of a good caddy?"

"Not at the moment," Jax told him.

"Smith, these people would like to speak with you."

The young man's brow crinkled as he looked from Biggins to Bella to Jax. "Why?" Suspicion roughened his voice.

"This is Miss Arabella Stewart. She's a co-owner of Ballantyne," Biggins said.

Chaz Smith looked at her. "Sure. I think I saw you last week."

"Probably so," Bella replied with a smile.

Smith looked at Jax. "Don't remember you. Are you the other owner?"

"No, I'm not." Jax kept his voice even and calm.

"This is Constable Jackson Hastings," Biggins inserted.

Smith's dark gaze narrowed as he took a step back. "What do you want?"

"Just to ask you a few questions," Jax replied.

"About what?" A note of challenge was in the young man's voice.

"About Cecil Laheene's death."

"I don't know nothing," Smith asserted, his tone surly and his expression hard. He crossed his arms over his chest and took another step away from Jax.

"Even so, I'd like to talk with you." Jax looked at Biggins. "Is there a quiet, private place for us to do so?"

"You can use my office. It's very small, but there are three chairs," Biggins said.

With that, he led the way into the golf shop and to a tiny room at the back. A huge desk took up most of the space but, as Biggins had said, there were three seats. "Bella, why don't you sit at the desk?" Jax suggested as he sat nearest the door. Although he didn't think Smith would do a runner, he couldn't be sure. If the kid ran, Jax didn't want Bella in the way.

After the three were seated, the pro said, "I'll be in the shop if you need anything."

Jax turned his attention to the caddy. The young man still looked tense and angry. "We won't take too much of your time."

"I hope not. I need to get out and caddy."

Jax cleared his throat. "As I said, this shouldn't take very long."

Smith's attention moved to Bella. "Why is she here? Shouldn't she be at Ballantyne?"

"Miss Stewart is taking notes for me," Jax replied. "I'm sure you've heard about Cecil Laheene dying in a car accident."

The boy nodded. "It was in the morning papers. We can't afford none, but some neighbors was talking about it in our building. Folks all know the Laheene name around here."

"I'm sure they do," Jax agreed. "Now, as I said, I want to ask you some questions since you two have a history. We know you and Laheene had words on Sunday evening."

Smith shrugged. "Yeah, we did, and that weren't

the first time. Since you know we have a history, as you call it, you must also know what he done to my little brother."

"We've heard about the incident, so I certainly understand why you hated Laheene," Jax offered.

"Do you really, constable?" Skepticism was in Smith's voice. "My brother still can't walk good. He needs therapy, probably surgery, too, but we can't afford none. My ma can't hardly get groceries and pay rent. She looks after an old lady at night, every night. She cleans houses during the days when me or someone else can be with Chipper cuz she's afraid he might fall and hurt himself worse if he was alone. That's why I don't caddy none until afternoon. Sometimes, it gives her a chance to sleep. Other times, she cleans somewhere. I've looked for a regular job but can't get none around here. The Laheenes are powerful, and no one wants to cross them. I'm lucky I can still caddy."

His tone remained hard, but his gaze was clouded with some softer emotion. Resentment, fear, frustration? Jax couldn't blame the boy for his hard feelings. Not after what his family had endured. "I suppose your father attacking Cecil Laheene has something to do with no one wanting to hire you," Jax suggested.

The boy's eyes widened. "Who told you about my pa?"

"When a man is arrested and found guilty of assault, it's hardly a secret," Jax said, "especially to a lawman."

Chaz's lips flattened into a grimace. "I suppose," the boy said, "but my pa only wanted Laheene to pay for what he did. Laheene wasn't arrested because his old man interfered. Both of them said it was my brother's own fault, but he wouldn't have run and fallen again if Laheene hadn't been cursing and chasing him. They coulda given us money. Chipper deserves good care, and they can afford to pay for it."

"I'd heard old Mr. Laheene provided funds," Jax observed.

Smith snorted derisively. "Only enough to pay the hospital bill, but there's not even enough to pay someone to sit with my brother when my ma works. That's why she took a night job looking after the old woman. That's why she can't even take regular cleaning jobs. Someone has to be with my brother all the time."

Sympathy filled Jax, but he didn't show it. He had a job to do and he couldn't let his emotions get in the way. "Witnesses said you threatened Laheene. Is that true?"

A sneer curved the boy's lips. "I said I hoped he got what was coming to him. I hoped he suffered like my brother," Smith readily admitted. "But I never said I'd kill him, and I didn't. Didn't cry no tears over him being dead, though." He paused before continuing. "My ma needs me. So does Chipper. If I went to jail, they might end up in the streets. I ain't takin' that chance, not even to hurt Laheene."

The boy sounded sincere, but Jax could hardly eliminate him based on that. Guy had also seemed earnest, but he remained a suspect. "No one seems to know when you left Moreley since you evidently parked in back of the hotel."

When Chaz shook his head, a lock of brown hair fell over one eye. With one hand, he hastily brushed it back. "It weren't only me. All the caddies parked there, but it ain't true that nobody saw me leave. Mick Carrier rode back with me."

Frustration filled Jax. Yet another name arose, and he'd only eliminated Ida as a suspect so far. A longer list meant more time to solve the case, and old man Laheene was close to hiring a detective. "Does Carrier caddy here?"

The boy hesitated before answering. "Yeah, he does."

"Do you know if he's here today?" Jax asked.

The boy shrugged. "He caddies here most afternoons, but he needs a ride. I usually pick him up, but I didn't hear nothing from him this morning. Sometimes, he comes with someone else, though." Smith shifted restlessly in his seat. "Look, I really don't know no more. Can I go now?"

"I have a few more questions," Jax told him. "I know your father was sent to jail, but he's out now. Do you know where he is?"

The boy looked away. "I ain't got no idea."

"Didn't he come home when he got out?" Jax asked.

Chaz clasped his hands in his lap and stared down at them. "For a few minutes, but Ma told him to get out and not come back because she was afraid of him getting drunk again. He said he'd dried out in jail. She didn't believe he'd stay off the bottle, though. He could get illegal hooch some place." The boy looked back at Jax. "I know my ma has her hands full, but pa needs help, too."

"Was your father drunk when he went after La-heene?" Jax asked.

The boy's gaze came up then. "I suppose. At least he were drunk when he came home from Laheene's place. I don't know if he went to no bar before or after."

"Did your father always drink a lot?"

Chaz shook his head. "Only after he got back from France. Then, him and the bottle was best buddies."

Surprise filled Jax. "Your father served in the war?"

"Yep. He didn't have to. He volunteered. Thought he should do his duty." A low, humorless laugh left the boy. "He got wounded toward the end. When he came home, he were still in a bad way. After a while, when he got better, he tried for his old job. They didn't save his place, and they didn't need no more help then. He looked for other jobs, but he couldn't find nothing. Lotsa men looking for work, and not much around. The leg bothered him some, so he couldn't do lotsa jobs. That's when pa really got to boozing. When Laheene went after my brother, my pa was furious." Chaz looked directly at Jax. "Laheene didn't go to France, you know."

"I know," Jax replied. He tamped down his own feelings.

"My pa said his father probably used his power to keep him home and that were wrong." He shook his head. "And it weren't right that Laheene got off after what happened to Chipper, but my pa went to jail. Chipper got hurt a whole lot worse than Laheene."

"Son," Jax began, his voice subdued, "many things

in life aren't fair, but that doesn't mean we should take justice into our own hands. That never works out well." He didn't try to explain the difference between the two cases to the boy. Laheene scaring and going after Chipper had led to the boy's injury, even if it wasn't a crime. Common decency should have led him to offer a lot more money, but no one had ever referred to Cecil Laheene as decent.

Chaz's answer was a shrug. Then, he said, "Can I go now?"

Jax ignored the question. "Do you know of any place that your father might have gone? Another relative's, for example, or a friend's?"

The boy shook his head. "My grandparents are dead, and we don't have no other family around here. As for friends, the ones who didn't go to France don't care and the ones who did have their own problems."

Since Jax couldn't deny the last comment, he went on, "You can go for now, but I may want to talk with you again after I interview Carrier. And, if you hear from your father, I need to know. If you tell Mr. Biggins, he can get in touch with me."

The boy gave a brief nod before leaving the office.

Chapter Twelve

After young Smith was gone, Jax turned to Bella. "He knows more than he said, I think."

"Probably, but we found out a lot about Mr. Smith and about Chaz's alibi witness."

Jax ran one hand over his face. "You're right, but it adds at least one more interview and, unless we can track Carrier down today, it means another trip here. Chaz was most likely lying when he said he didn't know where his father is, and Carrier might know something in that regard."

"Very possible," Bella agreed. "And, if Chaz didn't tell the truth about that, I have to wonder if Mr. Smith had something to do with the accident."

Jax drummed his fingers against his knee as he considered her statement. "If they are communicating, Mr. Smith and Chaz could both be involved. We don't know where Smith is, but what if he came to Moreley to see Chaz? If Mrs. Smith won't let the man into the house, it would have given them a chance to get together."

"I agree. Do you want to see if we can find the father today?"

Jax put his elbows on his knees and clasped his hands in front of him. "It would be like finding a needle in a haystack. We can ask if anyone else knows where he might be, but tracking him down today isn't likely. If he has no other family, he may be in a flophouse. Or go from one to the other. He may even live on the streets."

A soft sigh escaped Bella. "You're probably right." A man without decent accommodations was apt to be desperate, especially one who had served his country and come home to no job and then, to his young son being badly injured. Terrible insults had been added to grievous injury in Mr. Smith's life. Another thought came to her mind. "How would Mr. Smith get to Moreley? Do you think he could have a vehicle?"

Jax frowned. "That's a good question. One I should have asked Chaz."

"There's no reason to think he'd tell the truth about that, since he probably lied about not knowing where his father is. After all, a vehicle would make Mr. Smith more of a suspect, and the boy isn't likely to say something to implicate him," Bella pointed out. "Besides, Mr. Smith could have borrowed a car or gotten someone to take him, even if he doesn't own one himself. Chaz isn't apt to reveal that, either."

"Buying and maintaining a vehicle is expensive, so I'm guessing Mr. Smith doesn't own one. Chaz has a junker, but even that's unusual for a poor kid."

Bella chewed on her lower lip. "True, but it wouldn't be impossible for Mr. Smith to get a ride."

"We need to find out for sure."

"Maybe Preston Cherry can help," Bella suggested.

"I'll call him. He didn't know Smith was out of jail, but he could do some checking. I hope I can catch him now because we need to be at Etting's office by three o'clock. And there's also Mick Carrier to find." Once again, Jax sounded stymied.

"Maybe Carrier will show up if we wait a while. In the meantime, you can probably call Preston from here."

Jax nodded. "I'll ask."

Biggins said to make as many local calls as needed, so Jax contacted Preston Cherry. Bella waited while he did, but she learned little from hearing only one side of the conversation. When Jax hung up, she immediately asked what he'd found out.

"Preston doesn't know where Smith could be, but he'll call a friend in the district attorney's office who might be able to help. If he reaches him quickly, we may hear back in a short time. I also asked about the nature of Chipper's injuries, and if what Laheene told Ida was true. Preston said the boy was taken straight home from the golf course, and he didn't get medical help for a day or so. No one realized the extent of his injury, I guess. Evidently, Mrs. Smith was working two jobs and didn't get back until the following morning. Chaz wasn't sure what to do, which is understandable, since money is a big consideration. Anyhow, Chipper broke his ankle, and not getting immediate care affected its healing."

"That's terrible but understandable. Chaz wouldn't have had money to pay a doctor or hospital bill and probably felt he had to wait for his mother to get home."

"I'm sure he did. It makes me hope even more that neither Chaz nor Mr. Smith is involved in the crash. If they aren't, Laheene might pay more money, which would pay for additional care. That could make a big difference for Chipper."

"That would be wonderful," Bella said as she once again hoped Cecil caused the crash himself.

For the next fifteen minutes, Bella and Jax stayed in the pro shop. When Cherry called, Jax spoke while Bella stood nearby, trying to glean information.

As soon as he hung up, he turned to her. "Preston found out that the elder Smith has often been seen at a bar called The Shanghai. Other than that, his friend has no information."

"Maybe we should check it out," Bella suggested.

Jax immediately objected. "You're not going there."

Bella frowned. "I'd be perfectly safe with you."

Jax shook his head. "According to Preston, it's in a very tough part of town. Not only do criminals frequent it, but they also live in cheap hotels in the area. Rum runners do business there, too. Bars can't serve liquor legally, but many have secret hideaways. With all that going on, I wouldn't take the Chummy there, let alone you." With effort, he forced a note of amusement into his voice, but Bella still looked grim.

"Are you planning to come back by yourself another day?" she asked.

"I'm planning on talking with Mick Carrier today if we can, and I want to keep our appointment with Floyd Etting. There's not much point in talking to Preston in person. If he finds out anything more, he'll let me know. After we see Floyd, we can discuss what the next move should be." He added the last statement to mollify her. Not that Jax thought she wouldn't bring up going to The Shanghai again, but at least he could put her off for now.

"Then, we might as well go back to the putting green."

"You're right," he agreed. "If we're lucky, Carrier will show up soon."

While Bella and Jax spent the next hour on the putting green, Biggins came out a couple of times. Finally, he let them know he was teeing off shortly.

"We'll be gone by the time you finish your round, but I appreciate your help," Jax said.

Jax sounded more pleasant, which made Bella smile. His earlier behavior had been completely out of character. Of course, his admission about Laheene pushing him to the limit was, too. Jax had said, on more than one occasion, that war had changed him. Bella didn't disagree, but how much had he changed? Maybe more than she wanted to believe.

"Happy to do it," Biggins assured him, before turning to Bella. "I'll call when I have a free day to play Ballantyne. I'm really looking forward to seeing your course."

When his gaze briefly skimmed over her, Bella knew Ida had been right. The chic outfit definitely drew more male attention than her pre-war garb did. An added benefit was more freedom of movement, as Mary Rogers had said. "I'll look forward to that," she replied with a smile. Oddly enough, Bella found she meant it.

While they waited for Mick Carrier, Jax inspected Chaz Smith's car. Bella went along. As they approached it, Jax spoke. "This vehicle has seen better days," he said, glancing from one end to the other.

"With so many dents and dings, I'm surprised it made the trip to Moreley," Bella added.

"Me, too." A heavy breath left him. "There's no way to tell if any of the damage is new, so we might as well go back to the practice green and wait."

Less than thirty minutes passed before Biggins' young assistant came to get them. "Griff asked me to let you know if Mick Carrier showed up. He's here now, in the office."

Jax thanked the man before following Bella into the cramped space where the caddy waited. Jax introduced Bella and himself before they both sat down. "I appreciate you speaking to us."

The boy, who looked to be about fourteen, glanced uneasily from Jax to Bella and back. "I'm not sure why you want to talk with me. I didn't do nothing wrong while I was in Moreley or at Ballantyne." He plucked absently at the battered flat cap in his lap.

"You aren't being accused of any wrongdoing," Jax assured him. "I'm questioning everyone who was in the hotel on Sunday evening shortly before Cecil Laheene left. You've heard about the accident?"

"Yes, sir. It was in the papers. One of my neighbors is a newsboy, and he told me." Mick looked solemn.

"We heard you might have been at the hotel about the time Mr. Laheene left." Jax kept his voice well-modulated.

Carrier licked his lips. "Yes, sir, I was there. Several of us caddies shared one of the cheap rooms. Mr. Cooper was real nice about letting us do that. Otherwise, we would have had to drive back and forth every day. That's a long trip, and I don't drive yet, so I gotta go with someone. His wife even fixed sandwiches for us at no charge."

"Thad Cooper and his wife are fine people," Jax agreed. "Who gave you a ride to and from Moreley?"

"Chaz Smith. He gives me a ride here most times. Today, a neighbor dropped me off." The boy's pale blue gaze flickered from Jax to the cap in his hands.

"I see," Jax observed. The boy seemed nervous, but that didn't mean he was lying. As young as he was, being questioned about a homicide was enough to cause anxiety. "Did you and Chaz leave before Laheene?"

The boy shifted in the chair. "Yes, sir." He hesitated a moment. "We were on our way out when Mr. Laheene came into the lobby. He said nasty things."

"Like what?" Jax asked.

Color suffused the boy's cheeks. "He said he didn't know riff-raff was allowed in the hotel. That made Chaz mad. He said if anyone was riff-raff, it was Mr. Laheene. Then, both of them was mad. Mr. Laheene said Chaz should watch out, or he'd end up like his brother." Mick stopped and then, said, "Do you know about Chipper?"

"Yes, we've heard the story," Jax told him.

"Then, you know why Chaz hates—hated—Mr. Laheene. I was scared they'd get into a fistfight, but Mr. Cooper came out of the office and told them to stop."

"What happened then?" Jax asked.

"Chaz said he hoped Mr. Laheene got what he deserved. We left after that."

"Did Chaz say anything more in the car?" Jax asked.

Mick kept staring at his cap. "He was mad because Mr. Laheene said bad things about us."

"Were you mad, Mick?"

The boy's gaze came up to meet Jax's. "I didn't like being called no riff-raff," he admitted in a rough voice. "I'm not rich like Mr. Laheene, but my pa works hard, and I caddy as much as I can to make extra money."

Briefly, Bella and Jax exchanged a look. Then, she glanced at the boy's attire. Jax followed her gaze. While neat and clean, his clothing was worn and faded and his shoes, sporting broken and knotted laces, were badly scuffed.

"You're as good as anyone, Mick. Never let people make you feel like you aren't," Bella said in a soft but firm voice.

The boy studied her face for a moment. "Thank you, miss."

"You don't need to thank me. It's the truth," she told him. "People who belittle others usually aren't happy with themselves."

Mick's attention remained on Bella for several moments before he nodded. "That makes sense. I'll remember it."

"Good," Bella said with a smile.

Jax steered the conversation back to the matter at hand. "Did you leave town right away?"

Mick licked his lips. "Yes."

"And you came straight back to Cleveland?"

Mick again looked at the cap in his hands as if the answer might be found there. After several moments, he replied. "Yes, sir. My mother expects me to attend evening church services when I caddy on Sunday mornings, and Chaz knew I had to be back in time to clean up."

"Where do you go to church?" Jax asked. The boy named the place. "I'm sure your mother is happy that you attempted to be there."

"Oh, yes," young Carrier agreed, but his attention stayed on the cap in his lap.

"Do you know Mr. Smith, Chaz's father?" Bella asked.

The boy's head came up, and he looked from her to Jax. "Sure. I used to see him lots when they lived by us. Chaz's ma moved them after his pa went to jail."

"Have you seen Mr. Smith lately?" Jax observed the boy as he posed the question.

Mick started fiddling with his cap again. "Not lately."

The somewhat vague answer, along with Mick's startled expression, bothered Jax. "When was the last time you saw him?"

The boy shifted restlessly on the chair but said nothing.

"Mick, was Mr. Smith in Moreley over the weekend?" Jax asked.

The boy hesitated. "No, sir," was the delayed reply.

Jax felt sure the boy was lying, but he didn't know what else to say. Badgering Mick was unlikely to help. Boys his age were usually very loyal to their friends. If Chaz was seeing his father, he would expect his buddies to keep the secret. Undoubtedly, he wanted to keep the information from his mother. It wasn't lost on Jax that maintaining confidences was hardly limited to boys. After all, he was still honoring pledges to both Matt and Alan. "That's all for now. If I have other questions for you, do you have a telephone?"

"No, sir, but I caddy here most afternoons and on Saturdays. Some Sunday mornings, my mother wants me at church. She says even God took a day off."

Jax grinned. "It's good that you listen to your mother. I'll call Mr. Biggins if I have any other questions. He can pass along my message, and we can talk over the phone if he'll give you permission. I appreciate your time." Jax stood and extended his hand to the boy.

"Yes, sir. Can I go?"

Jax nodded. Once Mick was out of earshot, he looked at Bella. "What do you think?"

"He seems like a nice boy, but rather nervous. That's not unusual, though. He's probably never spoken with a constable before. What did you think? Did you believe him?"

Jax tapped his fingers on the edge of the desk. "I'm not sure. Mostly, but I don't know that he told the truth about Mr. Smith not being in Moreley. He seemed anxious and tentative, but Chaz probably said to keep quiet if Mr. Smith came around."

Bella leaned back in the chair. "If he was in Moreley, Mr. Smith would likely have maintained a low profile. He wouldn't have wanted Cecil to see him."

"True, especially since Laheene may not have known Smith was out of jail." Jax ran one hand over his face. "I hope we can get Smith's location. I want to talk with him, but we also need to check with the minister at the church, see what time the service was, and make certain Mick was there. Otherwise, I'm not prepared to remove Chaz as a suspect. The elder Smith might have talked Chaz into trying to run Laheene off the road. Chaz's old junker couldn't pass the Cadillac, but he could have swerved toward it. If they can't get money, they may have wanted to get even. Not logical but, when emotions run high, sense goes out the window."

"You're right about that. Chaz says he left before Cecil. Do you think he waited for the Cadillac to come along?" Bella asked with dismay.

"It's a possibility. Of course, I'm still not sure that either Chaz or his father is responsible. Guy could be, and I don't want to get focused too much on anyone in particular at this point. I wish we had one suspect, but it has to be the right one."

"I hate to think what will happen to Mrs. Smith and Chipper if Chaz ran Cecil off the road."

"Me, too, Bella. Me, too."

Luckily, the church was close to Etting's office, so they could stop on their way. Unfortunately, the minister was calling on parishioners. When the secretary said he wouldn't be back until late afternoon, Bella and Jax continued on to the next interview.

"Has Mr. Laheene contacted you again, Jax?" Bella asked. "I've been wondering if he just wants to keep after you, or if he'll really hire a private detective."

He grimaced. "He called the mayor early this morning and pretty much repeated what he told me. If we don't have a solid suspect by the funeral, which is day-after-tomorrow, Laheene is definitely planning to start his own investigation, not simply prod me." More than ever, Jax knew his job was in real jeopardy.

"What did the mayor say?"

Jax tried to keep the dismay out of his voice and expression. "He told Laheene that he completely understood, and he wants to be sure I do, too. After all, the man simply wants justice for his son." He hadn't revealed everything to Nolen, but it spilled out now.

Her gaze widened. "The mayor told you that?"

"Yes, he made a point of emphasizing how important it is to solve the case quickly. Of course, Cawlings also assured me he knows I will." Jax hadn't revealed the early conversation to anyone else, but it had been in the back of his mind all day. Pressure was building, and he felt the weight of it bearing down.

Bella scowled. "As usual, Mayor Cawlings isn't taking a strong stand. First, he said he supports you and that Mr. Laheene has no influence in Moreley. Now, you need to solve the case right away because the man demands justice for his son." A humorless laugh escaped her. "The senior Laheene wasn't concerned with justice when Cecil chased after a child and scared the poor boy so badly that the kid ended up with a badly broken ankle. Did you point that out to our mayor?"

"Of course not," Jax replied. "Cawlings is more-or-less my boss, and I understand he doesn't want adverse publicity for Moreley. We both know the town can't take more of that. Neither can Ballantyne. A lot of visitors used to come from the Cleveland area, and old Laheene could vent his complaints to the newspapers here. I need to be circumspect in how I talk to the mayor, and Cawlings has to be cautious in dealing with Laheene. We both do."

"I see your point, but you've been working the case very hard in a very short time. That's all you can do, Jax. Putting extra pressure on yourself won't help."

Some of the tension was internal, but a lot came from external forces—forces beyond his control. "The funeral is day-after-tomorrow. I need one primary suspect before then." His voice was rough with fatigue and exasperation.

"Jax, I know you don't want to deal with detectives, but give yourself some breathing space. We can go back to the church later and talk with the minister. Then, you can check on Guy's alibi witness on the way home. At that point, you should be able to eliminate one of them. Also, Etting may eliminate or incriminate himself. Let's see how things stand at the end of today."

"You're right," he admitted. "I just want to solve the case before private eyes get involved. And before Laheene's father makes trouble." The elder Laheene wouldn't hesitate to make good on his threats to besmirch Ballantyne and Moreley. Nor would he blanche at having Jax sacked. Mayor Cawlings wasn't apt to stand behind Jax, and neither would the councilmen who'd voted against hiring him. If he lost his job, where would he go? What would he do? Few options were available to a dismissed constable or to an infirm golf pro—and he'd be both if the worst happened.

"We don't need to worry about that now. Let's focus on getting as much information as we can today and see if any of it proves crucial."

"Good advice," he conceded, but taking advice was hard, especially when he didn't want to let anyone down. Or lose his job.

Chapter Thirteen

W hen they arrived at Floyd Etting's insurance office, his secretary asked them to sit down while she checked to see if he was free. Neither Bella nor Jax took a chair. She stood near the desk while he paced the width of the office. Bella wanted to tell Jax to relax but knew that would do no good. He was anxious, possibly too anxious, to solve the case. However, this was not a good time to point that out again. Although he listened to her concerns, Jax kept pushing himself hard.

The secretary returned in a few moments and ushered them into an office at the end of a long corridor. Etting, seated behind a massive and ornate desk, stood to greet them before telling the secretary that she was free to leave for the day.

After Bella and Jax took chairs across from Etting, who again sat behind his desk, the man asked, "How can I help you, constable?"

Bella, who was pulling her notepad out of her

pocketbook, glanced at the insurance agent in surprise. Floyd Etting had known Jax for many years, long before he was in law enforcement, so the use of his title, instead of his given name, seemed odd and off-key.

"As I said on the phone, I have some questions for you. I've been interviewing others today, as well," Jax replied.

"A fine idea. I gather you haven't found the culprit yet," Etting observed in a wry tone.

Implicit criticism seemed to underscore the statement and, as Bella glanced at Jax, she saw his jaw tighten and spoke up. "It's been less than two days, and Jax has narrowed the suspects down to a handful already." A dark flush rose in Jax's face. At the same time, he sent a scowl her way. She immediately flipped open her notepad and put pencil to paper. Obviously, he didn't appreciate her intervention. Not a surprise. Later, Bella might point out that she would have jumped to her brother's defense, too.

Etting's bushy eyebrows rose. "Really? That's good news."

"That's why I wanted to speak with you again," Jax said. "I'm hoping to cull the list even more."

"I'll help in any way I can. We don't want any killers on the loose."

"No, we don't," Jax agreed. "As far as physical evidence, there were two sets of tire tracks, but we can't be sure the other driver caused the smash-up. Even if he did, we don't know that he intended to harm Laheene. He may have only wanted to harass him."

"Really? What makes you think that?" Etting asked.

"Several things," Jax replied without elaborating.

Etting's lips flattened. "Why would someone want to harass Cecil?"

The insurance agent appeared to be genuinely puzzled, but perhaps he was a good actor, Bella thought as she briefly scanned his face. His expression gave away as little as his statement.

"The same reasons that someone might have wanted to kill him," Jax said. "It's common knowledge that Laheene antagonized many people. He enjoyed humiliating others, as you know."

Jax presented his points in a calm, professional manner that made Bella smile. Despite his self-doubt, he was proficient at his job.

Etting's placid demeanor disappeared. "I can't disagree with that, but I've never felt humiliated by him." He sounded defensive, even hostile.

"How did you feel? After all, he blamed you for your team not winning the fourball," Jax observed, "and he did it in front of a large gallery."

The older man leaned back in his chair, but tension was evident in the set of his jaw. "He played poorly himself, so he couldn't pin losing on me, although he tried. Everyone knows that, and everyone knows Cecil. I was aggravated at the time, but I didn't let it bother me much beyond the moment. I don't let him get to me. I know better."

"Even so, he made a scene when you left the eighteenth green. That couldn't have been pleasant," Jax observed. His voice remained calm, as did his expression.

Etting rested his elbows on the chair arms and steepled his fingers together as a laugh escaped him. "He's made many scenes. There's really nothing new to say on the subject. Cecil was a poor sport, a sore loser, and a spoiled rich boy."

"Then, why did you partner with him?" Jax asked.

"He was a substitute. My original partner had to back out. By then, I didn't have a lot of choices. Besides, Cecil was an excellent player, and we had a shot at winning," Etting replied. "I'd never teamed with him in the past, but I've had other difficult partners. I muddled along well enough with them, and I did with him until the final nine of the last day."

"You seemed furious with him when you left eighteen," Jax said.

A flush rose in Etting's cheeks. "Who wouldn't have been? He acted horribly." The man paused as he tapped his forefingers together. "We discussed all of this when we spoke on the phone, constable. I don't think there's anything more to add."

"I believe there is," Jax told him. "When we last spoke, you didn't tell me you threatened Laheene shortly before he left the hotel and on the golf course."

"Threatened him? I didn't threaten Cecil." His eyes widened as if in surprise.

Once again, Bella wasn't sure if Etting was putting on a front or revealing the truth. Before the war, the man had come to Ballantyne on a few occasions. Although she recalled him being courteous, Bella had never had a lengthy exchange with him.

"According to witnesses at the hotel, you said

you'd see Laheene pay for his transgressions," Jax pointed out. "And the boy who caddied for you heard you saying Laheene should get what was coming to him."

Surprise turned to stoicism, and Etting shrugged. "Right before we teed off on Sunday, I ran into a couple of the members from Cecil's club. One is an attorney, John Rylinger. He's helping the Smith family for free. Old Mr. Laheene gave them a pittance, but John is convinced he can get them a lot more. He only told me because he saw Cecil carry on at a couple of other tournaments this summer. Words of warning maybe, although I already knew about some of the issues. I was thinking of that when I said he should pay. I know the boy got injured falling in rocks, but he wouldn't have been running if Cecil hadn't been chasing and cursing him."

"How can I get in touch with Rylinger?" Jax inquired.

Etting hesitated briefly and then, jotted something on a slip of paper and handed it to Jax.

"Thank you." Jax put the paper into his pocket. "I still have a couple more questions,"

"I'm happy to answer them," Etting replied, although his expression appeared to be more resigned than pleased.

"A few people have said you like to play practical jokes."

Etting frowned. "What does that have to do with Cecil's death?"

Jax shrugged. "Maybe nothing. Maybe a lot. As I said, the other driver may not have wanted to kill

187

Laheene. He may have been trying to scare him, and maybe the poor weather conditions turned a prank into something deadly."

The other man shifted in his chair. "I'm a respected businessman. I wouldn't play a joke that might harm someone, let alone lead to a death. Rain started about the time I left Moreley. Heavy rain. Fog was an issue, too. Visibility was poor at best. Trying to scare someone by pretending to run them off the road would have been foolhardy. The other driver was lucky he didn't crash along with Cecil."

"You're right," Jax said.

"I know you have to question everyone who might have had a reason to get even with Cecil, and I'm sure you started with a long list." Etting paused as if uncertain how to continue.

"We've spoken with a number of people." Jax didn't deny the obvious.

Etting nodded. "I understand why you wanted to speak with me again but, if you talk with John Rylinger, he'll tell you we discussed him representing the Smith family in a civil case against Cecil. That's what I referred to, as I said."

"I'll try to contact Rylinger today," Jax said as he got to his feet. He put his hand out and the other man shook it. "I appreciate your time."

"I'm glad to help. Cecil wasn't a good man, but he didn't deserve to die like that."

"I agree," Jax replied. "Just to tie up loose ends, I'd like to look at your automobile."

Dismay flickered across Etting's face, but he provided the details about make and location before bidding them goodbye.

Bella and Jax made their way out of the building before either one spoke. "What do you think now?" she asked as they went to the nearby parking area and looked around.

"Etting will probably be off our suspect list soon. Let's take a quick look at his vehicle. I doubt we'll find damage. I think it's right over here."

Jax's statement proved to be correct. The Winton Touring car, the only one in the lot, had not the slightest imperfection.

"Are you eliminating Floyd Etting now?" Bella asked as they headed to the Chummy.

"I am. I thought his penchant for practical jokes might have combined with his anger over Laheene making a scene. That could have made him do something stupid."

"But now you don't think that."

He shrugged. "I always thought it was somewhat unlikely, but the possibility had to be explored, and I wanted to do it face-to-face, so I could gauge his demeanor. I can talk with Rylinger and confirm the rest of his story. With no damage on the Winton, and if what Floyd said is true, we can focus on Chaz and Guy. Possibly, Mr. Smith, too. What do you think?"

"I think the same thing, but I wish I didn't," Bella said. "Eliminating Etting means Guy or Chaz or the father is the most likely suspect. Both families have suffered so much. I hate to think about any of them being put through a trial and ending up in jail."

"I do, too, Bella," Jax replied, "but we can't let our feelings interfere. Besides, we still don't know that another driver was at fault. Laheene could have caused the accident himself." He pointed toward the right side of the road. "There's probably a pay-phone in that drugstore. I'll try to call Rylinger from here."

Bella pulled to the curb and waited in the car. After a few minutes, Jax rejoined her. "Rylinger confirmed Etting's story. He's working on a civil case for Mrs. Smith."

"Did he say if Chaz knows?"

Jax shook his head. "Mrs. Smith didn't want to tell him. She's afraid he'll get his hopes up and be even angrier if they lose. Rylinger said the family is really struggling. She and Chaz don't bring in enough money to keep up with expenses. Without a larger settlement, she'll have to send Chipper to a charity hospital."

"Oh, that would be terrible."

"Yes, it would be, but Rylinger is pretty confident he can help them. Even though, as we've already heard, Laheene didn't cause the actual injuries, the boy ran from fear of him."

Bella chewed on her lower lip. "I hope they win, and I hope Chaz isn't involved in Cecil's death, but I hope Guy isn't, either. I know that sounds foolish."

"Not really. I hope all the same things," he told her, "but someone is involved, although not necessarily guilty of anything other than leaving the scene of an accident. In any case, I can't let my wishes interfere with my job."

"I know."

For a moment, neither of them spoke. Then, Jax made a suggestion. "Since we missed lunch, why don't we find a place and have a bite? It'll be at least an hour before the minister is back at the church."

Bella's stomach growled and Jax laughed. "That's answer enough."

After a late lunch, they headed to the church. When they arrived, the minister was speaking with the secretary, who gestured toward Bella and Jax as she said, "These are the people that I mentioned, Pastor Summit."

After introductions were made, Summit—a short, trim man in his early forties—invited Bella and Jax into his office. "Please, make yourselves comfortable." Once they were all seated, he said, "Mrs. Park said you wanted to ask about one of my parishioners."

"Yes, we did," Jax told him. "I wanted to ask you about Mick Carrier."

Summit's kindly expression matched his response. "He's a good boy, and it's a fine family. They've had some tough times in the last few years. Mrs. Carrier was very ill with influenza, and she's never completely regained her strength. She already had some breathing issues, and the illness made them worse. Before then, she worked part-time, but now she can't work at all. Mr. Carrier works as much as he can, but his job doesn't pay well. Mick caddies in the summer and sets pins at the bowling alley in the winter." Summit rested his elbows on the oak desk. "His older brother died in France. Kenneth worked full-time and brought home his entire paycheck, so not having him is a terrible loss in more than one way. There are three girls, in addition to Mick and Ken. The girls are all too young to work at this point."

"I see," Jax said.

"I hope Mick isn't in trouble," the minister put in. He adjusted his wire-rimmed spectacles as if looking for the answer to his observation.

"Not at all, but he may be a witness to an accident." Jax briefly outlined the details of the case.

"My, that's terrible," Summit said. "And Mick saw the crash?"

"We aren't sure," Jax admitted. "That's why we're here. Mick rode to the tournament with Chaz Smith. Do you know him?"

"Yes, although I've not seen Chaz recently. The Carriers don't have a car, so I believe Mick often rides to the golf course with Chaz."

"Chaz said Mick rode home with him. They left before Laheene, forty-five minutes or a bit more. Unless they waited for him, Chaz couldn't be the one who forced Laheene off the road. The time frame that Mick gave us would mean they didn't lie in wait." Jax waited for a reply.

"How is that?" The pastor's brow furrowed.

"Mick said when he isn't in church on Sunday morning, his mother expects him to be here for the Sunday evening service."

The pastor chuckled. "She wants him to be here, but he doesn't always make it."

Bella and Jax exchanged a look before he spoke again. "What do you mean, pastor?"

"Mick has missed both services on a few Sundays this summer," the man replied. "I know he often caddies two rounds on the weekend, and I can't fault him for wanting to help the family."

"Did he miss Sunday evening's service?" Jax

asked.

The pastor leaned forward in his chair and put his elbows on the edge of his desk. For a moment, he appeared to be weighing his words. "I'm afraid he did. His parents and sisters were here, but his mother said he was caddying in a tournament out of town and would be home late."

"He wouldn't have come in and sat at the back where his family might not have seen him?" Jax inquired.

Summit shook his head. "No, the boy always sits with them, if hc's here. His parents treat the children to ice cream after services, and his mother wouldn't believe that he came in and sat in the back. He's tried coming at the end of my sermon, but she always found out the truth." The minister smiled and shook his head. "He is a good boy, but restless. Sitting in church can be hard for him and, as I said, his caddying is a big help to the family."

For a moment, Jax absorbed the man's revelations and asked another question. "You know Chaz. Are you also acquainted with the Smith family?"

Summit shrugged his narrow shoulders. "They were regular parishioners before the war. Since then, Mr. Smith has rarely attended services, although Mrs. Smith comes occasionally. Chipper doesn't get around well, so he's unable to make it to church, and she can't leave him alone. Chaz usually caddies both morning and afternoon on Sundays, which means she has no one to sit with Chipper then." The minister leaned back in his chair. "The boy had a bad bone break that wasn't quickly attended to. I've visited their home since he was hurt, of course. He can't attend school for the same reason he can't get here. I don't know how he'll ever manage on his own. Surgery might help, but the Smiths can't afford it. You know what happened?" he asked.

"Yes," Jax replied. "The man who died in the accident is the one who chased after Chipper."

"I see," the minister replied. His tone and expression became almost blank. He glanced at a point beyond Jax and Bella while clearing his throat. "I suppose that's why you suspect Chaz, but I don't believe the boy would do such a thing. He knows his mother needs his help. In fact, I don't know how she would manage without him. They barely get by as it is. The church can provide a little assistance, but no one in the congregation is wealthy. We have many needing help and few able to contribute."

Something in the man's demeanor bothered Jax, but he couldn't pinpoint what it was. Of course, Summit was concerned about his flock. Was he so concerned that he would shield one of them from the law? With the last thought in mind, he responded with restraint. "I'm simply conducting a thorough investigation, Pastor."

"Of course," the other man murmured.

Once again, Summit sounded noncommittal. "You said Mr. Smith rarely came to church. Has he been here at all since he got out of jail?" Jax asked.

"I suppose I shouldn't be surprised that you know he was in prison. He hasn't attended services, but he's been to see me a few times." His gaze moved from Jax to Bella, and back again. "When he returned from France, he struggled with a leg wound.

His old job was filled, and he couldn't find another one, which led to a drinking problem. I'm sure you know that Mr. Smith attacked young Laheene and served time. I don't sanction violence, but Laheene didn't take responsibility for what happened to Chipper. I suppose the police didn't see him chasing and cursing the boy as a crime. Perhaps, if Laheene wasn't from a prominent family, something would have been done. I don't know."

"We've heard about the elder Laheene intervening on his son's behalf in more than one instance," Jax told the minister, "and while I don't condone people taking the law into their own hands, either, I can understand why Smith was angry. Crime or not, Laheene shouldn't have gone after the boy."

Summit nodded. "If he hadn't been drinking, he wouldn't have done it. He is a good man who has had a lot of bad luck until he was released early. I'm hoping that will help turn his life around."

"When did you last see him?" Jax asked.

The pastor's nostrils flared with a sharp intake of breath, telegraphing reluctance to answer. "About two weeks ago. He'd been coming every week to see if we need odd jobs done. If we didn't, I'd make sure he had a good meal and some money in his pocket. Not too much because I feared he would spend some on bootlegged liquor." The man shook his head. "Even with Prohibition, people find a way to get alcohol."

Jax nodded. "You said he was coming every week, but you haven't seen him for two weeks?"

"That's right. The last time he came, he wanted train fare. He'd stopped at his family's home to see

Chipper and talk with Mrs. Smith. They only live a few blocks away. His wife wouldn't let him move back. In fact, she told him again to stay away from them entirely, according to what Mr. Smith said. I cannot fault her. He certainly wasn't the same man who sailed for France."

Jax didn't need to ask why. No one who had served in the trenches and survived was the same. "Was he drunk when he came here that day?"

"No, he wasn't. He dried out in prison, but I don't blame Mrs. Smith for not wanting him back at home. She has her heart and hands full. There's no guarantee that he won't go back to the bottle, although I pray he doesn't."

The good pastor probably prayed for many people since the war and pandemic, Jax thought with dismay. "Did you have work for him when he came two weeks ago?"

"He didn't want work this last time. He only wanted to borrow money, as I said. Mr. Smith has a cousin who offered him a home and a job. He said he'd send the money to me once he's on his feet, but I just wished him well. I hope it works out for him."

Jax focused on only one element of the statement. "Where does the cousin live?"

"Near Sandusky. I don't know the name of the town, though. I didn't ask."

Jax's pulse accelerated. "And this was two weeks ago?"

The minister's brow furrowed. "Yes, he was here two weeks ago on Monday."

"Was he planning to leave for his cousin's place

right away?" Jax asked. A sense of urgency filled him as his mind whirled with possibilities.

"I believe he planned to leave within the next day or so. Why do you ask?"

A few moments ticked away before Jax replied. "I hoped to speak with Mr. Smith while we were in town today, but that won't be possible now. I wish I had some idea of where the cousin lives."

Slowly, the other man's expression went from curious to calculating. "Do you think Mr. Smith had something to do with young Laheene's death?"

Uncertainty plagued Jax. If the minister had no way to contact Smith, answering the question posed no problem. Despite that, Jax hesitated to tip his hand. "As I said, I'm simply gathering as much information as possible at this stage. We have a long way to go before a strong suspect emerges, I'm afraid." Jax got to his feet and thrust out his hand. "Thank you for your time, Pastor Summit. I appreciate it."

Summit hesitated only a moment before shaking Jax's hand. Then, he bid both the young constable and Bella farewell before leading them to the door of the church.

Chapter Fourteen

As they walked toward the Chummy, Jax felt the minister's steady gaze on them. He kept walking but said nothing. Bella didn't speak, either, until they were almost at the car.

"You consider Mr. Smith a stronger suspect now, don't you?" she asked.

It was as much a statement as a question. "Yes, I do and I'm sure you do, too."

Bella nodded. "Sandusky isn't far from Moreley. Even if Mr. Smith doesn't have a car, his cousin most likely does. People in the city can manage without a vehicle. In small towns, it isn't as easy, especially if the cousin has some sort of business. I know not many shopkeepers in Moreley still use horse and wagon."

"Exactly. I only wish Summit had known where the cousin lives. Near Sandusky isn't much of a clue."

"Mrs. Smith would probably have that information," Bella pointed out.

Jax figured that was true, but he wasn't sure about going to the Smith house with Bella in tow. What if Mr. Smith was there, after all? His penchant for alcohol was troubling, especially since he now had to acquire it from criminal sources. And what about Mrs. Smith? How would she react to a visit?

When Jax didn't immediately reply, Bella spoke again. "You need to see Mrs. Smith. We both know that. You're not admitting it because you think I might be in your way."

Her observation made Jax look at her. The frown on her pretty face telegraphed dismay while the glitter in her dark gaze revealed obstinacy. Although he wanted to point out that going to the house could put them in a bad situation, Jax resisted. Instead, he focused on her last comment. "You're not in my way, Bella."

For several moments, she simply studied him. "Then, why aren't you suggesting we head to the Smith house? We have the address, and the pastor said it's only a few blocks away. You certainly don't think Mrs. Smith is dangerous."

A resigned sigh left him. "Not really, but there isn't a guarantee that Mr. Smith went to his cousin's place. He could be there, Bella."

"That doesn't seem likely," she pointed out. "Chaz and Pastor Summit both told us that Mrs. Smith wouldn't let her husband stay at the house."

Her points were perfectly logical, so refuting them was impossible. With real reluctance, Jax nodded. "You're right. I need to speak with her, and we need to do it before we head home."

The smile that lit Bella's face could only be called triumphant, but she said nothing. At least she didn't gloat when she persevered, Jax thought. Instead, once they were both in the vehicle, she headed the Chummy toward the Smith house without delay.

"What's the house number?" Bella asked once they were headed down the street where the Smiths lived.

Jax told her and said, "It must be on the opposite side of the road and down a few more blocks. You'll have to park on the street. If we're lucky, we'll find something fairly close."

A parking place was open right across from the house, which turned out to be a small apartment building. Crowded between similar-sized frame abodes, the structure's gray paint was chipping away while one dark shutter tilted sideways from a front window. The lack of a matching shutter on the opposite side contributed to the overall atmosphere of neglect and decline.

As Bella stopped the car and killed the engine, she looked up-and-down the block. The farther they had traveled from the church, the smaller and shabbier the residences had become. If this particular section had ever seen prosperity, it hadn't been recently, she thought with sadness. So many people had struggled since the Great War. Returning soldiers had surged into the labor force, making it harder to find work. Then, the recession changed to depression. At least her own stress and strain involved saving beautiful Ballantyne, not grubbing out an existence in a grimy apartment building.

She got out of the car and joined Jax on the sidewalk. When he didn't immediately head toward the Smith residence, she turned to look at him. "What's wrong?"

He shook his head. "Nothing. I just need to get something out of the trunk."

Her pulse rate accelerated. Undoubtedly, he'd brought his gun along. Bella hadn't seen it, which meant Jax had stowed it away before she'd gotten to town. No wonder he'd been standing by the Chummy as she'd driven up. When he returned to her side, Jax wore the jacket that he'd taken off earlier. Undoubtedly, he didn't want the weapon to show, but she didn't remark on it. Nonetheless, anxiety crept through her. What if Mr. Smith was home? What if Mrs. Smith was armed? What if other neighbors took exception to their presence? While their attire was perfect for the country club, they stood out on this block, and not in a good way.

When Jax took her elbow, she simply let herself be directed along the cracked sidewalk to the small stoop. "Be careful," he told her. "The wood looks to have dry rot in it."

Bella glanced down and saw that he was right. With his help, she avoided the bad planks and went to the door. When Jax held it for her, she stepped into the entry while he stayed close to her side. Like the exterior, the interior hadn't been painted in a long time. The color was so stained and faded that identifying the exact hue was impossible.

"Here's a directory. Looks like the Smiths live in number one. That must be on this floor." Jax glanced around. "There." He pointed across the narrow hallway.

As the pair crossed the short distance, Bella heard floorboards creak under their feet. After he knocked at apartment one, the sound of footsteps from inside easily carried to them. Evidently, the doors and walls were as thin as the floors.

A moment passed before the door opened to reveal a short, wiry woman clad in a shapeless, faded housedress. "What do you want?"

Not a hint of cordiality was evident. On closer inspection, Bella noted that the woman looked ashen and exhausted. No wonder she didn't welcome company. Perhaps, she'd been taking a well-deserved rest, and they had interrupted.

Despite the cold greeting, Jax smiled. "Mrs. Smith, I'm Constable Jackson Hastings," he said as he pulled his badge out of a jacket pocket, "and this is Arabella Stewart. We wanted to speak with you about a death that occurred in my jurisdiction late Sunday evening."

A sneering smile touched Mrs. Smith's thin lips. "I'm not talking to any coppers. No one here knows nothing about that, so git."

When she started to close the door, Jax put his hand on it. "Mrs. Smith, I won't take much of your time, but I need to speak with you. If I have to contact the Cleveland police and have one of their officers come with me, I will. I'd rather make this informal, though."

Something akin to hatred tightened Mrs. Smith's features, and her eyes blazed with fury. "I suppose you're here to blame my boy, and they'd help you do it."

"Ma'am, I'm only interested in information and

justice, not in placing blame on an innocent person," Jax assured her in a soft, composed voice.

Bella admired Jax for his restraint, but she wasn't surprised by it. Except for his reaction to Cecil Laheene, he was the most stoic person she'd ever known. Sometimes that bothered her, but it was an asset in his job.

"Ha!" The woman released a humorless laugh. "The authorities don't care about no justice. They only care about protecting rich folk. People like us are nothing to them."

"I care about justice, ma'am," Jax assured her. "May we come in? I promise that we'll only take a few minutes."

Her expression didn't soften, but she nodded. "I don't have much time. I need to fix an early supper, check on Chipper, and get ready for my overnight job," she said, stepping back and allowing them inside. "Take a seat."

A few footsteps carried Bella and Jax to a battered wooden table. When Mrs. Smith sat down, they did as well. A brief glance around the room revealed a broken-down, faded couch pushed against the far wall. Next to it was a small table with a lamp. One leg of the table must have been shorter than the others because the piece of furniture listed to one side making it look like the light was in jeopardy of sliding off. The only other furniture in the room was the scarred dining table and four chairs, none of which matched.

"What do you want to know?" Mrs. Smith asked, her voice sharp as nails.

"I already spoke with Chaz," Jax began, "so I'm not

here to ask about him. He said his father hasn't lived here since he got out of jail. I wondered if you had seen your husband lately."

"No," she spat out, "and I don't want to see him. We had a nice home and a decent life. Then, he had to go to war. No thought for us left behind. It weren't easy while he were gone, but I kept our house. When he came home wounded, he couldn't do his old job. He couldn't do most jobs. After that, he started drinking a lot. He spent all his time and most of our money in bars. We lost the house and ended up here." As Mrs. Smith glanced around the shabby apartment, her lower lip trembled, and she bowed her head.

Sympathy filled Bella, but she didn't know what to say. This woman had lost so much, and she might lose even more if her son was involved in Cecil's death. "I'm very sorry, Mrs. Smith," she murmured. It wasn't enough, not nearly enough.

Mrs. Smith looked from Bella to Jax before glancing around the room again. "I had to sell most of our furniture and anything else of value. Even with that, we barely get by. I don't need no drunken husband here to support along with my boys. I told William as much when he came after getting out of the hoosegow. I don't need no trouble with the law, neither. We already had too much of that."

Jax nodded. "We know about Laheene going after Chipper, ma'am. I'm sure that's what led to him taking a nasty tumble and breaking his ankle. Laheene should have made sure your son got proper care right then. It was a terrible thing, and I understand your anger. I'm not here to falsely accuse Chaz. In fact, I hope he wasn't involved, although I probably shouldn't say so."

Jax spoke with such sincerity that Bella felt tears prick her eyes. He really was a very good man.

For a moment, Mrs. Smith's tired gaze softened. "You're different, constable."

A half-smile tugged at one corner of his mouth. "Not really. I just believe in doing my job properly." He paused for a moment. "Right now, I'd like to find out if you know about your husband's cousin. The one who lives near Sandusky."

"Stanley?" she asked, her confusion clear.

"I don't know his name," Jax replied, "but we just spoke with Pastor Summit, and he told us that Mr. Smith had been to see him two weeks ago. Your husband needed train fare to get to his cousin's house. The minister said the cousin was offering a job and a home, so Mr. Smith only needed to get there. The pastor didn't know the exact town, though."

Mrs. Smith's brow furrowed as if in thought. "Stanley lives in Mohawk. That's not far from More-ley, is it?"

Jax and Bella exchanged a glance before he replied. "No, ma'am. It's only about twenty miles from us." He hesitated briefly before continuing. "I assume the cousin has a vehicle."

She shrugged. "I would think so, but I can't say for sure. Stanley farms, so a truck would be in order unless he's still using horse and wagon. He were always one for anything new, though, and the farm were a moneymaker. I haven't seen him in years, and we haven't had no contact since before William went to war. I'm surprised they're in touch now. Stanley never asked me if we needed anything."

Once again, anger was in her tone and expression, but Bella couldn't blame her. The woman had been dealt a series of bad hands, and she apparently had no support in handling her misfortune.

"What is Stanley's last name?" Jax asked.

"Harroll. Stanley Harroll." A long breath escaped her, and anger gave way to sadness. "My husband has lost his way, constable. The war, his wound, liquor, prison. They've all turned him into a different man than the one I married. You know, he went to jail because he attacked Laheene." When Jax and Bella nodded in agreement, she continued. "It won't surprise me if he went after the man again. William oughta understand that getting sober and finding steady work would do more for Chipper than attacking Laheene. I know he tried when he came back, and his leg is a problem, but he simply gived up. We was both angry about Laheene not paying more to help our boy, not when he were at fault for the injury. But I don't countenance no violence. William never did, neither. Not until he came home from that war."

"War changes people, Mrs. Smith." Jax's voice was low and rough, and his expression was troubled.

The woman studied him for a moment. "You went to war?"

He nodded. "Yes, ma'am."

"And it changed you," she suggested. Her gaze and voice were speculative.

"I think it changed all of us in one way or another," he replied.

His revelation didn't surprise Bella, nor did she disagree with it. Jax had changed, but certainly not as much as Mr. Smith evidently had.

For several moments, the older woman simply studied Jax. "But it didn't make you into a drunken, useless lout." She took a long breath. "It won't surprise me if my husband were involved in the accident, constable. As I said, he's a completely different man now. I don't know what he might do."

"He may not have been involved, Mrs. Smith. We have other suspects, and we're running down leads as fast as we can," Jax told her. "Do you have an address for Mr. Harroll?"

She shook her head. "No. He has a farm just north of Mohawk. That's all I know. He, his wife, and their boys came to the city a few times back before the war. William took our two to the farm, but I never went. Back then, my husband said I deserved to have a few days to myself." Her teeth caught her lower lip. "William were a good, kind man once. I wish I could have helped him to go back to that..." Her voice became hoarse and trailed off. She blinked hastily as if to clear moisture from her tired eyes.

"People have to help themselves, Mrs. Smith." Jax spoke softly, as if he was comforting a child. "Perhaps being at his cousin's farm will be good for him."

"I hope so, constable, I hope so."

He got to his feet. "I appreciate your assistance, ma'am. Thank you for your time."

Bella also rose from the table. "Yes, thank you, Mrs. Smith. I hope Chipper recuperates completely and soon."

Once again, moisture filled the woman's eyes. "Thank you." She looked back at Jax. "Good luck, constable."

When they were back in the car, Bella turned to Jax. "I feel very sorry for Mrs. Smith. She has so much on her shoulders."

"That she does."

"Unfortunately, Mr. Smith seems to be a strong suspect. His cousin is so close to Moreley. It's not hard to imagine that he, or maybe the two of them, came to town during the tournament."

"I agree," Jax said. "I feel pretty sure Chaz is still in touch with his father, which means they could both be involved in the crash."

"I hope not. It's obvious that Mrs. Smith needs every penny she and Chaz earn. Not to mention that having her son charged with a crime would be devastating." Bella's fingers tightened on the steering wheel.

Jax slumped back in the seat. "I don't want the kid to be guilty, but his father could have egged him on. Or Mr. Smith could be the culprit. There's no way to tell yet. I still need to clear both Guy and Chaz, since we don't have any solid evidence to put William Smith in Moreley, let alone at the scene of the accident."

"Do you want to try and talk to Mick again before we head home?"

"I think I should. I need to know why he lied about going to church. I hope we can catch him at the course because I'd like to check on Guy's alibi yet today."

"What are you going to do about Mr. Smith?"

"I definitely want to speak with him, but it will have to wait until tomorrow. As it is, we aren't likely to get back to Moreley until almost dark." He ran one hand over his face. "I'm sorry, Bella. I didn't think this would take all day."

"I have nothing else to do, Jax. I already told you that."

"You could be taking it easy or doing something fun," he pointed out.

"This is fun." When she saw his look of disbelief, Bella added, "I really find solving cases interesting."

He shrugged. "If you say so," Jax replied, but he didn't sound convinced. Or maybe he simply didn't want to encourage her. The latter seemed more likely.

On the way back to the course, they said little. Bella knew Jax was discouraged, and she had no idea how to ease his mind since she felt unsettled herself. With luck, they would get to the bottom of Chaz's lies, and Mick's, before they left the city.

But luck wasn't with them. Griff Biggins was back in the shop when they arrived, and he didn't provide good news.

"Neither Chaz nor Mick is here."

"What time did they go out to caddy?" Jax asked.

"They didn't," the pro said. "After you left, Chaz told the caddy master he couldn't go out today. Then, he and Mick took off."

A look of exasperation shadowed Jax's gaze as he glanced from Bella back to the pro. "Do you have any idea of where they went or places they hang out?"

"As far as I know, they caddy and go home. Chaz's mother works nights, and he stays with his brother. Mick's mother isn't well, and he usually helps with the younger children in the evening while she gets a bit of rest."

Jax thanked Biggins before returning to the car with Bella. After they got inside, she turned to him. "What do you want to do now?"

After looking at his pocket watch, Jax ran one hand over his face. "There's not much sense in trying to track down Chaz and Mick since we have no idea where to start. I'd like to check with Zeb to see if he saw Guy's car Sunday evening. That would eliminate one potential suspect, which would help a lot at this point. It's already late afternoon. If we leave right now, we won't get home until almost dusk."

"Mohawk is only a few miles off the main road to Moreley. We could stop and talk to Mr. Smith," Bella suggested.

"I can go tomorrow," Jax told her.

Bella shifted to look directly at him. "That's a waste of your time, and you said time is of the essence since you don't want Mr. Laheene hiring a detective agency."

His jaw tightened. "It wouldn't add that much time," he argued.

"It will take you over thirty minutes to get to Mohawk from Moreley and another thirty to get back. That's not counting time to interview Smith and his cousin. Besides, Richard might need to stay in Karston longer. If so, Nolen will have to be in the office tomorrow morning. Earlier, you said you want to move as quickly as possible. Stopping there today seems like a better idea." Bella studied Jax's expression.

He shook his head but said, "You're right."

A broad smile lit her face. "I love when you say that."

His lips lifted in a rueful grin. "I'm sure you do." Jax's humor faded when he went on. "When we get there, you need to do as I say. We don't know if Mr. Smith and his cousin were both involved, if only he was involved, or if he wasn't involved at all. If either one of the first two is the case, his reaction could be unpredictable. I don't want you in harm's way if Smith is angry and violent."

Bella knew without being told that Jax was think-ing of the Monticello murder case from April when the killer had abducted her. Jax had held himself responsible. A shiver rippled through her at the memory. Although she never discussed the kidnap-ping, Bella sometimes woke in the night feeling trapped and panicky. Once full wakefulness came, she was able to regain control, but memories of that rainy evening continued to haunt her. Knowing Jax, the incident wasn't likely to leave him, either. He'd certainly been distraught in the aftermath. Finally, she nodded. "I'll follow your orders."

"I love when you say that. Not that I've ever heard it before now."

When his lips twitched, Bella couldn't help but smile in return. "Very funny."

Chapter Fifteen

Jax and Bella exchanged small talk as she drove out of the city and toward their next stop. After a time, she returned to the case. "It sounds like Mr. Smith's cousin lives just outside Mohawk. It's too bad Mrs. Smith couldn't tell us exactly where or even what the house looks like."

"It's a tiny town, so we should be able to find someone to give us directions."

"That's likely to be true," Bella commented. In Moreley, finding a certain house was easy because people knew their neighbors. The same would happen in a smaller village. "I wonder if Chaz has visited this cousin recently."

Jax hesitated only a moment before responding. "I've wondered the same thing. He could have visited his father last week during the tournament. After all, Chaz wasn't angry with Mr. Smith."

"Boys usually want to be around their fathers and vice-versa."

Several seconds of silence filled the car before Jax spoke. "My dad would have liked for me to take more of an interest in his profession, but I never did. I imagine he'd be shocked to learn I have that same job now."

Once again, Jax had provided an opening into a more personal conversation. Bella knew there were hazards in following that lead, but she proceeded anyhow. "My dad and Matt would be shocked about you being constable, too," she suggested. Out of the corner of her eye, Bella saw Jax turn toward her, but she kept her attention on the road.

"I suppose they would. Sometimes, I'm surprised myself."

"You do a good job, but do you like it? I mean, I know you probably don't love it like golf. How could you?" Although he'd turned down the offer of a job at Ballantyne, didn't some part of him still love the game? Or maybe not. Jax seemed increasingly comfortable in his role as town constable. That could be a front or the truth.

"Spoken like a tried-and-true golf lover," he observed with a chuckle, but his amusement fled quickly, and his reply was serious. "I don't dislike being a constable, and it has its good points. I get a steady paycheck, for one."

"You could be a club pro and get a steady paycheck." The statement emerged without forethought, but she didn't regret it. Bella still didn't understand his refusal to go back to his previous career. His ideal career. Had he really relinquished his dreams? The thought made her profoundly sad.

"We've talked about this, Bella." His voice held a

sharp, cutting edge.

"You don't want to try." Bella heard the note of accusation in her words. She shouldn't feel so personally invested in his decisions, but she didn't apologize or back down. Understanding the changes in him was a Herculean task. Although Jax remained loyal to her brother, his decision to leave his dreams behind disturbed her in ways that she couldn't quite explain even to herself.

A harsh breath left him. "There is no point in chasing after vain hopes and old wishes. It's a waste of time and energy. I have a job, a good one, so that makes me a lot better off than many veterans. I won't live in the past. No adult should."

Bella flinched at his caustic tone and unyielding observations. "I'm being an adult," she protested, immediately taking his statements as criticism. "I'm simply trying to keep Ballantyne from failing, which will help Moreley. That's not living in the past. That's planning for the future."

"I'm not talking about that," he shot back. "I'm talking about how you continue to ask me why I don't go back to golf as a career. When you offered me the job at Ballantyne, I said you need someone who can represent the resort at big tournaments. I can't do that, and I don't appreciate you continuing to hound me. I've told you more than once that I'm not the same man who left for France. I can't be...not for you or anyone else."

His words stung so badly that Bella flinched. "I'm not asking you to do anything for me," she said in a muffled tone. "I just wondered..." Her voice trailed off. Obviously, he didn't cherish old memories as she did, so Bella hurried on. "I'm sorry I brought it up. Your life is your business."

"Yes, it is. Please keep that in mind." His icy tone fell between them like shards of sleet.

An angry, hot flush invaded her cheeks, while sadness gripped her heart. Bella focused on the road. "I most assuredly will."

Bella's wounded tone and expression forced Jax to look out the side of the Chummy. Clearly, she had no idea of how badly he wanted to accept her job offer or of how much he wanted to unwind the last few years. His shoulder and arm weren't the only issues. Maybe he could be a golf professional who didn't compete in big tournaments, but he couldn't look into Bella's face on a daily basis and continue hiding his culpability in her brother's death.

Jax shifted in the seat. If only going back to when Matt was still alive was possible, back to the last day that he'd seen his best friend. The memory of being in a field hospital, after the first time he'd been wounded, emerged with a fierce vengeance. He closed his eyes, but the images, noises, and words flashed in his mind.

The sounds of soft moans and beating rain filled Jax's ears. Unable to sleep, he shifted uneasily on

the cot and tried to find a more comfortable position for his arm. Four days had passed since he'd been shot, but he'd only been off morphine for one—his choice since he needed to get back to the line and his platoon. With grim determination, he swung his feet to the floor. Maybe sitting up would help, but sweat broke out across his forehead with the effort. His weakness was a hindrance. He needed to quickly build up strength. Once he stopped feeling dizzy, Jax would take a short walk.

"You look rather the worse for wear," a deep voice broke into Jax's thoughts.

He glanced up to see the familiar face of Matt Stewart, his best friend. Surprise hit Jax, but so did concern. Why was Matt in the field hospital? "Hey, buddy. What brings you here? You okay?" He scanned his friend's lean form and lined face. Although Matt's exhaustion was evident, he had no visible wounds. Had he contracted the Spanish flu? Worry assailed Jax. The two of them weren't just best friends. They were blood brothers. He smiled at the memory. At age six, they'd each nicked their thumbs, held them together, and let the red fluid from the small wounds mingle. Although it was a boyish gesture, their friendship had stood the test of time. It always would. Jax was an only child, but he and Matt were closer than many siblings.

Shaking his head, Matt sat on the stool next to Jax's bed. "I'm fine. A couple of my men were wounded, and I came to see them on my leave. I heard you were here, too." His dark gaze grew troubled as he studied the thick bandage around Jax's arm. "What happened?"

Before he replied, Jax marshaled his thoughts and tried to maintain a calm demeanor. "We were ordered to advance. There was a German sniper nest, and I got hit only twenty yards or so out of the trenches. One of my men dragged me back when we had to retreat. The wound has healed pretty well. I'm headed to the line later today or first thing tomorrow." It was hard to hide the emotions hammering at him. He'd been lucky, but the images of comrades who hadn't survived flitted on the edge of his consciousness. Asleep, the ugly visions rose like wraiths. Awake, they never completely retreated. The advance had been disastrous and far too many men had never made it back to the trenches.

A frown furrowed Matt's forehead. "The doctors approved you going back when you have an injury to your right arm? You need to be able to fire your pistol."

"It's my bicep, not my hand. Plenty of officers are returning to duty with worse wounds. Especially the British and the French, but ours, too."

Matt shook his head again. "You didn't answer my question. Did the docs decide you're ready, or did you convince them?"

Jax braced his elbows on his knees and folded his hands in front of him. "They have to okay my release. I can't just walk out of here. Not when they all outrank me."

"Which means you're the one pushing to return. That comes as no surprise to me. Ever since first grade, you've always been the first one to volunteer and the last one to give up, even when it's more obvious to everyone else that you should."

His jaw tightened. "I know you want to be with your men, but things are so jumbled up now, what with influenza and casualties, that we've all had changes in assignments. It's why I got a couple days of leave."

The last statement made Jax smile. "Good for you. You look like you need it."

A half-shrug lifted one of Matt's shoulders. "I think you need a couple of days more than I do."

The idea resonated deep inside Jax, and he bent his head to keep from letting his friend see how badly he wanted to be away from the line a little longer. So many men hit. So many left dead. So much suffering. Sweet heaven. He didn't want to return yet. He didn't want to lead soldiers, some just boys, to their ruin. Not again. Not ever. The feel of a hand on his shoulder made Jax lookup. The light weight of his friend's clasp grounded Jax, while the deep concern on Matt's face made him hurry to offer reassurance. "I'm okay," he muttered.

"Are you? I know you've lost several men in the past couple of clashes. Two from our hometown. That takes a toll as bad as a physical wound."

A shuddering breath left Jax. "You're right, but it's not an excuse to stay here."

Several moments of silence passed before Matt spoke again. "I don't think you're ready to be on the line yet, and I bet the doctors don't, either. Someone else will take your place if you're here a few more days."

The statement was accurate and appealing, yet Jax hesitated to agree. He didn't want just any officer leading his men.

And that's what had led to disaster.

An hour-and-a-half later, they reached the turnoff to Mohawk. Jax had feigned sleep for most of the time, and Bella was relieved. His rebuff left her feeling like an errant schoolgirl being taken to task by the principal, although she'd never had the experience.

"It's only a few miles down this road," Jax told her once he sat up straight again.

"You said you've been here a couple of times," Bella commented, trying to match his even tone. "How long ago was that?"

"When my dad was still constable," Jax replied.

Bella noted Jax said *when his dad was constable*, not *before my dad died.* Jax seldom spoke of his parents' deaths, about her brother, or about the war. But he rarely complained or talked about unpleasant things. The term stoic again came to mind because it fit him perfectly.

"I don't suppose there's a constable's office in Mohawk," Bella observed.

"No, it's basically four corners. A few houses in town and a one-room school. There used to be a gas station, a grocer, and a post office. I don't know if they're all still there, but I'm sure the church and cemetery are. The minister may be around unless we find someone else to guide us."

When they reached the town, Bella saw nothing had changed since Jax's last visit. "It is small," she said.

"Very small," he agreed. "It looks like the filling station is open. Let's get gasoline and ask the owner if he knows Stanley Harroll."

Bella steered the Chummy to the pump. Almost immediately, a rangy man of middle years came to the car. "How can I help you folks?" he asked with a smile.

Jax stepped out of the car to speak with the attendant. "We need a fill-up and some directions."

"I can definitely do the first, and I hope I can help you with the other," he replied while pumping gas. "Where you headed?"

"Actually, we're looking for someone who lives in the area. Stanley Harroll."

The man—according to his shirt, his name was Oswold—smiled. "Stan lives just outside town." He jerked his head to the right, indicating that they needed to continue to the far edge of the village. "He's lived here since his marriage. His wife were a local girl, but she passed a couple of years ago from influenza. Their kids was already gone. Not much for them in a town this size, and they wasn't interested in farming. Stan has a small place, so not big enough to support three grown sons and their families even if they'd wanted to stay. Nice farm for a single family, though. A cousin moved in with him a bit ago." He went about cleaning the windshield while continuing to talk. "Why do you want to talk with Stan?"

"We want to talk with his cousin," Jax told Oswold when the man finally stopped chattering.

A grimace pulled down the corners of the man's mouth. "He a friend of yours?"

Jax cleared his throat. "No, I don't know Mr. Smith, but we need to speak with him about an accident near Moreley the other day."

221

The man's gaze narrowed on Jax. "The crash where a man died?"

"Yes, sir. I'm Constable Hastings from Moreley, and this is Miss Stewart," he said, gesturing toward Bella who had gotten out of the car to join them. "We were in Cleveland talking with some witnesses and Mr. Smith's name came up."

"I see." The man topped off the tank, hung up the nozzle, and turned back to Jax and Bella. "Stan told me a little about his cousin before Smitty got here. Sounded like he had some tough times."

"I believe that's the case," Jax agreed.

"And you think he knows something about this accident?"

"I'm not sure he does. That's why we'd like to talk with him. His older son caddied in the fourball tournament at Ballantyne, and we understand that Mr. Smith may have gone to Moreley to see the boy while he was there. He may have witnessed something along the road that evening. I'd like to find out." Jax spoke calmly and casually.

"Smitty don't have a vehicle," Oswold said.

"Does his cousin own one?" Jax asked.

He nodded. "Yep."

"Does Mr. Smith ever drive it?"

"Sometimes."

Oswold's chatty demeanor had disappeared, and his current terse replies were not particularly helpful, but Jax maintained his friendly approach. "Would you know if Mr. Smith borrowed it on Sunday?"

For several moments, Oswold studied Jax. "You know that Smitty's had it hard. Got sent to jail for fighting with the rich man who went after his youngest. Man didn't pay hardly nothing. The police didn't help none."

Jax took a deep breath. "From what I know, the Cleveland police didn't want to pursue a case against Mr. Smith, but they had to follow the law."

"Why didn't they make the rich guy pay?" Oswold asked in a contemptuous tone.

A long, low breath left Jax. "That's not really up to the police, although I agree that the Smith family deserved a lot more money for their son." He paused. "I need to investigate the accident, sir. That's my job."

The other man studied Jax as if trying to determine his sincerity. Finally, Oswold nodded. "I understand. Stan's place is a white clapboard two-story on the right side of the road only a half-mile out of town. Porch on the front. They're likely sitting out there. Often are when I pass by on my way home."

Jax paid the man and offered his thanks before ushering Bella back to the car and getting in himself. "Let's see if he's right."

They were back on the road when Bella spoke. "I hope they aren't sitting on the porch with shotguns."

A laugh rumbled out of Jax. "You have quite an imagination. It's late in the day, so I'm guessing they're resting and cooling off after hours of hard work."

"Farmers usually have shotguns," she pointed out. "Sometimes, they have pistols, too."

"I am aware of that, but they don't usually relax on the porch with them," he replied, his tone still holding a note of humor.

"All the same, you need to be careful."

A moment expired before he spoke, this time in a more serious voice. "I will," he murmured.

Her gaze slid to him and back to the road. "You better be."

Chapter Sixteen

W armth spread through Jax at Bella's admonitions. Despite their earlier squabble, he appreciated her concern. "That must be the place," he said, pointing to a house that matched the filling station owner's description. "Stop at the end of the drive. I'll walk to the house from there."

Bella pulled off the road as he suggested before glancing at him. "They're on the porch." The house was only twenty feet from the road, so the pair was clearly visible.

"Yes, I see," Jax replied. Both men were clad in well-worn overalls, faded shirts, and battered boots. On the table between them sat two glasses. Spirits of some sort, he figured. He realized Bella had the same thought when she spoke again.

"What if they're drunk?"

"Even if they are hitting the bottle, I doubt if they've had much yet. Most farmers don't finish their chores until about this time. Besides, remember, Pastor Summit said Mr. Smith dried out in jail."

"That doesn't mean he didn't go back to drinking. Besides, it's not uncommon for country folks to have stills. Smith and Harroll might make their own booze since buying it is illegal."

When her anxious expression didn't lighten, Jax forged ahead. "If they seem drunk and disorderly, I'll return to the car quickly and come back here tomorrow with Richard or Nolen."

"Do you still have your gun on you? I didn't see you put it in the trunk when we left the Smith place. Needing to get it out now might put them on alert." Her attention riveted on the two men.

Jax laid one hand over hers, which brought her gaze to him. Her beautiful brown eyes were clouded with anxiety, which made his heart lurch. "I have my gun, but I don't think I'll need it. Just stay here in the car, so I don't have to worry about you." The last statement was usually his best argument. At least it should be since her kidnapping several months earlier, and her promise only hours ago.

A sigh escaped her. "All right. But what if something goes wrong?"

For several seconds, he held her gaze. "If it does, drive back to the village and get help." For a moment, Jax thought she would argue with him. Instead, Bella nodded. "And don't turn the engine off while you wait," he added as he slipped out of the car and headed toward the porch.

Trepidation filled Bella as she watched Jax go. Maybe she shouldn't have convinced him to stop here on their way home. If Jax had returned the next day as he'd planned, Richard or Nolen would have been with him. Of course, the senior constable might be delayed. Then, Jax would have been completely on his own. At least, she could go for help, if necessary. The thought did little to ease her mind.

"Good evening," Jax called out to the men.

"Evening," they replied in unison.

The blonde man went on, "How can we help you?"

"I'm looking for William Smith, and I was told he was staying here with his cousin, Stan."

The dark-haired man got to his feet. His belligerent expression made Bella's stomach knot. Even before he spoke, she knew he must be Chaz's and Chipper's father. He had the same chocolate brown hair as Chaz, and similar features, although his face was lined from time and experience, no doubt.

"I'm Smith. Who are you?"

His blonde cousin also stood, and both men went to the edge of the porch. Bella's fear mounted when she noticed a shotgun leaning against one of the porch posts. So much for farmers not sitting out with their weapons. At least, Jax had his service revolver, but could he get to it before one of the cousins put a bullet in him? Despite the sweltering heat, a chill rippled through her. Maybe she was letting her imagination run wild. She'd done that more often since her kidnapping, something she'd tried keeping to herself. No one needed to know about her occasional nightmares. They were less and less

227

frequent. Surely, eventually, they'd disappear un-less something happened to create new ones. Bella kept staring steadily at the cousins while silently willing them to cooperate. If Jax got shot because he'd listened to her...She couldn't let the thought develop completely.

Jax stopped. "My name is Jackson Hastings. I'm the constable at Moreley, and I'd like to have a few words with you, Mr. Smith."

Belligerence turned to anger in Smitty's dark eyes. "I don't like talking to coppers."

Bella frowned in consternation. The man's wife had said the same thing.

"Understandable."

Jax's voice was relaxed and respectful. Bella won-dered if that made any difference to Smith, who had every reason to dislike lawmen. For several moments, Smitty was still as stone. His cousin spoke to him, but Bella couldn't hear the words.

Finally, Smith said, "You know about my boy Chipper?"

"Yes, sir," Jax replied, "and it was a terrible thing. Cecil Laheene should have paid for the boy's ongo-ing care."

"Yeah, but he didn't, and I ended up in jail," Smith said.

"I know. I don't countenance people taking the law into their own hands, but I can understand why you did what you did." Jax hesitated before contin-uing. "If I had a boy and someone chased him after an accidental fall, I can't say I wouldn't be equally angry. At the very least, Laheene should have made sure your son got to a doctor right away and, like I said, he should be giving you more money."

Smitty stared at Jax for what seemed like an eternity to Bella. His expression had gone blank, so she had no idea what the man was thinking. She knew Jax was sincere but did this man believe him, or was he so sour on the police that he'd take his wrath out on any of them?

"Come and sit down, constable," the cousin said. "Your lady can come, too. Neither of you has anything to fear from us. Isn't that right, Smitty?"

Smith gave one nod of his head and went back to his chair.

Bella quickly slipped out of the car and caught up with Jax. When she reached his side, he turned to her with a scowl.

"Didn't I say to stay in the car?"

Her chin lifted a fraction. "I was invited to join you."

His frown didn't disappear, but he lightly grasped her elbow and guided her along the bumpy path to the porch. After they climbed the steps, he introduced her. "Miss Stewart sometimes takes notes for me when I interview folks. That isn't necessary right now. In fact, she could have remained in the car."

"Sorry, miss, I thought you were a couple. I'm Stan Harroll, Smitty's cousin."

"Nice to meet you, both of you," Bella replied, ignoring the reference to her and Jax.

"Please sit down," Stan said, gesturing to two empty chairs.

Harroll also returned to his seat. As Bella took the one next to Jax, she stole a covert look at William

Smith. He had a tan almost as dark as his older son's, giving him a healthy appearance despite his thin frame and shadowed eyes. Working on the farm seemed to agree with him, and she felt glad for that. Maybe he would get his life turned around—if he wasn't involved in Cecil's death.

"What do you want to know, constable?" Smith asked.

"I don't know if you heard or not, but Cecil Laheene died in a car accident on Sunday night. He was leaving Moreley after participating in the four-ball tournament at Ballantyne."

Bella noticed Jax referred to the event as an accident. Neither cousin reacted outwardly to the assessment.

"I heard about it," Smith replied. "Can't say I'm sorry he's dead. If he hadn't cursed and chased Chipper, my boy wouldn't have fallen and got so hurt. Then, Laheene said for him to git. Git on a broken ankle. My boy said he was crawling as fast as he could since he couldn't stand on his leg. A couple of the other men helped him, and so did some caddies. Thank the heavens, Chaz were at the course and took Chipper home, but can you imagine how scared he were?"

Smith's statements added new details that they hadn't heard from others. Bella's heart grew even heavier. Poor Chipper. Trying to walk on a broken ankle had to have been horrible.

"I can, and I'm very sorry it happened," Jax said, his tone still sympathetic. "There's no excuse for a man bullying a boy."

Smith gave a slight nod. "You said you want to

know something."

"I wondered where you were on Sunday evening, sir." Jax maintained the same placid demeanor.

Only a moment's hesitation preceded Smith's reply. "With my cousin."

Jax glanced at the other man. "Is that right?"

Stanley Harroll looked far from calm. Bella noticed that the farmer had gone pale. Her heart raced as they waited for an answer.

"Yes, we was together all day and all evening Sunday," Stanley said in a halting voice.

At that point, Jax focused more closely on him. "Did the two of you go see Chaz while he was in Moreley?"

Harroll looked at Smith as if he expected his cousin to answer. The other man's expression grew hard, but he said nothing. As silence ensued, Bella glanced at the shotgun. The weapon was closer to Smitty than to Stan. She wondered if he would try to grab it. She wondered if Jax could react quickly enough if that happened. When Bella felt Jax's attention move to her, the anxiety in his gaze made her wish she hadn't insisted they stop. While she was confident of her investigative skills, Bella would be no help in a gunfight.

"Gentlemen?" Jax used the word as a question.

Perspiration beaded on Harroll's forehead, but he continued to watch Smitty, whose expression and posture radiated tension, maybe anger, as well. A shiver rippled through Bella while sweat dampened her palms.

"What makes you think we were there, constable?" William Smith asked.

The man didn't deny being in town, which only increased Bella's trepidation. Smith wouldn't want to go back to prison. Who would? If he had purposefully run Cecil off the road, he'd likely be found guilty of murder and executed, so he had little to lose by killing Jax and her. She tried to rein in her galloping imagination, but fear gripped her.

"What about you, Mr. Harroll? Do you have anything to say? Your cousin doesn't have a vehicle, but you do. Isn't that right?" Jax inquired. His voice was still well-modulated, and his expression was composed.

Sweat poured off the farmer's face. He stopped looking at his cousin Smitty and focused on Jax. He licked his lips as if they were parched, but he didn't reach for his drink. "I have a truck," he murmured. "She's an old delivery vehicle that I fitted out for farm work. Better for moving crops and equipment than the horse and wagon."

"There were tire marks at the scene from a vehicle unlike Laheene's Cadillac," Jax observed. "It looked like the driver swerved onto the soft shoulder before getting back on the road."

Harroll tore his gaze away from Jax to look at his cousin. "We got to tell the truth, Smitty. It's the only way." His voice came out in a breathless rush.

Smith sent a glowering stare at the man beside him. "Shut up, Stan."

"No, I won't. I'm going to tell the truth. It's the best way, the only way. The constable here seems like a decent man. He'll understand it were an accident." Again, Harroll's words tumbled out rapidly. His breath was coming just as fast.

Bella was transfixed by his admission until Smith leaned toward the shotgun. His cousin moved faster, and Harroll grabbed it away. "No, Smitty. Don't make things worse."

For a moment, Smith stared at Harroll. Then, he collapsed back into the chair, braced his elbows on his knees, and put his head in his hands. Bella's pulse pounded in her ears. The staccato beat almost blotted out Smith's reply.

"You're right, Stan. You're right." His voice was soft and rough. He lifted his gaze. "We went to Moreley to see my boy. His mother won't let me around neither of our kids, and I can't blame her. Since I got back from France, I'm useless." A shuddering breath left him. "But I love my family, and I wanted to see Chaz again, if only for a few minutes. He'd stopped here on his way to Ballantyne, and I said I'd try to get to town before he left on Sunday night. We talked in the parking lot behind the hotel. He said Laheene had called him and the other caddies trash. Made me see red when Chaz told us, but none of us wanted to kill or harm Laheene. I knew better. I don't want no more trouble. I'm lucky my cousin is giving me a place to live and work."

The bleak expression on the man's face made Bella's heart turn over. She hoped he hadn't intended to harm Cecil but, even if that wasn't the case, both men might have left the scene of a fatal accident since it sounded like they knew more. Much more.

Jax looked from one man to the other. "I think we need to make this an official interview, which means we should head to my office. We can talk there," Jax put in before Smith could say more. "Let's get going."

Smith suddenly looked fearful. "Stan didn't do nothing wrong, and neither did I."

Jax held up one hand. "Please don't say any more." He glanced at Bella. "You can drive my car back to Moreley, and I'll ride with the cousins in the truck."

Bella's mind rebelled at what she considered a dangerous idea. What was to keep the men from overpowering Jax and even killing him? Harroll had wanted to tell the truth, but Smith seemed less interested in honesty. As she opened her mouth to object, Jax gave a quick sideways shake of his head. "I can follow you," she replied at last.

Some emotion flickered in his gaze before he replied. "No, you go ahead of us. When you get to Moreley, go into the constable's office. Nolen will be there, and possibly Richard. Tell them I'm with Mr. Harroll and Mr. Smith. And be sure to let them know no weapons or handcuffs are needed."

Bella nodded, but she still felt uneasy about Jax riding with the two men. She realized her dismay showed when Stan Harroll addressed her.

"Miss Stewart, we won't harm the constable or try to get away," the farmer assured her.

"No, miss," his cousin said. "I don't want no more trouble."

A slight smile touched her mouth, but anxiety still filled her. Both men seemed sincere and cooperative. At least, they did at the moment. Smitty had been angry earlier, though. He had reason to be, but Bella didn't like that Jax might become the target of his rage. She didn't like it at all.

Chapter Seventeen

The drive to Moreley shouldn't have taken more than thirty minutes, but it seemed interminable to Bella due to traveling at a low speed. As dusk fell, seeing the truck wasn't easy. Its headlamps were faint, so she drove much more slowly than normal. The battered, refurbished old vehicle didn't have the Chummy's power, which meant a lot of downshifting.

When the Moreley constable's office came into view, she breathed more easily. Light poured onto the sidewalk from the front windows, so someone was still there. Jax had seemed certain Nolen would be, but Bella hadn't been as sure, which added to her apprehension. Jax needed someone to back him up. She pulled into a parking place and waited until the truck stopped next to her. All three men were visible, but none made a move to get out. Assuming Jax was waiting for her to go into the office, Bella hurried inside. Despite Harroll's reassurance

235

and the safe arrival of the trio, she hated Jax was out of sight, even for a few moments. What if the cousins drove off with Jax as a hostage? Inwardly, Bella chastised herself for letting her imagination run wild yet again. That really wasn't like her. At least it hadn't been before the kidnapping.

"We were wondering when the two of you would be back," the senior constable said. "It's almost dark."

Bella shook off her troubled thoughts. "I know. Everything took longer than we figured." Briefly, she outlined their side trip to Mohawk and the result. "They're right outside, so they should be in soon. Jax insisted I drive the Chummy and he go with them."

Jenny, who stood with her husband and Nolen, moved to put a reassuring arm around the younger woman's shoulders. "I think that was a wise decision, and I'm glad you went along with it."

Some of Bella's tension drained away. "I didn't have much choice."

Nolen hurried to the front window. "Jax is getting out with two other men."

Relief filled Bella when the trio entered the office. Jax looked fine, and the cousins seemed calmer than they had at the farm.

Jax introduced the pair to Nolen, Richard, and Jenny before saying, "Sorry, it took us so long."

"I'm afraid my old truck don't have a top speed over thirty," Harroll said. "She's reliable, though, and a big help around the farm."

Jax looked from Nolen to Richard. "Mr. Harroll and Mr. Smith have some information about Sunday evening's accident. They've agreed to be interviewed separately, so one of us can stay out here with whoever isn't being questioned while two of us talk to the other."

"I can stay out here, Jax," Nolen offered.

"Thanks," Jax replied. "Richard, it's you and me for the interviews."

The senior constable nodded. "Perhaps one of the ladies will take notes."

Bella's heart leaped into her throat, but she said nothing. She wanted to be the one, but she preferred to be asked.

"None of us has eaten dinner. Why don't I go back to Jax's house and make sandwiches? I'll bring enough for everyone," Jenny said.

"That sounds good to me, my dear," her husband said with a smile before looking at Bella. "Feel like taking a few more notes?"

"Of course," Bella replied.

Once she, Richard, Jax, and Stan Harroll were seated at the battered table in Jax's office, Bella pulled her pencil and notepad out of her pocketbook.

Jax looked at the senior constable. "We didn't discuss the accident much at Mr. Harroll's farm and not at all on our way here. I told them that separate interviews are important. That way, we know neither is being influenced by the other one."

"It is important," Richard agreed. "So, Mr. Harroll, why don't you tell us what you know about the accident?"

Harroll swallowed convulsively. "It really were an accident. We didn't try to force Laheene off the road. We didn't even try to scare him." He glanced at Jax. "You know my truck don't go fast, and it don't handle well, neither. Especially not on a wet road in fog and rain." The man's attention went to Richard. "We been to see Chaz. He told us about Laheene getting nasty with some of the caddies who stayed in the hotel. Said trash like them shouldn't be allowed. Smitty were plenty angry when Chaz told us, and he might have gone after Laheene again if he'd heard it himself and seen the man. But he didn't."

"Did he want to follow Laheene?" Jax asked.

Harroll shook his head. "Laheene was still in the hotel, so I told Smitty that we needed to get back to the farm. I don't like driving the truck in bad weather. He agreed because I don't think he wanted to be on the road with it after dark, neither. My headlamps are weak, and we didn't need to take no chances of getting hit by someone going fast. So, we said goodbye to Chaz and started out."

"Do you remember what time it was?" Jax inquired.

"Around seven-thirty or maybe closer to eight. Not real sure. We shoulda had more than an hour of daylight, but the heavy clouds and thick fog made it darker. Then, drizzle began and rain followed," Harroll replied. "Anyways, we went toward home. Slow, but sure. We was only a couple miles down the main road when a car came up behind us fast. The highway is a little curvy there, so the driver couldn't pass and we was going at top speed for the truck." A shuddering breath left him.

"Take your time, Mr. Harroll," Jax told him.

Bella looked up from her notepad. The farmer

was once again pale, and who could blame him?

"The driver followed close, too close for comfort, and he started honking. I knew it weren't safe for him to pass, and there weren't no place for me to pull over. Not much of a shoulder between the road and that ravine. I kept my attention on the road as best I could." He paused briefly. "Both Smitty and I was a bit rattled, but he told me not to pay no attention and to keep on going, so I did." He laid his hands on the table and massaged one with the other in repeated motions. "It were hard to see, and my wipers don't work none too good, which didn't help. The other driver kept honking, and that were no help, neither. Made me nervous."

"I can understand that," Richard observed in a calm, easygoing voice. "The driving conditions were terrible on Sunday night. No one needed any additional distractions."

"No, sir," the farmer agreed. "But the honking kept up. I suppose he wanted me to go faster but I couldn't, and it wouldn't have been safe for me to wave him around us because I couldn't see far in those conditions. Another car could have hit him head-on. Finally, we got to a place where I thought I could safely go along the shoulder, but it were muddier than I figured, and my tires started to slide. About that time, the driver tried to pass. The road were still curvy, but not quite as bad. For a bit, I thought he'd make it. Then, he swerved back very quick and almost cut me off. It were all I could do to hang on to the steering wheel. He clipped my front bumper, and as he went, I hit his passenger side. I don't know if that's what made him lose control or not, but suddenly his car were careening off the road and into the ravine." Harroll bowed his head. "We figured no one could survive that, but we stopped. The car had gone about halfway down the ditch. Steam were coming out of the tailpipe and from under the hood. Smitty went to see if the driver were alive. He were able to look into the car. He shook the man and got no response. He started back toward me. Then, suddenly, the car slid all the way down, farther into the ravine and water. There weren't nothing no one could do then."

"Mr. Smith must have recognized Laheene," Jax said.

The man shook his head. "Nope, he didn't. The other night, darkness were coming quick. Neither of us knowed it were Laheene until we heard about the accident on Monday afternoon. We only found out then, cuz a couple of folks who stopped at the filling station told Oswold." He took a deep breath and went on. "Neither of us had no idea what kind of car Laheene drove, and a lot of people was still in town but getting ready to leave when we took off. Coulda been anyone."

"Why didn't you come back to Moreley for help?" Richard asked.

Harroll sat stiffly, as if awaiting a blow. "We knowed it was a Cadillac when he started to pass. Smitty were scared because the driver had to be rich, and I were scared, too. We was both afraid of being blamed. Smitty even more than me. I know we shoulda come back but, like I said, we knowed the driver was beyond help and we was worried about getting into trouble."

"Both the constable and I were at the scene," Richard said, "and I can't deny your assessment. We thought he might have died on impact, and the coroner agreed."

Some of the tension ebbed from Harroll's broad shoulders. "I'm sorry it happened. I really am. But I didn't do nothing to cause it."

"It certainly sounds that way," Jax agreed. "We thank you for speaking with us, Mr. Harroll. You can go to the outer office and wait. I'll be out to get your cousin soon."

The farmer nodded and quietly went on his way.

Jax looked at Richard as soon as the door closed behind Harroll. "What do you think?"

"I think most of the story is quite credible. I'm not sure Smith didn't recognize Laheene, but that's not a crucial piece of information. All along, we haven't known if it was accidental or intentional and his explanation was quite detailed, as well as logical. I can definitely see it happening exactly as he said." The senior constable glanced at Bella. "You have good insight. How do you feel about Mr. Harroll's explanation, Arabella?"

"I agree with you. He was thorough and mea-sured. He didn't seem like he was grasping at straws or making up a tall tale. It was more like a retelling of what he experienced," she replied, pleased to be asked for her opinion. "But I also agree that Mr. Smith probably knew it was Cecil, which would have added to his anxiety. With that in mind, it's not hard to understand why they didn't report the accident."

"That's a good summation," Jax said, "and I think

both of you are right. Now, let's hear what Mr. Smith has to say."

When he entered Jax's office, Smith looked drawn and wary, but he sat down at the table without protest. Bella knew he must wonder what his cousin had said. Although she should be unbiased, she hoped the pair told the same story since that would go a long way to clearing both men and closing the case without Mr. Smith returning to jail.

"Mr. Smith, we won't take much of your time, but we do have some questions we need answered," Jax told the man.

"I know." His tone was emotionless, but his eyes were pools of anxiety.

"Can you tell us what happened when you left Moreley on Sunday evening?" Jax asked.

Smith started slowly and carefully. For a minute or two, Bella wondered if he would deny, unknowingly, everything his cousin had said. But he didn't. As Smith continued to speak, his voice grew stronger. "You've been in the truck, constable. It ain't easy to steer under the best of conditions. I don't know how Stan controlled it that evening. Laheene honking so much were distracting, too. Course, we didn't know who were behind us at the time." He folded his hands on the table and stared at them. "That's a tough stretch of winding road, and we couldn't figure if the driver were drunk, impatient, or crazy."

"It sounds like a dangerous situation," Richard suggested.

Smith nodded. "Very dangerous. Eventually, Stan tried to get over on the shoulder when it were wider. Tried to let the other car pass, but we started to slide then. I honestly thought we was going off the road and down the hill but, somehow, he kept going and got two tires back on the highway. Everything woulda been fine if the other driver had dropped back, but he didn't. He tried to pass even though Stan couldn't keep the truck going straight." He shook his head. "When I saw it were a Cadillac, I figured it were some young, rich kid who had played in the tournament. I didn't want no trouble and told Stan to do what he could to let the car go by. He just couldn't cuz the car swerved toward us."

"You didn't know it was Laheene?" Jax asked.

Bella silently noted that Jax wanted to ensure the cousins' stories matched completely. Again, she held her breath in hopes they would.

Smith looked incredulous. "How would I know? I didn't have no idea what kind of car the man drove, and it were impossible to see the driver. He were just a dark figure as he sped by. I couldn't see him much when I went to check, neither."

"If he was in the other lane passing you, how did he end up going into the ravine?" This time, Richard made the query.

Smith released a harsh breath. "I think he wanted to bully us or show off. He had to see that the truck was old and beat up. It's an old milk delivery truck. Stan made some changes, like closing the seat in, but it ain't fast. Maybe he figured he could force us over farther, give us a fright, and speed on past. After all, the Cadillac has a more powerful engine and better handling. The problem were that the truck's right two tires were still in the mud with little traction. When the Cadillac clipped our front bumper, the driver were going pretty darn fast. After that, he swerved over. He maybe lost control, but I think his front right tire got into the mud, too. Stan were struggling to get us back on the road, and we hit the back bumper and then, the passenger side. It's a blur cuz it happened fast. Suddenly, the other fella were going down into the ravine." Smith bowed his head.

"Why didn't you stop to help him?" Jax asked.

His head came up, and his eyes were wide with dismay. "We stopped, but we could see that we couldn't help. I went down and looked into the car. No one coulda helped. He were dead."

"Are you sure you didn't recognize Laheene?" Richard inquired.

Although Bella knew the lawmen had to confirm what Harroll had said, she felt as anxious as Smith looked. His family had already suffered terribly.

Smith ran one hand over his face. "No, sir. Like I said, it were dark and I could hardly see. The Cadillac were partway down the ravine. Once I started up to the road again, it went crashing to the bottom. Maybe I made that happen. I dunno."

"Is that why you didn't come back to Moreley and report the accident?" Richard took his turn again.

"I just got out of jail for beating a man up, and I were scared to death that I'd be blamed even though I weren't driving. I didn't want to cause no trouble for Stan. He's trying to help me out—giving me a home and a job." Smith shook his head. "What happened weren't Stan's fault, senior constable, but because he's the cousin of a convicted criminal, I figured he'd get blamed along with me. I'd rather die than go back to prison." Defeat and dismay combined in his expression. "Are you going to arrest us now?"

"No, we aren't," Jax said without hesitation.

Surprise flickered in Smith's dark eyes. "Why not?"

"You and your cousin tell the same story and, along with the evidence from the scene, it's completely logical," Richard replied.

"I can definitely attest that the truck couldn't have kept up with the Cadillac," Jax said. "I could also easily see that it handles poorly in dry conditions. It's a bit of an odd vehicle, but I'm sure it's helpful on the farm. In any case, your cousin couldn't have passed Laheene. If Stan had tried to pull alongside and force him over, Laheene could have sped away. In fact, knowing Laheene, I doubt if he would have let you catch up with him, so it makes perfect sense he was attempting to pass you because you weren't going fast enough to suit him."

"I agree with the constable," Richard said. "Neither you nor your cousin is guilty of anything other than leaving the scene of an accident. I wish you had reported it that night, but it's not a reason for us to arrest you."

"Will I have to go to court?" Smith asked. "If I do, if we do, we'll both end up in jail."

"I won't kid you, sir," Richard began, "because Jax will have to consult the local judge and prosecutor. Vehicle laws are quickly being enacted, and I'll admit I'm not up-to-date with them. But I think, under the circumstances, we can get any possible charges dismissed. I don't like that you didn't report it, but I understand."

Smith looked from Richard to Jax. "I can't believe the two of you are lawmen. You're like regular folks."

"I know your son Chipper was ill-treated by Laheene, and I'm truly sorry about that," Jax said. "But a lawyer has agreed to represent your family in a civil suit. At no charge. That should bring enough money to keep Chipper well treated for the rest of his life, and enough for surgery, if it's needed."

Smith stared at Jax in disbelief. "Truly?"

"Yes, and I think the case will succeed," Jax assured him. "If I need to file charges against you, and that may be beyond my control, I'll contact him. Maybe he would represent you and your cousin in court, if necessary."

For several moments, Smith stared at Jax. "Thank you ain't enough, constable," the man murmured, his voice tremulous and his eyes bright.

"It's more than enough, Mr. Smith. You and your cousin are free to go for now. I'll be in touch when I know how we need to proceed." Jax got to his feet and put out his hand.

After expressing his appreciation again, William Smith—his eyes suspiciously damp—walked out of the office. Jax glanced at Richard. "I think they'll both come back if we have to have a trial." A trace of anxiety entered his voice. Maybe he should have held the pair in jail at least overnight. The senior constable nodded in agreement. "You handled it perfectly, and I'm sure they will return. Now, I'm going to call my wife and see if she's bringing food here or if we're all eating at your place."

Chapter Eighteen

Once Richard was out of the room, Jax glanced at Bella. "It's been a long day, and you must be tired." Although it was still Tuesday, he felt like more than a-day-and-a-half had passed since Laheene's body was found.

She smiled. "I enjoyed going to Cleveland today. It was fun to see The Woods again."

Jax stiffened as he recalled Griff Biggins' cheerful flirtation and Bella's reaction to it. The memory of her invitation to the golf pro surfaced. Biggins would undoubtedly come to Ballantyne sooner rather than later, and why shouldn't he? Why shouldn't Bella welcome him? Most of her friends were already married, so she had to be thinking about a husband and family. A family could be even more important to her now that her parents and brother were gone. One errant reflection after another surfaced until her voice broke into his thoughts.

"It ended well, so all the effort was worth it."

Jax studied her face for a few moments. "Yes, it did, and I'm glad of it. Everyone will be."

She nodded. "I'm relieved that it was an accident and not another murder. Neither Moreley nor Ballantyne needed any negative publicity."

"No, they don't," he said. "The past week has been a real boon to the area. I think things will only get better from here on." Jax tried to sound optimistic. He should be happy about solving the case and probably saving his job.

"I believe you're right." Bella glanced at the notepad. "I can get all the information from today typed up by tomorrow."

Richard's reappearance at the office door interrupted their conversation. "Jenny already has everything packed up, and she'll be here shortly."

Bella got to her feet. "I should be going."

"Nonsense," Richard said. "Eat with us. Jenny will bring more than enough, and we can go over the case as a group."

Although he could have echoed the invitation, Jax debated whether or not to do so. If he was really her brother, he'd join in suggesting she stay. "That's a good idea."

"All right," Bella agreed.

Ten minutes later, the group was assembled around the old table in Jax's office, where Jenny had laid out sandwiches and cookies. A pitcher of lemonade and a pot of coffee sat to the side.

"Thanks for bringing food, Jenny," Jax said after taking a bite of his sandwich.

"It's already well past supper time," the older woman pointed out. "I'm sure you and Bella were ready to eat, and I know the rest of us were."

"That's for sure," Nolen said between mouthfuls.

"I appreciate you going to all this work, but I didn't expect to even see you here," Bella said, voicing the question that had been in the back of her mind since returning to the station. "In fact, I was surprised Richard was back already. How is your mother?"

The older woman smiled. "She didn't break a bone after all. It's a sprained ankle, and a friend offered to stay with her until we get home. I didn't think the case would be over quite so soon. Of course, I'm glad it is and happy I could contribute something to the effort, even if it was only a meal."

"You helped a lot yesterday," her husband said.

"I'm still surprised Mr. Smith told you everything, Jax," Nolen put in. "I figured he'd put up a struggle."

A half-shrug lifted one of Jax's shoulders. "I wasn't sure myself." He didn't further elaborate, but moved to a related topic. "We learned a lot from Mrs. Smith, too." Jax summarized what the woman had told them.

"This is such an interesting case," Jenny observed. "I would have liked to be more involved."

A low laugh left her husband. "You've said that after all of my major cases." He glanced around the table. "I've said it before, and I'll say it again. My wife has better instincts and intuition than most of my colleagues did." His gaze met Bella's. "And you're on a par with her, Arabella."

Heat crept into Bella's face, but she smiled. "Thank you. That's high praise."

"You were a major help again," Jax said. "We all appreciate it."

At least Jax acknowledged her contribution. "Thank you," Bella said again. "I'm glad the case was solved so quickly, and I'm sure Cecil's father will be, too."

Jax frowned. "I doubt if old Laheene will be happy to hear that we're ruling it an accident."

"Probably not," Richard concurred, "but we've been consistent in saying it could be. Just as important, Doc Smedlay agreed from the start that it could be an accidental or intentional act. He also said Cecil most likely died on impact, so Smith and Harroll leaving the scene shouldn't weigh heavily against them."

"I hope not," Jax said. "I may have to file those charges tomorrow. I'll see what the judge and local attorney say. Mayor Cawlings will also have something to add, I'm sure."

"He can talk," Richard said, "but he won't control the judge. I believe any decent jurist will suspend the sentences or drop the charges entirely."

"I hope so," Bella put in. "The Smith family already has a world of troubles."

"They certainly have," Jenny agreed. "If they get enough money to properly care for Chipper, maybe Mr. Smith will be able to go home."

"Or Mrs. Smith and the boys could move to Mohawk," Bella said. "That could be a good place for all of them."

Nolen frowned. "What about Chaz caddying? They may still need extra money."

"He could drive over to Ballantyne. With additional play, we need more caddies," Bella said. "He could be very busy during the season."

"He needs to be busy," Jax put in.

Richard nodded. "I agree."

"He wasn't involved in the accident, was he?" Jenny asked.

"Not according to what his father and cousin said," her husband replied.

"I'm going to call the course where they caddy tomorrow morning. I want to talk with Chaz and Mick again," Jax added.

Bella frowned. "Do you think they were involved?"

Jax shook his head. "I don't, but I want to tie up all the loose ends, like why Mick didn't show up for Sunday evening service. It's probably not a big deal. The boys could have stopped a lot of places on their way home."

"Yeah," Nolen agreed. "Someplace more interesting than church." When everyone chuckled, he flushed to the roots of his red hair. "I didn't mean anything bad about going to services."

"We understand," Jenny said with a smile.

"We certainly do," Richard added. "Having been a young boy once myself, I'll admit that I missed a few church services doing something with my buddies."

"I did that when I caddied at Ballantyne," Nolen said. "A lot of Sunday evenings, the older boys played cards somewhere. I didn't go very often, but a few times. I never wanted to lose my money, so mostly I stayed away."

"Played cards and gambled?" Surprise was in Bella's tone and expression. She turned to Jax. "Did you know some caddies gambled on Sunday evenings?"

He glanced away from her penetrating gaze before answering. "Yes, I knew."

"And my brother knew, too?" she asked.

"He did," Jax replied.

Consternation hit Bella as she mulled the revelation over. "Did the two of you go?" When red crept into his lean cheeks, she had her answer. "You did and never told me."

"Like Nolen, we only went a few times," Jax replied.

"I understand why you didn't reveal it to my parents, but why hide it from me? I wouldn't have said anything." Indignation was in her tone and probably in her expression. The three of them had been a tight-knit trio—or so she had thought.

Jax shook his head. "Maybe not, but you would have nagged us to take you along, and Matt didn't think it was any place for his little sister." Bella opened her mouth to object, but Jax hurried on. "You know you would have and, when we didn't take you, you would have been mad."

As she glanced around the table, Bella saw Richard and Jenny exchange an amused look, while Nolen seemed to study his plate. Embarrassed, she hurried to defend herself. "You make it sound like I was a terrible pest."

His lips twitched before Jax managed a more solemn expression. "Not really. You just wanted to do what we did. The problem was that girls don't get to do everything boys do."

"Sadly, that's true," Jenny put in. "Although gambling is not the best activity for boys or girls."

The older woman's comments made Bella feel better, but she remained aware of Jax's repeated references to her independent streak, and his insistence that he needed to play big brother. No sense in arguing, especially in front of an audience, so she moved the conversation to a different topic. "What about Guy? He seemed like a possible suspect, especially when he said no one could have seen him on the road Sunday evening after mentioning that he passed another car. Why do you think he said that? It made him look guilty."

"He could have been nervous about getting blamed even when he wasn't involved, but I'll call him in the morning. I want to let him know about the outcome of the case anyhow," Jax told her.

After that, Bella finished her sandwich and glanced around the table. "I can take notes if there's anything to be added," she said before a yawn overtook her. "Sorry."

"You've already done enough for today, Bella," Jax said.

"Yes, you have," Richard said. "Jax and I can finish the notes in the morning. Jenny and I won't head home until tomorrow afternoon."

"I'll type everything from today and get it to you

as early as possible," Bella told the group.

"Sounds good," Jenny added. "I'll type whatever is discussed in the morning. That will give you a bit of a break."

"Thank you, Jenny," Bella managed before another yawn escaped her. "I don't know what's wrong with me."

"You're tired," Nolen said. "You've had a busy week and a long day."

"I suppose so," Bella admitted.

"You need to get some rest," Richard observed.

"I think you're right," Bella said. "Thank you for making supper, Jenny, but I should get home now."

Alarm spread through Jax. Bella's dark lashes kept fluttering down before she forced them open. Combined with her yawning, it did not bode well for being alert on the drive to Ballantyne. "I'll drive you back," he offered, getting to his feet. "Nolen, if you follow in the Chummy, I'll take the Model T, so it's at the resort."

"Sure thing, Jax," the deputy replied.

Jax got to his feet. "Are you ready, Bella?" For a moment, he was sure she would object outright. Then, Richard spoke.

"It's a good idea for you to get a ride, Arabella. We don't want you dozing at the wheel and having an accident."

"What if Jax dozes off?" she asked. "He's had as long a day and week as I have."

"Yes, but he just had three cups of strong coffee while you drank lemonade," Jenny pointed out with a soft smile.

"I suppose you're right," Bella said, getting up herself.

Her enthusiasm was less than reassuring, but Jax said nothing more. Although the trip to the resort was short, the chance of her going to sleep at the wheel frightened him.

The group said their goodnights before Jax and Bella headed to her Model T. Nolen followed shortly after them.

An uneasy silence filled the car as Jax headed down Main Street toward the highway. He wasn't sure what to say, so he said nothing. When Bella didn't speak, he glanced at her. Her dark head had fallen forward. A closer inspection revealed that she was sound asleep. A slight smile touched his mouth.

She stayed that way until he pulled to a stop in front of Ballantyne Inn. At that point, Bella sat straight up. "Sorry, I guess I was more tired than I thought," she murmured.

"I guess so," Jax replied, glad he had driven her home. "I'll see you inside."

Bella said nothing in return. Instead, she preceded him up the steps and into the lobby. There, they found Mac and Ida sitting on either side of the empty grate.

"Tis glad I am to see the two of ye back," the old pro said with a smile.

"Yes," Ida agreed. "Even though you called from town to say you were running late, we wondered when you'd get here."

"I'll tell both of you all about it tomorrow," Bella assured them. "Suffice it to say that Cecil's death was a complete accident."

"Good news," Mac said.

"I agree," Ida added. "It's a relief to know someone didn't intend to harm Cecil, even though most people won't be sad that he's gone."

"His arrogance certainly earned him a lot of enemies," Bella agreed. "Did anything important happen here today? I know we're closed, but there weren't any cancelations for later this week, were there?"

Jax heard the undercurrent of anxiety in Bella's tone and knew she was still concerned about the future of Ballantyne. He wished he could do something to help her and Mac, then chastised himself for such foolish thinking.

"Nay," Mac said. "We actually got a few more reservations for later in the summer and even into the fall."

"Yes, and several ladies called to see if the women's fourball will be reinstated," Ida added with a grin.

A broad smile lit Bella's face. "That's wonderful. As for the women's tournament, we definitely need to discuss it."

"There was a personal message for you, Bella." Her friend pulled a slip of paper out of her pocket. "Griffith Biggins, the pro at The Woods, called a bit ago. He figured you'd be home by now."

Jax stiffened at the announcement. His attention went to Bella, but her expression revealed very little.

"Did he say what he wanted?" Bella asked.

"Evidently, the two of you met today?" Ida paused to let her friend respond.

"Yes, we did," Bella replied. "He was very cordial

when we were at the course to interview Chaz Smith."

"He said you invited him to play Ballantyne, and he wanted to set a date." Her friend smiled again.

"Oh, I see," Bella began. "Yes, we talked about him coming to play a round."

The flush in her cheeks and the sparkle in her eyes made Jax feel sick at heart, but he carefully controlled his expression. Only ago, he'd realized Bella would want to move ahead with her life. If Griffith Biggins could help her do that, who was he to get in the way? As a substitute big brother, he should be pleased.

"Wonderful," Ida said. "I met him at a tournament last month, and he is a charming, handsome man."

Jax felt Mac's steady gaze on him. The old pro looked pensive, almost troubled.

"He seems quite nice," Jax said, hoping Mac wouldn't see through his phony observation. But it was Bella, not Mac, who stared at him in disbelief, making Jax hurry on. "Nolen will be here momentarily to pick me up. Let me know when you have a chance to type up your notes, Bella. There shouldn't be a hurry. I can go ahead without them." He nodded to Ida and Mac. "Bella can fill in the details for you, but I want to make sure Nolen gets home soon. He's had a long week." The excuse was weak because they had all had long days, but Jax needed to get away. He couldn't stand listening to Ida and Bella discuss how amiable and good-looking Biggins was.

Once Bella said she would bring the typed notes in the morning, Jax headed out. He stopped on the top step of the porch and took a deep breath. Keeping his distance from Bella again wouldn't be as hard as he figured. Not when she would soon have a gentleman caller.

Chapter Nineteen

The next morning, Bella drove into Moreley. When she parked in front of the constable's office, she didn't see the Chummy, and conflicting emotions hit her. Jax knew she was coming, so he'd likely made himself scarce on purpose. Not that she cared. Or rather, she didn't want to care. Bella knew better than to let Jax's hot-and-cold attitude bother her. The case was about to be closed, which meant he would quickly move back behind the barriers he'd erected in France. The ones he kept in place by supposedly playing big brother. A mostly absent big brother. Despite Ida's observations, she and Jax were not together, never really had been, and never would be. Sadness nipped at her. She'd lost her entire family. Now, a childhood friend seemed to be slipping further and further away.

With a sigh, she grabbed the neat stack of papers from the seat and headed into the office. Surprise stopped her just inside the door when she saw Jax behind the counter with Richard.

"Good morning, Arabella," the senior constable said with a smile.

"Good morning," she said, crossing the room to where the men stood. "I have the notes." Bella laid them on the counter.

"Thanks, Bella. These will help me wrap up the report today," Jax said, with markedly less enthusiasm than Richard.

"Great," Bella replied. "What happened as far as charges?"

Jax shook his head. "First thing this morning, Richard and I spoke with the judge who would have heard the case. We asked if he would go along with no charges being lodged. After he heard everything, he agreed that was the best course of action."

"That's a relief. Do Smith and Harroll know yet?" she asked.

"I called them right away. There's no phone at the farmhouse, but Oswold, the filling station owner, was happy to send his son to get them and let them use his telephone to call me back," Jax told her.

"What about Cecil's Cadillac? Is it still in the ravine?" she asked.

"No. The guys from the Moreley filling station were able to drag it up early this morning," Jax replied. "There are a number of dents and dings. They don't make much difference now that we know what happened, but it's out."

"All-in-all, it's a job well done, and another case wrapped up," Richard said. He glanced at the papers on the counter. "Now, you have everything you need to finish your report, Jax."

"What about Mr. Laheene?" Bella asked. "Does he know yet that no charges will be filed?"

A long breath left Jax. "I talked to the mayor right after the judge, and old Laheene had already called today. That meant I needed to get in touch with him, since he was still threatening to hire detectives."

Anxiety knotted Bella's stomach. "Did you talk to him?"

Jax nodded. "I let the judge call him first. Evidently, they knew one another in college. That paved the way for me to contact the man. He isn't happy, but the judge was firm and clear, so Laheene won't make trouble. And he's agreed to give the Smith family more money for Chipper's ongoing care. I also spoke with Rylinger. The money will pay for ankle surgery, and that should help the boy get back to normal."

"That's wonderful," Bella said with a smile. "The two of you accomplished a lot this morning."

"Jax did most of the work," Richard put in.

Color rose in Jax's face. "The case was a team effort."

"Every good team has a strong leader," Richard pointed out.

"Yes, it does," Bella agreed, mostly because she didn't know what else to say. Jax had barely looked at her, which signaled—as expected—his withdrawal. Before that happened, she wanted to get the last details, or loose ends, as Jax had called them. "Were you able to speak with Chaz or Mick?"

He nodded. "I called the course, and they were both waiting to caddy. Biggins let them use the telephone."

"That was kind of him," Bella commented, not knowing what else to say.

"Right." Jax's tone still held little emotion. He cleared his throat. "Both boys admitted they stopped at a card game on their way home. Evidently, Chaz goes almost every week. Mick had never been before, but he went along. Not surprising. I also called Guy Brewster. It was like I thought. He said he wasn't sure about the other car and wished he hadn't mentioned the color or type. Mostly, he was worried that he'd get blamed for the accident, which would have been hard on his parents, especially his mother."

"That's understandable. They've been through a terrible loss, and I believed Guy when he said he didn't want to add to their grief." With no further reason to stay, Bella went on, "I need to get back to Ballantyne, but it was lovely to see both you and Jenny again, Richard. I hope you'll come back to play soon and bring her with you."

"She would love that, and so would I, but why the hurry? I thought the resort was closed again today," the older man said.

"It is, but Ida and I are going to play with someone I met yesterday. Griff Biggins, the golf pro at The Woods." Bella kept her attention on the senior constable, but she waited for a response from Jax. He provided none.

"Ah, the course where Chaz caddies," Richard said.

"Yes. Griff has never played Ballantyne, so it will be fun." She glanced at Jax, but he was looking at her typed notes. If he had any reaction at all, it wasn't visible. Only the gold wavy hair on the top of his head was. Silent dismissal. "If you'll both excuse me, I'll be on my way."

"Certainly," Richard said. "Enjoy your round."

"Thank you." Bella turned toward the front door when Jax spoke.

"Yes, have fun."

Something in his voice made her look back. Richard was smiling, but Jax wasn't. If anything, his expression could be called stoic. "I heard you've played Crystal Lakes a few times." The words were out before Bella considered them. "You're welcome to join us today if you can get away." As she studied his face, Bella saw resignation turn into surprise.

A heartbeat passed before Jax replied. "Thanks, but I can't. Nolen is checking on Mrs. Adams and another of her complaints. Richard and Jenny want to get on the road, and I need to finish my report. Maybe another time."

"The invitation is always open, and you don't have to play with me to play Ballantyne. You can come any time and play with anyone you want." She bid farewell to both men before quickly leaving.

Jax stared at her retreating figure for long moments. The invitation caught him off-guard. Even worse, his desire to accept it was a palpable force.

"You must have a good reason to turn her down," Richard said, his tone and expression serious.

With one hand, Jax massaged his temple. "It's like I said. I have work to do."

"But you'll play golf with Arabella another time."

Jax recognized it as the question it was. Briefly, he considered lying, but his respect for the senior constable evoked candor. Her offer dangled in front of him like bait to a starving fish. It was only with the greatest effort that Jax kept from grabbing at it. He'd gone to the other course twice and hadn't even made nine holes before his arm started to ache. Jax had no intention of revealing the extent of his weakness to Bella, but her invitation still appealed to him. So did the job offer. Foolish and futile to consider either one. Finally, he quelled the mental meanderings and responded to Richard. "Probably not," he replied at last.

"There may not be another case that gets her involved any time soon, or at all," Richard pointed out. "You might want to consider that."

His nostrils flared with a sharp intake of breath before Jax released the air in a rush. "I have, and I hope there isn't. Bella needs to move on with her life, and I need to let her." Saying the words made his throat hurt. His head knew moving on was the only way, but his heart yearned for the past and its possibilities.

Richard didn't speak for several moments. "I had the impression there was something between you and Arabella before the war."

Jax ran one hand over his face. Again, he wanted to change the subject, but Richard Jenkins was a kind man and a good friend. One of the few Jax had now. They'd had a short talk about Bella a few

265

months ago, so he repeated his story. "There was the possibility of something, but the war changed that. It changed me."

"It's none of my business, Jax, but your father is gone and you're pretty much on your own now. I know you spent a lot of time at Ballantyne before the war. I know you and Matthew Stewart were best friends. I've had the feeling that you and Arabella were going to be more than friends. I can't believe the war changed you or your feelings that much." A soft smile touched his mouth. "Remember, I was young once and, lucky man that I am, Jenny and I are still in love."

The last statement made Jax's heart race, and he fought against revealing everything to this man. What good would it do? "I have changed, Richard, more than I ever thought I would or could...and not for the better." He bit hard on the inside of his lower lip before going on. "I grew up with both Bella and Matt. We were all close, but she and I never courted." He'd escorted her to town and college events as a friend, not as a sweetheart.

"What if the war hadn't come along?" Richard asked.

Jax ran one hand over his face. "I'll never know what might have happened," he admitted in a hoarse voice. "I only know that Bella and I are heading in different directions. I can't even make nine holes now, which means we have little in common other than memories."

The older man's gaze narrowed on Jax. "You mentioned the possibility of surgery a while back. Is that still a consideration?"

Jax shrugged. "It probably isn't a complete solution. Nothing is." The admission cost him. However, Richard was concerned, which Jax appreciated.

"I know it's unlikely they'd get all the shrapnel out, but wouldn't it help?"

A few days ago, Jax had confided in Mac, and there was no reason not to tell Richard the entire story. "It's not just shrapnel," he said before revealing the gunshot wound to his bicep.

"I see," Richard said in a solemn tone. "Evidently, Arabella doesn't know how bad it is, or perhaps she doesn't know about it at all."

"No, she doesn't. I only told Mac about being shot in the upper arm last week."

"Is there a reason that you haven't revealed the truth to her?"

Jax leaned back and folded his arms over his chest. "Not really," he replied, although that wasn't true. "Maybe I should say there's more than one reason now. Bella and Griff Biggins hit it off very well, and he's the perfect kind of man for her. He'd be an asset to Ballantyne, too. I hope it works out for them." Again, his words burned his mouth, but they had to be said. Eventually, he'd be able to say them and mean them. While his wounds were handicap enough, his role in Matt Stewart's death was a far more substantial barrier. If she knew...Jax didn't let his mind pursue that idea. He couldn't bear for her to hate him.

Long moments passed before the senior constable spoke again. "If that's what you want. But be sure, very sure." Richard glanced at his pocket watch. "Jenny and I have to go. If you need us in the future, you know how to reach me."

When Richard put out his hand, Jax shook it. "Thank you for your help and Jenny's, too. I hope her mother heals quickly."

The older man nodded and left the office. When the door closed behind him, Jax bowed his head. Richard was right. Another major case wasn't probable. He ought to be glad of that. After all, both Moreley and Ballantyne could use an extended period of serenity. He could, too. But Jax was already missing Bella. Already thinking about how her brow furrowed in concentration when they discussed suspects. Already wishing he had some problem or another for her to confront. Already hoping that some outside force would bring her back into his life. He brushed away the imprudent thoughts and set about finishing his report. Long ago, on the day his best friend died, Jax had known he'd lost any chance to court Bella. Every day since then, he'd tried to put the past behind him and move forward. Too bad doing it wasn't as easy as thinking it.

When Bella got back to Ballantyne, Ida immediately intercepted her on the porch. "Did you ask Jax to join us?"

The question didn't surprise Bella. After all, her friend had made the suggestion earlier and with emphasis. "I asked, and he declined."

"That sounds quite formal. What actually happened?"

"As I said, I invited him to play with us, and Jax said he's busy with work."

"You don't believe him." Ida made it a statement, not a question.

"I don't know whether to believe him or not. He played at Crystal Lakes, even though he had to know he could come here." Bella didn't quite keep the hurt out of her tone.

Ida studied her friend for a moment. "Did you ask if he finished eighteen holes?"

"No, I didn't," Bella replied.

"Since he has trouble driving and writing, it seems likely that he can't and, if Jax can't play an entire round, he may not be playing very well. Golf would surely be more of a challenge than either of those," Ida pointed out. "Isn't being unable to play competitively one of his big reasons for not becoming a head professional?"

Bella mulled the idea over. "Yes, so I suppose you're right. But I wouldn't care how he played. Neither would you and why would Griff?"

"It isn't about how we'd react. Playing poorly could embarrass to him, especially with another golf pro in the group."

Bella chewed on her lower lip. "Maybe so. In any case, this investigation is over, and I won't be seeing much of him any time soon, which is probably for the best."

"For the best," Ida echoed, disbelief in her tone and expression.

"Yes," Bella reasserted, "for the best. Jax and I are not on the same path any longer. He's made that clear."

Ida shook her head. "That's a front on his part, nothing more."

The urge to believe her friend was powerful, but Bella resisted. Trying to hang on to the past was useless. "We've discussed this already. More than once. I can't pin my hopes and future on Jax changing back to the person he was before the war." Or in their friendship, possibly growing into more. They hadn't been courting before leaving for France, and they might never have done so. Once again, the image of him standing by the French nurse came to Bella. "I need to focus on the resort, and he needs to focus on his job as town constable. He's moving on. You've made the same decision in your life. I have to do that, too."

For several silent seconds, Ida studied Bella's face. Finally, she nodded. "Maybe I want the happy ending for you and Jax that Alan and I can't have."

Her friend's admission tugged on Bella's heartstrings. "It's not the same, Ida. You and Alan courted and fell in love. You planned to marry. Jax and I never had a relationship like that."

"He escorted you to events around here and at college."

"As my childhood friend. As Matt's best friend. Nothing more."

Ida's hazel eyes narrowed. "It seemed like you two were headed toward courtship. At least until the threat of war came along."

Although Ida was like a sister to her, Bella didn't want to admit she'd thought the same thing three years ago, but not now. "Once it looked like America would enter the war, Alan proposed, so it didn't stop him."

"Jax is more reserved than Alan was, but I see your point. And you're right about moving on. If Jax keeps pushing you away, his feelings—whatever they are—don't really matter. You deserve a husband and family, with or without him."

Her friend's comments took Bella aback. "I'm not looking to get married right away. Ballantyne comes first. Besides, I'm not even stepping out with anyone."

A grin curved Ida's lips. "You might be soon. Griff Biggins is driving a long way to play golf with you."

Heat rose in Bella's cheeks. "It's a friendly game, not a social engagement, and certainly not a romantic date."

"Romance can bloom from playing golf. It did with Alan and me." Ida winked.

"I like Griff, but I barely know him."

Ida's good humor remained in place. "You'll know him better after several hours on the course."

"Perhaps." Bella turned and gazed across the inn's front yard and to the golf course, dock, cottages, tennis courts, and creek winding through the resort. Ballantyne wasn't back to normal, but not even a highly successful season could accomplish that feat. The Great War had changed the world, including her little corner, almost beyond recognition. Now, the only path led forward, and Bella had to follow it without a backward glance. Day-by-day, step-by-step, she could do it. She had to.

Thank You!

Thank you for reading <u>A Lethal Arrogance!</u> I hope you enjoyed it. If you have time, please rate or review it. Comments from readers are helpful and appreciated. I am on Goodreads and BookBub. Most retailers also accept reviews. If you purchased from my website, there is a review option.

https://www.goodreads.com/author/show/21325652.D_S_Lang

https://www.bookbub.com/profile/d-s-lang
For more information, please go to my website or Facebook page.

https://dslangbooks.com

https://www.facebook.com/profile.php?id=100064024056297
You can sign up for my newsletter on my website.

I share other authors' work, news about my books, a peek into the writing life, historical tidbits, and more. Your email will never be shared, and you can unsubscribe at any time!

What's next for Bella and Jax?

Bella's amateur sleuthing does not end in <u>A Lethal Arrogance</u>. In the series' fourth book, <u>A Baffling Absence</u>, she faces new challenges, as does Jax, who finally reveals why he feels guilt about her brother's death in the Great War.

A missing teacher. Old grudges. Disappearing suspects.

What happens when a teacher from a nearby girls' boarding school does not return from vacation? Arabella Stewart is asked to substitute, but she finds the position involves more than lesson planning. Her sleuthing skills are needed, so Bella and her friend Ida Byington, a faculty member, start investigating. Soon, Constable Jax Hastings is also on the case, and the trio work against time to solve more than one *baffling absence*.

The book is available at many digitial retailers: https://dslangbooks.com/books/a-baffling-absence/

About the Author

D.S. Lang started making up stories to entertain herself as a child, and she still is making them up. Now, she puts them in writing!

After obtaining Bachelor's and Master's degrees in Education, she worked as a golf shop manager, teacher (junior high, high school and college), program manager, tutor and mentor. Writing is currently her main job. Taking care of a very spoiled dog is her other vocation.

D.S. loves hearing from readers. You can email her at: dslangbooks@gmail.com and learn more about the Arabella Stewart Historical Mystery series at https://www.dslangbooks.comYou can buy her other books directly from the website or connect to a variety of digital retailers.

In addition, you read/rate books and check her reading recommendations on:

https://www.goodreads.com/author/show/21325 652.D_S_Lang

https://www.bookbub.com/authors/d-s-lang

Arabella Stewart Historical Mysteries

The Arabella Stewart Historical Mystery series is set in small-town Ohio after the Great War. Bella returns home from serving as a U.S. Army Signal Corps operator to find her family resort and home-town in dire straits, and the murder of a neighbor adds to the trouble. Much to the dismay of Constable Jax Hastings, Bella turns amateur sleuth to solve the case. As the series continues, Bella and Jax vanquish the shadows of the war, while solving a series of whodunits with a team of colorful characters. If you love history and mystery mixed with touches of humor and drama, this series is for you!

Books in the Arabella Stewart Historical Mystery series:

Doro Banyon Cozy Historical Mystery series

The Doro Banyon series has a cozier tone than the Arabella Stewart books. History and mystery still mesh as amateur sleuth Doro solves whodunits with a team of colorful characters in small-town America during the 1920s. Travel back in time to a college campus and crack cases with them!

Prequel-<u>The Lost Exam</u> (free when you sign up for my newsletter)
<u>Book 1-The Catalogued Corpse</u>
<u>Book 2-The Murdered Matron</u>
<u>Book 3-The Jammed Judges</u>
<u>Book 4-The Problem Professor</u>
<u>Book 5-The Bottled Bootlegger</u>

Book 6-<u>The Doomed Doctor</u> (coming in April 2025)

A Valentine's Day short story, "The Vintage Valentine," is available to my newsletter subscribers. In it, college librarian and amateur sleuth Doro takes a break from detective work as she prepares for a romantic evening at the annual Sweetheart Ball with her would-be beau, Everett Mallow. Will this be the night when they go from stepping out to courting? Or will a snowstorm interfere? A vintage Valentine plays a role in this standalone story, which is not a mystery but has a thread of suspense.

You can sign up for my newsletter at https://dslangbooks.com